Anytime Soon

TAMIKA CHRISTY

Alpharetta, Georgia

Published in the United States by BQB Publishing
(Boutique of Quality Books Publishing Company)
www.bqbpublishing.com

Printed in the United States of America

978-1-937084-95-0 (p)
978-1-937084-96-7 (e)

Library of Congress Control Number: 2013932829

Book design by Robin Krauss, www.lindendesign.biz
Cover illustration by Leah Jennings

This book is dedicated to

My daughters for inspiring and motivating me;

My dad for guiding and nurturing me;

And my sweetie for the unconditional love and support.

Mom, you are still the most amazing and loving person I've ever known—Rest in Peace.

ONE

The sound of my parents talking woke me out of my sleep. I sat up and looked around my bedroom. It looked like the room of a twenty-four-year-old college senior, but lately, it didn't feel like I was in college. I often had to remind myself of why I made the decision to live at home instead of on campus. Granted, at the time that I made the decision, it had seemed like a good idea. Living at home was comfortable and affordable. Once I started school, however, I often questioned my decision to continue living at home. Shortly after I decided to get my own place, my only brother, Andrew, was killed. We were a close family and devastated at his untimely death. At that point, there was no way I was going to move out. I thought my parents and sister needed me home with them. But, as time passed, I realized they really didn't need me at all—I was the one who needed them.

Andrew and I were as close as any two people could ever be and when he died, part of me died too. He and I had gone to a house party one night and we separated at some point—me hanging out with some friends and Drew going outside for some air. I was still talking with a friend when I noticed everyone headed outside. I followed the crowd and gasped, only to discover my beloved brother lying on the ground, bleeding. It was frustrating because no one stepped up to say they knew anything. It was a mystery then and, over a year later, it remains a mystery. There were different rumors going around. One was that some guys were walking by and got into a verbal altercation with Drew and shot him, but none of the stories were ever corroborated. It was hard for my family to deal with the loss and even more so because of the lack of clarity surrounding his death. We all grieved, but we grieved differently. My mom ate, my sister Ava fasted, my dad drank, and I sank into depression. As time moved on, however, so did my family. I, on the other hand, still struggled with losing Drew and my mom "gently insisted" that I see a therapist. Some woman named Dr. Judy. I was resentful at first, but I eventually learned to appreciate having Dr. Judy sit for an hour and listen to me gripe and pontificate. Mom paid for it and, depending on my mood, sometimes she got her money's worth and other times she didn't.

Some days, I enjoyed the comforts that home had to offer. Other days, however, I would have shaved off my eyebrows to have my own place. Between my overbearing mom, and the issues of my extended family and friends, there were days I struggled just to hear my own thoughts.

I showered and dressed before heading downstairs. On the way down, I peeked into my sister's room. Ava was buried under her comforter, with one foot hanging off the side of her bed. I shook my head at the chaos. Given that my mom and dad were the tidiest people I knew, Ava's sloth often caused me to question her paternity.

I walked into the kitchen, where my dad, Roscoe, was fussing at my mother. He was bent over, looking in the cupboard. I sat down at the table quietly.

"When did you start buying *Diet* Dr. Pepper?" he complained. "And, Anita, where are the cinnamon rolls?"

"The cinnamon rolls are at the store, where they belong," Mom replied, not bothering to turn away from the cantaloupe that she was cutting.

"Wrong answer," he told her. "Where they belong is right here in this kitchen, so I can pack them in my lunch."

Mom turned and rolled her eyes at him. She had battled the

bulge for as long as I'd been on the Earth, probably even before that. This means I grew up on every diet known to humanity. When she dieted, we all dieted with her—whether we wanted to or not.

"Come on, Roscoe, you know I don't have that kind of willpower," Mom explained. "You don't need those cinnamon rolls. Take some of this cantaloupe to work. I'm taking some with me. You'll like it. It's sweet."

"I don't want cantaloupe, Anita. I want a cinnamon roll." Roscoe kissed Mom on the cheek, picked up his lunch off the counter, and kissed me on the forehead before walking out of the kitchen.

She called out to him, "The banquet is in a month, and I need to fit into my dress. I can't fit into my dress with cinnamon rolls lurking around the kitchen, taunting me."

She looked over at me. I was still sitting quietly. I looked over at the small television on the counter. I wanted to avoid a conversation about food and eating habits. There were many things that Mom and I didn't agree on, and weight management was at the top of the list. I'm size two, but I'm healthy. It seemed that my mom had developed a rare form of amnesia and forgot the countless diets she raised me and my siblings on. Now she thought I didn't eat enough.

"Where are you headed?" she asked me.

"I have an appointment with Judy," I responded.

"Okay," she said, still cutting the cantaloupe. "Are you going to complain about the cinnamon rolls, too?"

"Nope," I said, heading to the cabinet for oatmeal.

"That figures," she said. "You don't eat enough anyway."

Here we go.

"I eat, Mom. Just in moderation. Healthy weight management, remember?" I said.

"More like weight obsessed," she said, pouring a cup of coffee.

"I'm not weight obsessed, I'm healthy," I said, instantly regretting the comment. I should have just kept my mouth closed.

"Bulimia isn't healthy, honey," she said.

"You're right, Mom. Bulimia isn't healthy. It's an illness—an illness I don't have."

She glared at me over the top of her glasses. "You need to eat more," she said, putting the cantaloupe in the refrigerator. "You're as thin as a rail."

I wanted to tell her that she needed to eat less, but I didn't. I wanted to live to see the end of the day.

Roscoe walked back into the kitchen before I could defend myself. He was wearing his work uniform and still had his lunch in his hand.

"Remember, I have my meeting tonight after work," Roscoe has worked for the electric company for at least twenty years. He loves his job and has often said that he has no plans to retire. He said working kept him out of trouble. Although that could be true at times, there were plenty of other times when he almost lost his job because of his drinking. That's why he frequented a sober support group. As hard as he tried to stay on the wagon, there were times when he slipped up. Too many slip ups, in my humble opinion.

"Okay," Mom said. "See you later."

Mom sat down and started watching a news report about a black business executive who had been indicted for fraud.

"Surely they know he wasn't behind it. There's more to it," Mom said.

"Yeah," I said sarcastically. "Greed."

"No. He was under somebody's direction," Mom said.

"So that makes it okay?" I asked. "He did it because he wanted to, because of greed."

"He did it because he wanted to keep his job," she said.

"He did it because he was greedy," I repeated.

Mom glared at me. "Anaya Goode, how in the world do you go to college smart and come out stupid?"

"Mom," I said, "you think everything is a conspiracy, but this is not someone else's fault. The man is guilty, plain and simple. They have e-mails of him admitting his wrongdoing."

"So I'm a conspiracy theorist?" she asked.

"I didn't say that," I argued. "It's just that sometimes you sound a little . . . paranoid."

"Don't start that," she exclaimed. "Don't you call me paranoid until you've lived a day in my shoes. You couldn't have survived one day in the life I had when I was your age."

Not this morning, Mom; not the story about the twelve-mile walk!

"Do you realize that my sisters and I had to walk twelve miles to and from school in the heat of summer and in the dead of winter, and after school to help my mama clean houses? You need to respect the struggle."

"Mom, I *do* respect the struggle. I'm just saying, everything that happens to Black people is not a conspiracy. People make choices, knowing there is a consequence, and it's no one's fault but their own."

She looked at me as if I had grown a third eye.

"People do what they have to do to survive. And there are always two sides to a story."

"I get that, Mom. But at some point, we have to be accountable for who we are and what we want to be. We have the same opportunities for education, the same opportunities for prosperity, and the same opportunities to raise our families. But what is happening?" I gestured at the television as if to prove my point. "We have more black men in prison than in college. So who's teaching young boys how to be men? Who's showing girls what kind of man to look for? We need to wise up and get educated. We need to move forward. Heck, it would be nice if we started voting."

Mom stared at me a long time before she finally stood up and spoke.

"There's a story in the Bible about Jesus and a blind man," she began. "The blind man comes to Jesus and asks to be healed. Jesus spits on some dirt, mixes it up, and puts it on the man's eyes. Then he tells the man to go to the water, rinse his eyes out, and come back. When the man returns, Jesus asks him what he sees. The man says he sees men as trees. Jesus spits on the dirt again, rubs it on the blind man's eyes, and tells him to go and rinse his eyes a second time. When the man comes back, Jesus asks him what he sees now, and the man says he sees men as they are. You, Anaya, see men as trees, and I see them as they are."

What?

"I don't know anything about men looking like trees," I said, "but I do know that we live in a society where we can do anything we want. This is not the old days, Mom. We can move forward. We do not have to hold on to the past, singing old Negro spirituals all the time."

She stood up, and I ducked.

"Old Negro spirituals? Where's the child I birthed into this world? Girl, you don't have a clue. You millennials are privileged and ignorant. You think this family is struggling because we have only one premium cable TV package instead of two. Your two best friends drive cars that are worth more than most people will earn in a lifetime. You aren't doing so badly, either. Get a clue. One day you will see for yourself."

She walked out of the kitchen. I followed behind her, but not too closely.

"See you later," I called out.

I was five minutes late for my appointment with Judy. I'd been seeing her since Andrew died, and she never gave me grief about being late. I sat down in the obnoxiously massive leather chair in her office. She sat across from me, looking like The Joker; she had small red lips, over-arched eyebrows, pasty skin, and heavy black eyeliner.

"So what's going on?" she asked me. "Have you made the decision to move out of your parents' house?"

"No," I said.

"Why not?" she probed.

"I keep thinking that my family needs me there," I said, surprised to have said it so bluntly.

"For what purpose would they need you there?" Judy asked, writing on her little yellow pad.

"I don't know."

"Have you talked with your parents about moving out?"

"Nope."

"Why not?"

"I don't know. My mom still hasn't cleaned out my brother's room. I think she needs closure."

"What do you think that has to do with your gaining independence?"

"Nothing."

"Have you spoken with her about cleaning out your brother's room?"

"No. I don't think she's ready."

"Has your mom said that to you?"

"She doesn't have to. I know her."

"Say more," Judy encouraged.

"It just doesn't feel like the best time. Things feel strange in my house. Mom is not herself, my sister spends all of her time in church, and my dad seems oblivious. Things just don't seem right."

"How does that make you feel?"

"Sad. Insecure. Lonely."

"What can you do about that?"

"Drugs."

"What else?" She asked, ignoring my sarcasm.

"Move out."

"Alone?" Judy asked.

"I thought about moving in with one of my friends, but she's going through something. I know she's using drugs, and I don't know what to do." I let out a heavy sigh before I continued. "Life is turning upside down right in front of my face, and there's nothing I can do about it."

"You feel like life is hard for you right now?"

"Yes. Home is in turmoil since Andrew died. My extended family is overwhelming me with their issues, and even my friends seem to be leaning on me pretty hard right now. Lately, I don't even recognize my life, and it doesn't feel good. I thought I knew exactly what I wanted to do after college. I had my entire life planned out. Now I have no idea what I want to do." I started to cry.

The session drained me. But when I left, I suddenly realized that somehow, in the rich chaos of my family and friends, I needed to find my own voice. The question was—who was I, apart from them? What did I want to do with my life?

When I got home, I found my best friend, Sophie, sitting in my room, waiting for me.

"Hey," I said, surprised to see her. "How long have you been here?"

"Not long. I was in the kitchen talking to your mom for a few minutes. I had to make a phone call, so I came up here. That's okay, isn't it?"

"Of course, it's fine. You are family, anyway. You practically used to live here when we were kids."

When she smiled, I noticed that she looked different. I couldn't put my finger on why she looked different, but she did. Even though we grew up like sisters, there was a growing distance between us. A big part of it had to do with her not returning my calls and her newfound coke habit. I wasn't into drugs and didn't tend to entertain the company of those who did. Sophie was my friend though, and I needed her just as much as she needed me. I wasn't going to abandon her, but I wasn't going to pretend her drug use was okay. Lately, it had become a source of tension.

"I've been calling you," I said. "Why haven't you called me back?"

"Busy," she said.

Sophie was beautiful, with her dark eyes and small, button nose. Her naturally curly hair was a wild mixture of dark- and light-brown highlights. She had full eyebrows and thick, pouty lips.

"Where have you been?" I asked her.

"Just around," she murmured evasively. "Been busy doing . . . stuff."

"What kind of stuff?"

"Just stuff," she repeated vaguely. "What's been up with you?" she asked, changing the subject. I didn't want to fight. I walked to my closet and pulled out a bouquet of roses.

"Whoa. Who did those come from?" she asked, startled.

"Someone sent them to me."

"I can see that. Who?"

"Guess," I said, with my hands on my hips.

"Okay, Ny, I'm not trying to be funny, but I don't have a clue. Have you even dated anybody since Justin?"

I looked at her and smirked.

"Justin sent these to you?" she said, incredulous.

I nodded my head.

"What the hell for?"

"I don't know. I haven't talked to him in ages," I said. "Well, you know, we dated a few years ago. After he cheated on me three times and broke my heart, I finally broke it off. Hadn't heard from him since. Then yesterday, this bouquet of roses shows up at my house." I waved the roses around in a flourish. "Justin—the love of my life, the scum of the Earth."

"Wait. Justin is gay," Sophie said.

"No, he's not."

"You sure?" Sophie asked, chuckling.

"Yes, I'm sure."

"What does he want?"

"I don't know," I said.

"Well maybe you can start hanging out with him again. I mean, you haven't been out with anyone since you broke up with him. That's not really normal, Ny."

"I have been out since Justin!" I exclaimed, defending myself.

"Really?" she countered. "Name two people you went out with since you and Justin broke up." She looked at me with her arms folded across her chest.

"Remember that guy that used to be in Jack and Jill with us?"

"What guy?"

"The tall one."

"Really, Ny? The tall one? That could be anybody. What's his name?"

"Reggie," I said.

"I don't remember him," Sophie said.

"Well, I went out with him."

"Sure you did," Sophie said, pulling a compact out of her yellow Chanel tote.

A silver vial fell out of her bag. Sophie hurried to put it back in her bag, but I had seen it already.

"What's that?" I asked.

"Just a little powder," she said defensively. "Don't start on me today. I told you I only use it when I party. It helps me to stay awake."

I looked at her sharply.

"I have it under control," she said.

"Are you on your way to a party?" I asked.

She looked at me blankly.

"Are you going to a party?" I repeated.

"No."

"So why do you have it, then?"

"I said, don't start, Anaya, okay?"

"According to what you said, you only use it when you are

going out. So, if you have coke in your purse, you must be going to a party."

"I went out the other night. I forgot to take it out of my purse."

I didn't want to look at her, because she was lying to me. Lately it was hard being her friend. She was moody, didn't call when she said she would, and canceled plans. I had always admired Sophie for having famous parents, a fancy wardrobe, and the best things life had to offer.

We've always envied each other. She always said how wonderful my parents were, and I was impressed at how rich and sophisticated her parents were. Sophie likes that my mom cooks dinner almost every night, and I like that she has a live-in cook. She always wanted a younger sister, and I wanted to give mine away.

Before the conversation about her coke habit got heated, my other best friend, Catie, breezed through my bedroom door, smelling like flowery perfume.

"Hey, you guys," she said.

"Hey, Catie," we both chimed.

She gave me a big hug and handed me a large shopping bag before plopping down on my bed.

"What are you doing here?" I asked.

"What do you mean? I can't come visit my very best friend in the world?" she asked with mock hurt.

"Yeah, but you normally don't just pop up," I said.

"My car got towed," she said. "I had to get a ride downtown to pick it up. It's a few minutes away, so I decided to come and see you."

As I looked through the bag, I felt astounded at the stuff Catie gave to me. I pulled out a pair of jeans that I had recently seen on a fashion blog. Catie rolled her eyes at me when she saw me smiling. I walked over and tried to hug her, but she backed away. She reminded me so much of my mom. I immediately tried on the "Young, Rich, & Skinny" jeans in front of the mirror.

"Girl, you gonna have your mama's hips," Catie said.

I cringed.

"What's up, Sophie?" Catie said, playfully punching Sophie on the arm. "When is your dad having another party?"

Sophie's dad, Terry, is a music producer. He used to throw huge parties and invite all of his celebrity friends. Sophie always invited me and Catie. Among the three of us, we had pictures with some of the biggest names in the music industry. But Terry hadn't thrown a party in a long time. In fact, I hadn't seen him in a year. Every time I asked Sophie about him, she said he was traveling.

"I'm not sure," Sophie said to Catie. "I heard you've been to some pretty good parties lately."

Catie smiled with satisfaction. She stood up and smoothed her skirt. Catie was a five-foot-nine beauty. She had thin, straight hair that hung down to her waist, sharp features, and flawless skin. "Actually, my favorite Oakland Raider is throwing a party tonight," she said. "You guys wanna go?"

"I'm down," Sophie said softly.

I looked over at Sophie, surprised. She hated going out with Catie, because Catie was too high strung and loud, and that didn't mesh with Sophie's low-key persona.

"Sweet," agreed Catie. "You got something to wear?"

"I have something," Sophie said.

"Of course you do," Catie grinned.

"What time and where?" Sophie asked.

"It's at his house. Invitation only. So we roll together. Got it?"

"We can roll together," Sophie said, "but I'm not staying at a party until four a.m. I'll take a cab home if I have to."

"Shut up, Sophie. Just call me when you're ready, and I'll come swoop you up. What about you, Ny?"

I opened my mouth, but I didn't get a chance to answer.

They both groaned in unison. "We know. You need to study."

"Girl," Catie said, pointing at me, "you're gonna wake up one morning, realize you're forty, and wonder what the hell happened to your youth."

With that, she grabbed her huge, red, patent-leather purse, which probably cost more than my Honda.

"You act as if I've never been to a party before," I said. "I don't have to go to every party I'm invited to."

"Pu-leaze!" Catie exclaimed. "I can't remember the last time you went to a party."

"Did you tell Catie about the roses?" Sophie asked.

"No," I said tightly.

"What roses? Someone sent you roses, Ny? Who on Earth did that?"

"Excuse me?" I countered. "You act as if I'm not worthy of roses."

"I'm not saying you aren't worthy. I'm saying in order for someone to send you roses, you have to give them the time of day. So, who is the lucky gentleman?" Catie asked.

"Justin," Sophie blurted out with a grin.

"Justin? The guy you used to date?"

"Yes," I replied.

"Wait. He's gay."

"He's not gay!"

"Ny, the boy wore a thumb ring and arched his eyebrows. Now I love the gays just as much as anyone else, but he wasn't into you. He was gay."

I sighed.

"What does he want?"

"For me to call, but I'm not," I said.

"That's fine, he's not for you anyway," Catie said firmly. "I will say that you need to hurry up and get your groove on. I mean, give that little kitty cat some action down there. Those little toys you have can be fun, but you need real stimulation. You know what I mean? Like a man? You don't want your coochie to shrivel up and fall out, do you?"

Sophie smiled, as if the demise of my private parts amused her.

"Leave her alone, Catie," Sophie said. "She's got her priorities right. There's nothing wrong with that."

Catie frowned.

"Just trying to help."

"What are you wearing for the party?" Sophie asked Catie.

"I saw this pink Narciso dress that hugs every curve I have . . . and creates some I don't."

Her cell phone rang, and she took it in my walk-in closet.

I looked over at Sophie. We both shrugged.

"Why does she need to go in the closet?" Sophie asked.

"That's a good question," I said.

Catie came out of the closet and grabbed her purse.

"I thought we were going to a party tonight?" Sophie asked.

"We are," Catie replied. "I'll be at your house by eleven. We should get to the party by eleven-thirty. Anything earlier looks desperate."

She blew us a kiss as she disappeared out the door.

But then, peeking her head back in, she said, "And, Sophie? Do something with that hair, will you? You look like Carrot Top, for goodness sakes."

"Hooker!" Sophie called after her, before Catie closed the door completely.

"Sophie!" I exclaimed.

"What?" she asked, shrugging her shoulders.

TWO

I worked part-time in an interdisciplinary department at the University of California. My official title was Administrative Assistant of the School of Arts, Letters, and Sciences. But my job was basically to do whatever the faculty members asked me to do.

Most of the time, I liked my job. The hours were flexible, the pay was pretty good, and the work wasn't demanding, so I was able to focus on my college coursework.

One morning when I got to work, I found out the department had hired a young woman as extra help in the front office. Initially, it seemed like a good idea, until she started dogging me daily with questions and hadn't absorbed any of the training that I gave her. I was patient, though; in fact, I was patient and nice, even when she told me she couldn't focus on what I was saying because she had been partying the night before.

I didn't let her drive me crazy. Graduation was around the corner, and I had bigger things to focus on. I had recently decided not to go directly to grad school. I planned to work for a year and then start applying to programs. I wanted to get my own place and settle in before starting school again.

The day seemed to drag on with the new girl forgetting things and making the same mistakes over again. Late in the day, I decided to walk over to the accounting office to pick up my paycheck. I smiled to myself when I noticed that I had received an hourly increase.

The day just got a little better.

I took the long way back to the office. As I sat back at my desk, my phone rang. It was Catie.

"What up, Cow?" she said.

"You have great timing," I said. "Guess what?"

"What?" she asked.

"I got a raise!"

"Wow," she said. "I knew all those hard hours would pay off. What do you make now—three dollars an hour?"

"Excuse me, don't make fun. I make an honest living. Respect me." I almost immediately regretted the comment. Catie's chosen profession was one that the average woman could never be proud of. Catie wasn't the average woman though. She managed her career—or her dates, rather—like she did everything else in her life: with spontaneity and chaos. I didn't ask her a lot of details about what she did. I just hoped and prayed every day that she would come around and decide to do something different with her life. She was a beautiful, smart girl. Why waste all of that?

Catie was quiet for a few seconds too long. Then she said, "I have the utmost respect for you, my dear." The sincerity in her voice made me smile. "I called because I wanted to ask you about your school."

"What about it?" I said.

"Do you know what it would take for me to get back in?"

"Not really," I said, "but I can find out. Why do you need to know?"

"Because I'm thinking about going back to school," she said, sounding exasperated with me.

A lump formed in my throat, and my eyes filled with tears. I couldn't say anything, so I just remained quiet.

"Call me when you finish crying," she said. "Bye, crybaby!"

"I'm not crying."

"Whatever, Ny. Get me the info, and call me tonight. I have a date at eight, but after that I'm free. Can you drive me?"

That's what she was really calling for.

I didn't like driving Catie on her "dates." I didn't even like for her to go. In your wildest dreams, you just never think that one of your best friends will become a prostitute. We had some of the worst fights over her chosen profession, and I finally decided to stop fighting her about it. When she first started, I thought it was just a phase. I figured she was trying to find a way to deal with her parents' deaths. I wasn't happy with what she did, but she was my best friend and I loved her. Whenever she went out, she had this guy named Sam drive her. But when Sam got in a car accident a few months ago, Catie started having a hard time finding someone else to drive her to dates.

"Catie, what am I gonna do if something happens?" I asked.

"You're gonna help me, that's what you're gonna do," she said, matter-of-factly.

"Help you how?"

"Trust me, if I need help, you'll figure out what to do."

I knew better than to ask her any more questions over the phone.

"Okay," I said hesitantly. "You want me to meet you at your house? I can be there by four-thirty."

"I won't be ready until about six. I'm getting my highlights touched up today. Why don't you just meet me at Jazzie's?"

"Okay," I agreed.

"Good. You need something done to that hair anyway!"

"I'll see you there," I said.

"Good." With that, Catie hung up on me for the billionth time. She never said goodbye.

So I called her back.

"Hello?"

"You didn't say 'bye,'" I said.

"We don't say 'bye' in my culture," she said and hung up again.

I laughed to myself.

A moment later, Irwin Klein, the sociology professor, walked into the office with a big smile on his face. He was in his early forties, single, and very handsome. He looked like an older version of the actor Paul Walker. I liked him because he was always pleasant. No matter how crazy it got in the office, he smiled and stayed calm. He didn't have any children, but he had two dogs that he treated just like kids. Despite his good looks, it was obvious that his wardrobe was at the very bottom of his list of priorities. He wore the same jeans almost every day and the same shirt almost every other day. I once heard him tell someone on the phone that he owned one suit, which he had bought ten years before. He was nice to chat with, but I think he had a touch of adult attention-deficit disorder. Whenever he came to my desk to talk with me, he'd always pick something up and start fiddling with it.

The students were crazy about him. He had more student appointments than the other faculty members combined. Whenever I summarized his student evaluations, most of them were rave reviews.

"How are you today, Goode?" he asked as cheerfully as anyone possibly could.

"I'm fine, Professor. How are you?"

"I'm great. I just picked up my dogs from their annual physical."

"Is everything okay?"

"Everything's fine, and they were on their best behavior. I'm gonna take them out for a long walk after work today."

I smiled but went on with my work, not daring to ask any questions. If I showed an inkling of interest in those canines, he would have talked to me for twenty minutes. I didn't have even one minute to spare for dog talk—not today, anyway.

When he was gone, I cleared my inbox the best I could. I am generally a neat person, and my work space reflected it. I had everything in neat piles—one for responses I was waiting for from the professors, another for stuff that needed to be filed, and a third for callbacks I needed to make. Behind my desk, I kept a stack of things I didn't want to deal with and some stuff that needed to be signed and mailed out. I could work in clutter for a little while, but I started to lose my concentration if my work space stayed muddled for too long. I think I got that from Mom, who claimed to be allergic to clutter and mess. She liked everything neat and orderly. She dusted our blinds and wiped down the windowsills almost as often as most folks wash their dishes. I think she would have dusted the roof if she could have gotten up there. The fact that Mom and I were at least alike in that area gave me some comfort.

After three o'clock, the traffic in the office died down, so that was a good time to get work done. Professor Jeffrey Alexander had six phone messages waiting for him. When I put them in his mailbox, I realized he hadn't been in all day, so I sent him a short e-mail, telling him which things seemed urgent.

When I shut down my desk for the day at five, Professor Klein was still in his office, with his door closed, so I sent him a quick e-mail, telling him I was going.

I met Catie at Jazzie's, and the hair appointment took only two hours of my life. I didn't spend a moment of it waiting around. When it was time to leave, Catie paid for both of our fabulous hairdos and gave her hairdresser a tip.

Catie had extreme mood swings, maybe even multiple personalities. She could be happy and upbeat one minute, but down and depressed the next. When we pulled into the garage of the luxury, high-rise condominiums that Catie lived in, the attendant helped her out of the car. She didn't speak or thank the gentleman, or even look at him. That was certainly a clue that she was in one of her darker moods. I let myself out of the car and met her at the elevator. She lived on the thirtieth floor of her building.

Each floor past the twenty-fifth had its own key, so the elevator let us out directly into her condo. Without a word, she went straight to her bedroom and closed the door.

Catie's condo was really nice. It looked like it could be featured in a magazine. It originally had three bedrooms, but she had converted one into an office and another into a workout room. There were three bathrooms, a laundry room, a formal dining room, and a gourmet kitchen. The girl couldn't make noodles, but she still insisted on having a gourmet kitchen.

I sat on her brown leather couch, looking through her photo albums. She always had new pictures from the parties she went to. I was still impressed by some of the people she had met.

She finally walked out of the bedroom, wearing tight, red-leather pants, a red-sequined halter, and a short, red mink. She was holding her shoes in her hands, and when I saw how high the heels were, I knew why.

"How many inches are those shoes?"

"Six."

A pair of silver drop earrings had taken the place of her diamond hoops, because she never wore her best jewelry to appointments. She smelled like flowers, had on too much blush, and was wearing way-too-long fake lashes.

"Ready?" she asked. Her expression was blank, but there was irritation in her voice.

We had fought about her work far too many times. She knew I thought she was letting all her potential go to waste.

I didn't want to go with her, but I didn't want to leave her stranded, either. Anything could happen to her. I loved Catie, but I hated what she did. I felt like she had given up. Somehow, she had convinced herself that no one cared about her—except her.

"Catie, you know you don't have to do this," I said cautiously.

"Do what?"

"Live like this."

She looked around her condo and spread her arms.

"Like a queen, you mean? I don't have to live like a queen?"

"Catie, you know what I mean. This is not you. You're too good for this," I said, walking closer to her.

"You've always had it easy, Ny," she said. "You don't know what survival is about."

"Maybe I don't know what it's like to live in foster home after foster home. But I do know what it's like to care about someone. You have people who care about you," I said. "This life is not for you."

I knew for sure that Catie was not raised to live this kind of life, because I knew her parents. Catie originally came from Fresno, and moved to the Bay Area to live with foster parents when she was a little girl. She was biracial, but she would never tell us what the other race was.

She had been sexually abused and was moved in and out of foster homes until the Johnsons adopted her when she was seven. When Catie moved in with the Johnsons, she finally got some stability. The Johnsons lived a few houses down from us, across the street. They were nice people. Before Catie came around, Mrs. Johnson used to talk to Mom about having kids, but she couldn't get pregnant. Over the years, they had fostered more than a dozen kids. They got on a waiting list for an infant. While they were waiting, the lady at the adoption agency asked if they would consider foster parenting Catie for a few months. The Johnsons agreed to take her, and Mrs. Johnson told Mom they knew Catie was going to be their child from the moment they saw her—said that Catie was sent to them from God.

There was adjustment when Catie moved in. She had been abused and neglected so much that she didn't trust anybody. She also didn't like to clean, do homework, or go to church. The

Johnsons had a hard time getting her to be respectful. They went to private counseling and church counseling, but Catie was defiant. Nevertheless, they were eternally patient.

Catie tested their boundaries to the fullest. She ran away from home one time when she was ten, and the Johnsons didn't know what to do. Finally, the police found Catie up north somewhere. She had apparently gotten on a Greyhound bus and was on her way to Reno. When they found her, she claimed that the Johnsons were trying to force religion on her.

The social services worker suggested to the Johnsons that it might be better if Catie was placed in another home. But her parents persuaded the worker to give them another chance. In an attempt to get Catie to settle down, they took privileges away from her and continued to make her go to church. Mom used to force me to go over and try to play with her, but Catie was downright mean. Whenever I said anything to her, she just sat there with her arms folded and stared me down without saying a word. Finally, I told Mom I wasn't going back, and I didn't. At least, not for a long time.

Eventually, Catie warmed up to Mrs. Johnson; but she still had issues with Mr. Johnson, as she seemed to have with all men at the time. The Johnsons were very patient, and Mr. Johnson was cautious in dealing with her. It took a while, and there were plenty of times when Mrs. Johnson came to our house in tears. Mom worried about them out loud. She didn't know if the Johnsons were tough enough to handle Catie. Her parents reasoned that she would be okay with prayer, love, and a churchgoing home. After eight or nine months, everything came together, and Catie became closer with Mr. Johnson than she was with Mrs. Johnson.

After that, life was good for them. They went on vacations, Catie's grades improved, and they were genuinely a happy family. When Catie was eighteen, the Johnsons were killed in a car accident. I didn't think Catie was going to make it through that time. Sophie and I couldn't get her to leave the house at first. She barely made it to the funeral, and everybody wondered what would become of her.

She would talk to me about missing her parents, but she didn't cry much. The Johnsons had left her their four-bedroom house, three insurance policies worth over three hundred and fifty thousand dollars, and a Mercedes-Benz coupe. My parents helped her to sell the house and put the money in a trust. Catie moved in with us for about a month; during that time she was accepted into several colleges, but she opted for the University of Santa Cruz.

Mom was excited. She helped Catie get all of her financial aid paperwork filled out and found grants and scholarships to pay for Catie's education. Mom paid for most of Catie's other expenses, because she didn't want Catie to get accustomed to spending the money the Johnsons had left her. Mom's biggest disappointment came when Catie dropped out of school after one semester. We couldn't figure out what had happened, because Catie had gotten A's in every class. She told Mom that school just wasn't for her, and she wasn't going back. Shortly after that, Andrew died, and Mom wasn't able to keep up with Catie anymore. Mom would not be happy if she knew Catie's current situation.

"Look," Catie said, pointing a manicured finger at me. "I have a date in forty minutes, and you agreed to drive me. Can you just do that, please?" She blinked her eyes a few times, looking as if she wanted to cry.

I didn't pry. Keeping my word, I drove her to the appointment, which was somewhere in San Bruno, north of the airport. We just stayed quiet. I don't know what she was thinking, but I didn't want to do small talk, and I didn't want to get into a serious conversation, so I just kept my mouth shut.

When we pulled up in front of a huge house with beautiful landscaping and a red sports car parked in the driveway, Catie added some lip gloss, sighed, and got out. I watched her clop up to the front door in her six-inch red sandals. When the door opened, she quickly disappeared inside.

It didn't really make sense for me to be driving her. I wondered what would happen if she came running out and needed my help. What if I couldn't get the car started fast enough? Or what if the man came after me? Also, it was just irritating as hell, sitting in that car and knowing what she was doing inside. Of course, leaving wasn't an option, and I had forgotten to bring along something to read.

I tried to call Sophie, but she didn't answer. This was the third time that week that I had tried to reach her but didn't get through. I checked my voicemail and played a card game on my cell phone. I must have dozed off, because I woke up to knocking on the window.

"Open the door!" Catie growled, irritably.

That was fast! Or was it? How long had I been asleep?

When she got in, she threw her shoes into the back seat and stared straight ahead. I wanted to know what had happened, but she seemed so moody. When I asked if she wanted something to eat, she ignored me. When I asked her how to get back to the freeway, she pointed.

"What happened in there, Catie?" I asked her as we headed toward the freeway entrance.

She didn't say anything.

"Catie?"

"He wanted Greek, and I said no," she finally said in a nonchalant tone.

"Why?"

"Because I don't do that."

"I thought you did everything."

"Well, I don't!" she yelled.

I looked over at her sharply. She had asked me to drive her out here, had ignored me almost the whole way down, had an attitude on the way back, and now she was yelling at me. I wasn't going to keep putting up with that.

"Contrary to what you and anybody else might think about me," she said, "I do have rules and I do *not* do everything. Okay?"

That did it!

"Catie!" I snapped. "I drove you out here. You know I don't like doing this, but I did it because I'm your friend and because you asked me to. You acted crappy all the way down here. I don't have to be here, and I don't appreciate you talking to me like that. All I've ever been is a friend to you, and when you get in these moods, you take your frustrations out on me. I don't care if that man in there wanted you to be Greek, Iranian, or French. You don't get to take that problem out on me."

"Are you kidding me?" she asked.

"What?" I asked, irritated.

"Greek is a *position*, Anaya, not a nationality."

Who the hell knew that?

"Well, whatever. I don't know about all that. Why are you so mad? And why are you leaving so early?"

"I'm mad because he's one of my regulars. That was four thousand dollars." She smacked her teeth like a little kid. She always had been a pouter.

"Well, it just wasn't meant to be," I said dryly.

Did she say four thousand dollars?

"Catie, do you get paid by the hour?"

I knew it was off-subject, but I was curious.

"What?" she shrieked.

"Do you get paid by the hour or by . . . the things you do?" I sounded like I was in grade school.

"It depends," she said after a long pause.

"And do you have sex every single time you have these appointments?"

I could feel her glaring at me.

"Yes, I do," she said slowly. "I could try to make it sound all glamorous, and tell you sometimes they just wanna talk or have somebody keep them company, but that's not true. I deal with men who have people around them who listen all damn day to what they have to say. They don't want that. They don't want conversation. They don't need companionship. They have wives, kids, and employees for that. They want sex, Ny! Every time I see them, they wanna have sex with me, in one way or another. They wanna fondle me. They wanna kiss me. They want me to be their whore. Sometimes they want me to be their mama. Hell, one wanted me to be his damn third-grade teacher."

I held up my hand. "Too much information, Catie."

"Well, *you* asked," she said, and pushed her seat far back.

We were quiet the rest of the way home.

Catie showered as soon as we got to her apartment. I sat in the living room, looking at some pictures she had on the table. She was on a beach somewhere, looking gorgeous. There was a whole pile of pictures, but they were all of her. I wondered who had taken them. In contrast to the photos, she finally came into the living room in sweats and a tank top, with her wet hair in a high ponytail, looking exactly like she did when we were in high school.

"Anaya," she said, handing me two hundred-dollar bills and a fifty, "thank you for driving me tonight."

"No big," I said, taking the money.

"No, it is a big deal. It's a big deal to you, and it's a big deal to me. I know how you feel about this. Thank you for putting that to the side, to be there for me. You're the only person I know who cares about me like that. Everybody else only comes around because they need something from me. People always got their hands out for something. You aren't like that. You never have been. You're a good girl, Ny. I've never met anybody like you. I know I don't say this much, but I'm glad we're friends."

This was a rare moment for Catie. She was a lot of things, but hardly ever vulnerable. I knew it was hard for her to say all this, so I didn't interrupt. I just let her talk.

Finally, after she was quiet for a while, I asked, "Why do you wanna go back to school?"

"I'm tired, girl. Tired of being used. Tired of getting screwed. Tired of being tired." She got quiet again.

"So, what do you wanna do?"

"I don't know. Event planning maybe? I could open up a small office downtown once I build up a clientele. But I wanna do it right. I don't wanna have to hire a bunch of people to do stuff for me. I wanna know how to do it myself. But first I've gotta finish my education. It would mean a lot to Mama and Pop."

This was only the second or third time I ever heard her mention them. And as she did, her eyes filled with tears. When she stood to go into the kitchen, I gave her a hug.

"I'll call you tomorrow," I said.

"Okay," she said, hugging me back.

"Love you," I said, stepping into the elevator.

She didn't respond.

THREE

Sometimes I went to the faculty offices after hours to study. The offices had only recently closed for the day, so the lights were still on. I made a cup of coffee and set up my books. I studied for only five minutes before I started thinking about Catie.

School would be a big change for Catie, in a good way. For the past few years, she partied with celebrities and shopped in places that most folks can only dream of. Living the life of a student would almost make her average again. I didn't know how she would handle that. My heart ached for my friend. When I heard my tears hit the textbook, I didn't bother to wipe them away.

"Anaya?"

I almost jumped out of my skin.

"Hi, Professor Alexander," I said, absent-mindedly wiping my face with the back of my hand. "I didn't realize anyone else was here. I'm just here studying for my microeconomics class."

He gave me a funny look.

"That's fine. I thought everyone was gone already. I'm gonna step out for a bit. I will be back."

"Okay," I said.

"Get back to the books," he smiled, then walked away.

"Thanks," I said. I was worried that he had seen me crying. After studying for about an hour, I got restless and wandered into his office. He still hadn't gotten back.

He was apparently very busy, because his office looked as if he had slept there. Disheveled papers littered his desk, and there was a pair of shoes in the corner by the couch. Instinctively, I started to clean up the mess. As I sorted through the papers, I found all of the graded student assignments and piled them together. All of his office-related memos and documents went into another pile, and all of his assignments in progress and ungraded papers went into two separate piles. As I cleaned the desk, a woman and a small child stared at me with big smiles from a picture frame on the wall. Aside from the shoes and a pair of socks, his office was now tidy. I put the shoes under his desk and placed the socks in the desk's bottom drawer.

"Is everything okay, Anaya?" Professor Alexander asked, walking into his office.

I jumped. As I closed the drawer, I slammed my finger. I searched my brain for words, but it was all I could do to mask the sharp pain in my finger.

"I straightened up your office a little bit." I moved toward the door. My finger still throbbed.

He looked around the room, back at me, and then at his desk drawer.

"You had some socks over in the corner," I said, still embarrassed. "I put them in the desk drawer."

He didn't say anything.

"I'm sorry," I stammered. "I came to take a break from studying, and when I came in here, it looked a little . . . well, it looked like you had been busy. I know you don't normally keep your office like that . . . I mean, messy . . . so I tried to straighten it up a bit."

"Thank you for straightening the place up for me," he said. "Believe it or not, I'm normally a pretty neat person."

He smiled, but he looked tired. He put his briefcase on a chair and sat down at his desk.

"Did you get the e-mail I sent about helping me with that assignment?" he asked.

"Yes, I got it."

"And?"

"I'll look it over and get back to you by Friday. Is that too late? Professor Klein has me working on a project. I should be finished with it by Friday."

"That'll be fine. There's no rush, so if you have other things going on, I understand. I know the university fair is coming up, and I'm sure the Young Dems want to get a booth prepared."

How does he know I'm a member of the Young Democrats?

I looked at him to see if I could find the answer in his face; nothing.

"You're right," I said. "We want to get a booth set up, but we haven't been able to get approval yet. The Student Services office in charge of the fair is trying to limit the booths to on-campus organizations."

"Oh, really? Is that a new policy?"

"I don't know, but it sure sucks."

He smiled. I did, too.

"Well, I guess it's always good to be passionate about something," he said, looking down at his desk. "Anyway, I have to get some work done, so—"

"Right. Me, too. See ya."

I turned around and almost tripped over a box of files.

He smiled. I didn't.

I straightened up and got out of there as gracefully and as quickly as I could.

The next morning when I got to work, I continued Professor Klein's project. As absorbing as the work was, it was not hard to notice that the cute mail-delivery guy had breezed into the faculty offices as cheerful as ever. He was always singing or humming. I don't think I ever saw him in a down mood. I couldn't figure out why it irritated me a little that he was so happy all the time. You'd think I'd be more appreciative of his appearances; after all, he was the cutest guy who ever came into that office, with great biceps and a Colgate smile. I'd never seen him anywhere around campus and never had him in a class, so I figured he was a freshman. I was always polite to him, but we never really talked. I didn't even know his name. He was one of those people who smiled so much that he looked like a different person when he wasn't smiling.

After leaving his cart at the door, he brought the mail over to my desk.

"Good morning," he said.

"Good morning," I responded. "How are you?"

He smelled like cinnamon.

"Good. You?"

"I'm good."

My tone was formal, but my smile was warm. At least, I hoped it was.

"So, do you go to school here?" he asked. "Or you just work here?"

"Both."

"Me, too. What year are you?"

"I hope this is my last year. How 'bout you?"

He was still beaming, but the smile was not so broad anymore.

"This is my first year here," he said. "I transferred from a junior college in the valley, so technically I'm a sophomore."

"Oh. What's your major?"

"Psychology."

Now I was curious.

"Really? What do you plan to do with your degree?"

"Run group homes."

"Oh."

"Not just any group homes. Ones that help prepare young men for life and for success. I don't want to do it for the money only. A lot of people open group homes with a vision, and then they end up losing the vision and focusing on profit, instead." When he spoke, his hands carved the air, accenting his words, and his eyes lit up. "What's your major?" he asked.

"Same as yours," I said. "Psychology."

"Interesting," he said. "I guess I'll be seeing you in some classes, then."

"Probably not. I've already taken most of my required courses."

"I'm gonna turn your question around on you. What do you plan to do with *your* degree?" he asked.

He seemed genuinely interested, but I was at work and didn't want the conversation to get too personal. Just then, Professor Alexander walked by.

"Well," I said to the mail clerk in a more hushed tone, "I had thought about employment therapy and counseling. But I'm not so sure anymore. It seems like the closer I get to finishing, the less sure I become about what I wanna do." I was surprised at how honest and open I was being with him.

"Okay, wow," he said. "That's good." He gave me another one of his patented smiles. "Is it cool working in this office?" he asked. "I actually applied for a position here recently, but I heard somebody beat me to it."

I frowned. "Yeah," I said, "we just recently got somebody to work in the afternoons. It's okay working here. Not a lot of stress, and the professors are nice."

There were a few seconds of silence. Then he smiled, tapped the top of my desk, and turned to leave. "I'll let you get back to work," he said. "I guess I'll see you around."

"Maybe." I smiled again.

"Can I ask you a question?"

"Sure."

"What's your name?"

"Aaah, finally. That's the first question you should have asked," I said with a grin.

He smiled.

"Anaya Goode," I said, reaching out to shake his hand.

"Well, it was nice meeting you, Anaya Goode. You have a nice day."

"Are you gonna tell me your name?"

He had gotten cuter and cuter as the conversation had progressed.

"Carl."

"Just, Carl, huh? Well, it was nice meeting you, too, Carl with-no-last-name."

"See ya," he said, and left.

No lunch invitation, no last name. It had been a while since I had been on a date, and even though I wasn't looking for a boyfriend, it would have been nice to at least be *invited* on a date. I turned to look in the mirror to see if something in my teeth had precluded a potential invitation. Nothing.

"Hey!"

I looked up, and Carl was back, smiling. I didn't respond because I had a fingernail stuck between my teeth.

How embarrassing!

I quickly dropped my finger.

"Would you like to have lunch with me sometime this week, Ms. Goode?"

"That might be nice."

He walked over and handed me a piece of paper with his phone number and e-mail address written on it. He had a nice little swag in his walk.

"Holla at me, Ms. Goode," he invited.

I smiled. There's no shame in admitting that I needed a little dating action. I'm also not ashamed to say that Carl with-no-last-name might have been just what I needed to get my groove back.

This time I'm gonna be cool, I promised myself. *Just enjoy dating and have a little fun.*

I think Mom was right when she extended my therapy with Judy. I have always been an intense thinker. People often respond to something I say with "I never thought about it like that." Or,

"I hadn't thought about that at all." I certainly picked the right major. I love delving into other people's minds and thoughts and trying to figure out why they react or don't react the way they do. So I'm easily drawn into the daily problems of my friends and family. But at the same time, I am unsure of where my own life should be headed.

Because I was in my last year as a psychology major, all of my classes were related to psychology—particularly female-related issues. My favorite class had been "Women in the Workforce." Recently, we discussed the typical woman who worked a day job and then had to go to her "home job." I was sure that I didn't want to get stuck in that trap.

Through the psychology department, there were lots of opportunities to train under licensed therapists. Even though getting such an internship position was highly competitive, I was sure I could get one. But I didn't apply, because those therapists were mainly helping rich married women who were bored with their housework. I didn't want to do that kind of therapy.

I wanted to do worthwhile therapy. I wanted to reach out to children who didn't understand why their moms were unable to care for them because of some addiction. I wanted to listen to young girls who had been abused or neglected and couldn't understand why they were unable to find happiness anywhere. I believe we were all put here for a purpose, and my purpose was to hear the hearts and minds of those kids no one else has time to listen to. Talking is not therapy. Being *heard* is therapy.

I went to the student lounge for lunch. Normally, I brought food to the office, but every once in a while I liked to sit in the lounge and watch the other students. Sitting down at one of the tables that faced a TV set, I watched music videos as I ate my salad.

Wanting to get a little more comfortable, I decided to go into the faculty lounge, which was right next door. It wasn't officially open to students, but some of us who worked in the faculty offices had a key. I was one of the lucky few.

"Hi, Anaya!" a familiar voice greeted me.

"Hey, Professor Alexander," I replied. "I never see you in here."

"Well, I'm normally too busy for lunch, but today I needed a little something to keep me going, and I had to get out of that office. I come here every once in a while, myself. How's microeconomics going?"

"It's going," I groaned. I didn't like talking about subjects that were hard for me. "It will be behind me soon, though. The semester's almost over. I could use a break."

"Yeah, I hear you," he said, sitting down across from me. "I definitely need a break, too. A long one, actually."

"Can I ask you a question?"

"Of course," he said with a warm smile.

"How do you find time to teach *and* practice law?"

"Teaching is my passion," he said. "I started out as an adjunct and really enjoyed it. It took a lot of prep time, and a *lot* of time reading homework and exams. But I loved it. At about the same time, there were some issues with the law firm I worked for. Things didn't work out, so I left and started my own firm. The university offered me two more classes to teach, and I accepted."

By now, I was half-finished with my salad, and he hadn't even touched his soup yet. Because I was trying to figure out what I wanted to do in life, I wanted to ask him why he had decided to become a lawyer. But for some reason I couldn't ask him because I felt shy. I let him go on about grading papers and the stress of finals. He didn't say much about his work at his firm, and I wondered if he enjoyed teaching law more than practicing it.

"I'm boring you, aren't I?" he suddenly said, looking embarrassed.

"No, you're not," I said. "I like listening to people talk."

He gave me a strange look. Then he said with a laugh, "I guess that's your nice way of saying I'm talking too much."

"No, I just meant I'm interested in you . . . I mean, I'm interested in what you are saying."

You are a bumbling idiot, Anaya.

He looked at something behind me, and I followed his glance. Carl had just walked into the lounge.

"Hey, you," he called to me.

"Hey, yourself," I responded with a smile.

"How's it going, Professor Alexander?" he asked.

"I'm hanging in there, Carl. How about yourself?"

"I'm good," he said, still looking at me.

"What are you doing in here, Carl?" I asked.

"Oh, I come in here sometimes. I have keys to all the rooms in this building, so I come here to chill or even study. Staff is okay with it . . . right, Professor?"

Carl hadn't taken his eyes off me since he came in the room.

"That's right, Carl. Well, I can see it's time for me to go. I'll see you back at the office, Anaya."

"Later, Professor," Carl said.

"Bye," I said.

When Professor Alexander left, Carl continued staring at me.

"What?" I asked.

"Why don't you have a boyfriend?"

"What?"

"You heard me. Why don't you have a boyfriend?"

"How do you know I don't?"

"*Do* you have a boyfriend?"

Slick.

"No, I don't."

"Can I be your boyfriend?"

Wow.

"How about we start with that lunch?" I said.

"I'd rather start with being your boyfriend, but I'll settle for lunch. What do you do for fun, Ms. Goode?"

"Fun? What's that?" I laughed.

We ended up talking for half an hour. His smile had grown on me, and I was enjoying his company.

"Well," I said, "I do have to get back to work, you know."

"Yeah, I gotta get outta here, too," he said.

We stood up at the same time and found ourselves facing each other up close.

"It was nice talking to you, Anaya Goode," he said with that famous smile.

"It was nice talking to you, too, Carl with-no-last-name."

For a few seconds, we just stood there. It was awkward, but neither of us moved. Finally, I picked up my bag, hoisted it to my shoulder, and walked away.

"I'm gonna call you so we can have that lunch," he said.

"You don't have my number."

"Well, can you call me, then? You have mine."

"I'll think about it," I said over my shoulder.

FOUR

"I don't know why Merle can never make it anywhere on time," Mom fussed. I was peeling sweet potatoes, and she was making cornbread dressing. Aunt Marie had changed her name years ago, but Mom always called her "Merle" anyway.

"I should have just asked her to bring plates and napkins again," Mom continued.

For as long as I can remember, Aunt Marie's contributions to the family dinners had been chips, soft drinks, or utensils. This was going to be the first time she actually prepared a dish.

"Ny," Mom fussed, "get your Aunt Merle on the phone. By the time she gets here, cabbage will be out of season."

"I didn't know cabbage had a season," I said, smiling at her.

"Well, that shows how much you know. Call her cell phone." Mom was clearly irritated now. "Tell her to get here, so we can eat. Riley will be here soon." Mom meant their younger brother, who was coming with a date.

Before I could call Aunt Marie, she walked into the kitchen.

"Well, there you are!" Mom exclaimed.

"Oh hush, Anita," Aunt Marie said. "Hi, Anaya, sweetheart," she said in her usual formal tone.

"Hi, Auntie Marie," I said, looking at the covered dish. "Smells good."

"Well, thank you, dear," she responded, as her two teens, Amber and Adam, followed behind her.

"Hey, Amber!" I said. She gave me a quick hug before heading into the living room, where Roscoe was at his post in front of the TV set.

"What's up, Adam?" I said to Adam.

"I'm just hangin', Anaya. What's up with you?"

He gave me a fist bump and a huge grin. In his baggy jeans, oversized red t-shirt, and red sweatband, he looked much older than his fourteen years.

"What's hangin', Adam," said Aunt Marie in a dour tone, "are those huge pants. Will you pull them up, please? And go get the chocolate cake out of the car."

"What took you so long, Merle?" Mom barked. "That's why I don't ask you to bring anything, because you are always late. You're gonna be late to your own funeral."

"I'm doing fine, Anita. And yourself?"

Aunt Marie gave Mom a peck on the cheek before Mom had time to move away. When Aunt Marie saw Aunt Deb was already at the party, she shrieked and gave her a big hug.

"Auntie Deb! It's so good to see you! How was Palm Springs?"

"There are some great opportunities for financial growth out there, sweetheart," Aunt Deb said, giving Aunt Marie a big hug.

"Really?"

"Oh, yes. I'm gonna start investing in commercial real estate."

"Commercial real estate?"

"Definitely. Especially because financial independence is in my chart this year. I'm gonna invest wisely, and the Creator will provide."

"You sure believe in them stars, Aunt Deb, don't you?" Mom said over the mixer, while preparing her sweet potato pies.

"I sure do. The stars have never failed me, Anita."

Aunt Deb, the family matriarch, was Mom's favorite. She didn't have any children of her own, and she had always lived out of a suitcase with an astrology book in one hand and a candle or incense in the other. When we were kids, I used to joke to Ava that

Aunt Deb was a witch. She always wore flowing dark dresses, and her wiry hair scared us. But she was a sweet lady, and although she and Mom were so different, they got along beautifully—which was rare, because my mom hardly got along well with anyone.

"I told you six thirty, Merle," Mom continued to argue. "We were gonna eat at six thirty. Didn't I say that? Six thirty! And here you come pulling up at a quarter to eight. What's that perfume you're wearing?"

"You like?" Aunt Marie asked with a big grin.

"It's okay. What is it?"

"I'll take the name of this perfume to my grave," Aunt Marie teased.

"Yeah, well, take it, then," Mom said. "And take that dress you're wearing, too. Where's Allen?" Mom asked, referring to Aunt Marie's husband.

"He's running an errand. He'll be here shortly. And this dress is a Stella McCartney, thank you very much."

Aunt Marie twirled in a circle to show off the dress that hugged her figure.

Mom turned up her nose at Marie's snootiness, and Marie turned up her nose at Mom's crassness. Their personalities couldn't have been more different. The similarities came in their physical appearance only. They both had wide hips and big butts. Mom was thicker and curvier by about four sizes because Marie worked out religiously. But although one was thinner, their shapes were basically the same. They also had the same big, brown eyes, brown hair, and (originally) the same nose.

Aunt Deb chuckled at the two of them going at each other. I was used to it, so it wasn't so funny to me.

"Hey, Auntie Nita," Adam said as he walked back into the kitchen and gave Mom a big hug. Mom hugged him, too, and gave him a big kiss on the cheek.

"Hey, boy! Where you been?" she asked, rubbing his head.

"I've been going to school and just chillin'," he said.

"Chillin', huh? Yeah, okay. Chillin' is fine, but you make sure you call your Auntie sometimes. You hear me? You know your mama won't let you and Amber come around family like she should."

Aunt Marie made a face, but she didn't say anything.

"Yeah, I hear you, Auntie," Adam said. "Did you make greens? I've been dying to get some of your greens!" He rubbed his hands together.

"I sure did. I have some right over there in that plastic container for you to take home. You know Auntie is gonna look out for her baby."

"All right!" he said with a big smile, and walked out of the kitchen.

Aunt Marie swirled over to Mom.

"Anita, why on Earth would you make greens when you knew I was bringing cabbage?"

"It doesn't matter, Merle. Whatever's left over, you can take home with you. Those kids are tired of eating Chinese takeout. Feed them some *real* food."

Aunt Marie looked thoroughly confused.

"Chinese takeout? Anita, that has *nothing* to do with the fact that you made greens when you *knew* I was bringing cabbage. You are so rude!"

"Rude? Well maybe I'm rude, but at least I'm not a prude," Mom gave her a dirty look.

"What is that supposed to mean?" Aunt Marie asked.

"You know what I mean," Mom said. "You sent my niece and nephew to that all-white school."

Aunt Marie sighed. "Not this again, Anita. What exactly is wrong with giving my kids a better life and putting them in a good school? I would love for the students at the Academy to be more diverse, but unfortunately I don't have any control over that.

What should I do, Anita? Put them in the local public school, so they can be inducted into a gang?"

"First of all," Mom said, "you don't get *inducted* into a gang—you get jumped into a gang. Get with the program, Merle, you have pre-teens in the house. Second, if you had your preference, your children wouldn't interact with any Black people besides yourself and Allen." Mom pointed her finger at Aunt Marie. "I'm surprised," Mom hissed, "that you even let them come around us."

"And I'm surprised," Aunt Marie countered, "that Roscoe has been hanging in there with you for so long. You are so closed minded and old school, Anita. We were raised in a different generation. Get over it already. You're intimidated by people who are intellectually superior to you. It's pretty sad, Anita."

Uh-oh.

"Intellectually superior? Sad?" Mom exploded. "Just because you picked up that European diction from God-knows-where doesn't make you better than me, Merle. I graduated from college, just like you, and I even went back to graduate school, which you *still* haven't done." She tossed a spoon into the sink with a clunk. "I don't know where along the way you felt like our upbringing was beneath you, and you were above us. You were embarrassed about the family nose, so you pulled a Michael Jackson. You were embarrassed about our great-grandmother's name, so you pulled a Tina Turner. You're a phony, Merle, nothing but a phony, with a phony nose and a phony name."

Aunt Marie's new nostrils flared.

"What's wrong with changing what you don't like about yourself, Anita? Who says you have to accept what life throws you and just deal with it? I always hated my nose, even when we were kids. And it was *not* the family nose." Aunt Marie gestured what its former length was like. "It was twice the size of everybody else's. You know that, because you used to tease me mercilessly about it. And the name *Merle*, Anita? *Merle?* Give me a break. I'm not walking around with that name. I've asked you a thousand times to stop calling me that. I changed my name over twenty years ago!"

"Whatever, *Merle*. I don't have time for this."

"Yeah, let it go." Aunt Deb chimed in.

"I'm over it already," Aunt Marie said.

Uncle Allen walked into the kitchen with a case of beer.

"Hey, girl!" he called to Mom. "You got it smelling *good* up in here!"

His voice boomed. Uncle Allen had the deepest bass voice I've ever heard. It was like James Earl Jones and Barry White mixed together.

"Hey, boy!" Mom said, giving him a big hug. "I wouldn't have it smelling any other way up in here."

"You make any of them greens to go, Anita?" Uncle Allen asked, rubbing his hands together exactly as his son had just done. He always tried to get as many leftovers as he could when he came over. Aunt Marie did a lot of things, but cooking was not one of them.

"You *know* it!" Mom said, and they both laughed.

Aunt Deb got up and gave Uncle Allen a long hug.

"You sure are looking good, girl," he said to her.

"Thank you, Allen. You're looking good, too. No wonder Marie's keeping herself together. She's got to."

She winked at Uncle Allen, and we all laughed.

"So, how was Palm Springs, Deb?" Uncle Allen asked. "You were just down there on business, weren't you?"

"Allen," Mom interjected, "take this macaroni salad and put it on the table for me, will you?"

I guess she didn't want to hear any more financial freedom speeches from Aunt Deb.

"Sure, I'll take it," Allen said. "I'm gonna check out that game with Roscoe while I'm at it."

"Hey, Anaya," Adam said, peeking his head in the kitchen door, "Can I hang out in your room?"

"Adam," Aunt Marie said, "don't eat any more of those cookies. We're gonna be eating dinner soon."

He just nodded.

"I don't care," I said. "Just don't make a mess in there."

Whenever he came over, Adam liked to go to my room, look at pictures from Terry Beat's parties, and use my computer. There had been two parties since the last time he had come over, so I had new photos for him. He flashed me the peace sign and walked out of the kitchen.

I heard Roscoe and Uncle Allen in the living room, laughing and talking. The two of them had no issues with each other. They were debating which sport Blacks were going to dominate next. Uncle Allen said hockey, and Roscoe said swimming.

Uncle Allen chuckled. "Black folks," he explained, "worry too much about their hair and ashy skin to be swimming all the time."

"Maybe so," said Roscoe, "but we'd rather be a little ashy and throw a hot oil treatment in our hair than be skating on that damn ice. You know we don't like to be cold, man!"

Ava walked into the kitchen. She walked over and gave Mom and Aunt Marie a kiss.

"Hi, Mom. Hello, Aunt Marie. It's been a long time since I've seen you."

"Well, hello, Ava," Aunt Marie said. "How have you been? You sure are growing up."

Aunt Marie still greeted Ava as if she were twelve years old.

"I'm good, Aunt Marie, the toils of life will not defeat me," Ava replied.

I rolled my eyes.

"Mom, you need help with anything?" Ava asked.

"No, thank you, baby. Anaya's been helping me out. How was Bible study?"

"It was enlightening. When will dinner be ready? Are you making greens?"

Aunt Marie frowned. "Your mom claimed that dinner was ready over an hour ago," she said, "and everybody was just waiting for me. But the funny thing is, I'm standing right here, and she's still putting cheese on the macaroni."

"The macaroni and cheese is done," Mom announced. "I'm just adding Velveeta for extra flavor. It'll take three minutes. But you don't know much about extra flavor, do you, Merle? All that bland food you cook. Do you still season your meals with only salt and pepper?"

Everybody laughed except Ava, who apparently didn't think it was very funny. She was wearing nothing noticeable—a long, black skirt; black turtleneck; and black-and-white Pumas. No makeup or earrings, and her hair was piled on top of her head in a tight ponytail. But dare I say that my sister still looked beautiful?

"How have you been, Ava?" Aunt Deb asked. Aunt Deb was sitting at the small table near the door, so Ava hadn't seen her yet. Or, at least, Ava *acted* as if she hadn't seen Aunt Deb.

Ava turned to Deb with a pause that was just a few seconds too long.

Rude!

"I'm good, Aunt Deb," she responded. It was no secret that Ava disapproved of Aunt Deb's belief in astrology. She called it sacrilege.

"Let me know when the grub's ready, Mom," Ava said. "Oh, hi, Ny," she said my way, pretending she had just noticed that I was in the room.

She left without waiting for my response.

Ava had been doing some bizarre things since joining her new church. To begin with, she was always protesting something. It was strange to me.

Ava and I weren't close, but we were cordial, and I figured that was as good as it was ever going to be between us. Whenever I talked to her for more than five minutes, I had to fight the urge to pin her down and pluck her eyebrows. I loved her, but sometimes I wished she were a little more normal. She was a great student and never got in any trouble, but there was no doubt that she was a head case.

Sometimes it was hard to believe we were related. I liked clothes, music, shopping, and hanging out with my friends. Ava never shopped, she only wore black, and she went to prayer meetings for fun. I accepted her, though. We were definitely different, and sometimes I wished we were closer and had been able to work together through losing our brother, Andrew.

"Is that girl okay, Anita?" Aunt Deb asked Mom.

Aunt Marie looked over at me, and then at Aunt Deb.

"Yeah, she's fine," Mom said. "Just on the quiet side. Why do you ask?"

This was the first time I had ever seen Mom play dumb.

"Her rising sign is Venus, Anita. It's awfully strange she takes so little care in her appearance."

"So?" Mom asked, putting her hands on her hips.

"People born under her sign tend to be weak-willed and easily led," Deb said in a hushed voice. "Doesn't that worry you?"

"What are you trying to say, Deborah?"

"I'm not trying to say anything. I'm saying you should keep a closer eye on that girl and find out what kind of church she's going to. Even the strongest people can get caught up with the wrong thing."

"Deborah, my child is not a part of some cult, if that's what you're thinking. I taught my kids to be strong. Ava loves God. She's not a part of some cult. You hear me?" Mom was shaking a spatula and raising her voice.

"Who said anything about a cult?" Deb asked.

The doorbell rang, and both Mom and Aunt Deb looked at me to get it.

Shoot!

I didn't want to miss anything, so I ran to the door as fast as I could. It was my Uncle Riley and some super-tall woman I had never seen before. I thought it was going to be Wanda, who had been his girlfriend for the past three years, but this woman was definitely not Wanda.

"Hey, Ny! How you doing, baby?"

"Hey, Uncle Riley!"

I gave him a quick hug and held my breath, because if I didn't, the Cool Water cologne would have made me faint. When I stepped back to let him into the house, he let his friend go first. It was nice to see that Uncle Riley had picked up manners from somewhere.

Aunt Marie came out of the kitchen and gave Riley a big hug.

He eyed Aunt Marie up and down, saying, "Hey, girl, you looking *good!*"

She put her hands on her hips and gave him a quick pose. "Well," she said, "I certainly can't complain, Riley." She looked up at Riley's date.

"Marie, this is my friend, Troy. Troy, this is my sister, Marie."

"It's a pleasure," Aunt Marie said, extending her hand.

"You, too," Troy said, offering a limp hand that looked more like a dead fish. Then Troy leaned into Uncle Riley, who put his arm protectively around her waist.

I didn't know what was more shocking—the fact that Troy was an entire head taller than my uncle, or that she sounded like Darth Vader.

"You two make yourselves comfortable," Aunt Marie said, pointing to the living room. "Dinner will be ready shortly."

Uncle Riley and Troy went into the living room, where Roscoe and Uncle Allen were watching TV.

Uncle Riley introduced Troy to Uncle Allen and Roscoe, while Aunt Marie and I exchanged curious looks. Aunt Marie was different from Mom. She didn't judge people—not with her mouth, at least. But one of her looks was worth a thousand words. Before I could speak or laugh, Mom came out of the kitchen.

"I *thought* I smelled Cool Water cologne," Mom said in her loud voice, walking to the living room. "What's going on, baby boy?" She gave Uncle Riley a hug.

"Hey, Anita, how you doing, girl?"

Uncle Riley was closer in some ways to Mom than he was to Aunt Marie. Whenever he had a problem, he called Mom. Whenever he needed advice, he called Mom. But whenever he needed money, he called Aunt Marie.

"Well," Mom said, "I'm doing much better now that my brother's here. And who's this pretty lady you have with you?"

Troy stood up and extended her hand.

"Anita, this is Troy. Troy, this is my other sister, Anita."

"It's nice to meet you, Troy," Mom said politely.

"Nice to meet you, too, Anita. Riley has nothing but nice things to say about you."

This was the first time Uncle Allen or Roscoe had heard Troy speak. They both stopped looking at the TV set and stared at her. Uncle Allen looked at Uncle Riley, then at Roscoe. Over his glasses, Roscoe looked Troy up and down, stopping at her feet.

When in doubt, they say, check out the feet.

"Well," Mom said when she finally recovered her own voice, "dinner will be ready shortly. Make yourself comfortable. Ny, come in here and fix Miss Troy something to drink."

No matter how old we got, Mom insisted that we call our elders "Miss" or "Mister." That is, unless they were family or close enough to be family—in which case, our family elders could be called "Uncle" or "Aunt." It was an extreme contradiction on mom's part because I'd been calling Roscoe by his first name for years. When I was ten years old, Roscoe's drinking was at its worst and it took quite a toll on my family. He and mom weren't getting along and my siblings and I were in the middle of the craziness. Roscoe had ruined countless family outings and birthday parties with his drinking and, unless absolutely necessary, I had all but stopped communicating with him. I had become so tired of all the unhappiness Roscoe's drinking caused our family that I decided to stop calling him dad. The first time I did it, he was lying on the couch drunk and throwing up. My mom asked me to get him a towel and I yelled to Andrew to get "Roscoe" a towel. I remember her shooting me a look, but she never commented. I never called him dad after that day and what surprised me the most was that neither of my parents confronted me about it. In retrospect, I imagine they felt guilty and let it continue for so long, so they couldn't go back. As time passed, I learned to deal with my anger toward Roscoe. I didn't hate him, and my anger had subsided, but there were still times when I was disappointed in him. I guess along with age comes tolerance and wisdom.

I went to the kitchen to fix Miss Troy a glass of lemonade. I wasn't in there ten seconds before Mom whispered something to Aunt Marie, but I heard every word.

"That's a *man*, Merle!"

"Shh! Anita! What's wrong with you?"

"Your brother walks into my house with a man in a jean skirt, and you have the nerve to ask what's wrong with *me*?"

"Anita Goode! You don't know Troy's a man. Besides, what would that make Riley?"

"I didn't see," Aunt Deb interjected, "but I heard, and what I heard sounded like a man!" Aunt Deb was clearly enjoying the red wine that Mom had sitting on the counter. "I'm gonna go see for myself." She stood up and wobbled out of the kitchen.

"Merle," Mom said, "stop playing games. Troy sounds like he played high school football. I don't know what's going on now, but she wasn't born a woman. And why did you let Deb get hammered? You know she doesn't know how to act when she gets that vino in her."

"Deb's an adult, Anita," Aunt Marie said with a laugh, and she walked out of the kitchen.

Mom looked at me with raised eyebrows. I held in my laughter and walked out, too.

Dinner went nicely until Aunt Marie had downed one glass of wine too many.

"Merle, you might want to slow down on that wine," Mom said.

Aunt Marie gave Mom a wicked smile as she stabbed her steak with her fork.

"No, no," Aunt Deb said out of nowhere. "I think we need *more* wine."

"Perhaps the Goddess of grapes can provide you with some," Ava chuckled.

"Ava, watch your mouth!" Mom snapped. "Don't be disrespectful."

"I apologize," Ava said.

"Apple doesn't fall far from the tree, does it, Anita?" Aunt Marie said. Mom waved her hand and stuffed a spoonful of Aunt Marie's cabbage into her mouth.

Conversation over.

Uncle Riley whispered something in Troy's ear, and she laughed out loud.

"You are so silly, Pookie Bear," Troy said. Uncle Riley blushed. *Pookie Bear?*

The rest of dinner was largely uneventful, aside from when Troy spilled her wine in her lap and started laughing hysterically. She laughed so hard that Roscoe and Aunt Marie started laughing, too. I didn't find anything funny about it and neither did Mom, who shot Roscoe a look that clearly said so.

It turned out that Mom and Miss Troy had more in common

than anyone would have suspected. For one thing, they both loved celebrity gossip.

"Did you hear about that basketball coach who's getting stalked by his mistress?" Troy asked.

"Oh, yes!" Mom said. "I heard she went to school with one of his kids!"

"Scandalous!" Troy said.

"Oh, you two!" Aunt Marie cut in. "You can't believe everything you see in those rags. They say a lotta stuff without confirming whether it's true or not."

"Shut up, Merle!" Mom commanded.

"What? It's true. Half of those stories are made up."

"Well," Roscoe said, in between bites of greens, "I know one thing. I can't wait to get some of that peach cobbler."

The last thing Roscoe wanted to do was talk gossip at dinner. Mom knew that and broke off the banter.

"Dessert, anyone?" she asked.

Aunt Marie had made a lopsided double chocolate cake, and Mom had made the peach cobbler. Everyone opted for the cobbler, including Aunt Marie herself.

After dinner, Ava went to her room, Adam went to my room, and the rest of us went to the den with our drinks and desserts.

"That's the problem with those Hollywood types," Troy said. "They have too much going on and can't stay in a marriage."

Roscoe pursed his lips together.

"No offense, Twinkie," Uncle Riley said to Troy, "but maybe the problem is people like you, who care about other people's lives more than they care about their own."

"Amen, Riley!" Aunt Marie said, holding up a spoon filled with peach cobbler. She didn't hold her liquor any better than Aunt Deb did, and she was already beyond tipsy.

Troy looked like she wanted to cry.

She can't be that sensitive.

Uncle Riley leaned over and put his hand on hers. "I'm sorry, sugar plum, but it's true. If you keep reading what those magazines say, they'll keep turning out those stories."

"Yeah," Troy wailed, "but you don't have to embarrass me in front of your whole family!"

"I didn't mean to embarrass you, sweetie pie." Uncle Riley sounded like a mom trying to talk a toddler into getting a vaccination shot.

"Yeah, Riley," Uncle Allen said, chuckling. "Don't be so insensitive, man."

Aunt Marie looked at him hard, but he just ignored her and stuffed his mouth with more cobbler.

"I don't think it's funny, Allen," Aunt Marie said. "That's your problem, you can't seem to figure out when people are really hurting."

"Yeah, and *you* can't seem to figure out when to shut your mouth! I wasn't even talking to you, Marie. Besides, I *did* tell him she was hurting."

"Yeah, but you were joking about it."

"Hold on!" Mom said. "Everybody calm down. We were just having a harmless conversation. Miss Troy, Riley didn't mean to hurt your feelings. Just everybody calm down."

"I'm sorry," Troy said, sniffling. "It's that time of month, and I get a little emotional."

When he heard that, Uncle Allen choked on his cobbler.

"That's quite enough from you, Allen," Aunt Marie said.

"And that's quite enough from you, Merle," Mom said. "Hush, girl!"

I'm sitting with a bunch of loons.

Things calmed down a little after that, and between the gossip, grunts from Roscoe, and Troy's voice sounding like gravel, I had had enough and went up to my room.

Adam was looking through my pictures again.

"How are Aunt Marie and Uncle Allen getting along?" I asked. That was probably a dangerous question, but I asked anyway.

Adam just shrugged his shoulders. Everybody in the family knew that Aunt Marie and Uncle Allen fought like the Bloods and the Crips. It wasn't just your regular get-in-a-fight-and-make-up-the-next-day kind of thing, either. Aunt Marie and Uncle Allen had fights that lasted for days.

"Do they still fight?" I asked.

"Not like before," he said. "They hate each other, though."

I just looked at him. For a brief second, he looked angry. I didn't know what to say, but I wouldn't have been able to say anything anyway, because at that moment Aunt Marie came into my room. She was flushed and smiling, which meant that she had had too much to drink. When she walked in, she picked up some of the pictures that Adam had been looking at. She flashed one of my friend Sophie in front of my face.

"You know J.Lo?" she asked, slurring her speech and wobbling a bit.

"Mom, that's Ny's friend, Sophie," Adam said.

"Who?" she asked, blinking.

"Sophie, Mom." Adam was impatient.

"Don't you remember my friend Sophie, Aunt Marie?" I asked.

"Oh! Carmen and Terry's daughter! Wow! She sure turned out to be beautiful. Who woulda thought?"

She put the picture down and walked out of the room, never stating why she had come in, but Adam and I had already figured that out.

"Time to go," he said to me, and gave me a fist bump before heading downstairs.

My cell phone rang. When I looked at the number, I knew it was Carl. I hadn't called him, but we had exchanged text messages earlier that day.

"Hello?" I said, pretending not to know who it was.

"Hello, Anaya Goode!"

I smiled.

"How did you get my number?" I asked playfully.

"I found it on the bathroom wall. It said to call you for good conversation and a pretty smile."

I beamed.

We talked for two hours. I can't remember the last time I talked to somebody on the phone for two hours straight. He was interesting and liked to talk. We covered every topic from kissing to tithing.

"Why do you think you should give your money to a church," he asked, "when you don't know what they're gonna do with it?"

"Because that's what the Bible says for us to do. It doesn't matter what the church officials do with the money once you give it. What matters is your heart."

He didn't agree. He had issues with religion, he said. Bigger issues than I had. Finally, we ended the conversation with him inviting me to dinner. I told him I would think about it, and we got off the phone.

When I went back downstairs, everyone had gone home. Roscoe was sleeping upstairs, and Mom was still in the kitchen. I started putting the dishes away. Mom had always given us chores when we were kids. She kept a list on the refrigerator, so there wouldn't be any question about who was supposed to do what. She never let the list get outdated. Now cleaning up and helping were like second nature to me. Ava had a cleaning disability, but that's another story.

"Hey," Mom said. "You don't have to help me, honey, I got this."

But I just wanted to be in the kitchen with her and listen to her ramble about the night. She was so funny after a few drinks, especially when her sister and brother were around. She already had everything put away, just as I knew she would. The leftovers were neatly packed in containers, and she was bleaching the sink when I walked in.

"Did you enjoy dinner?" she asked me, wobbling a little to her left. I smiled.

"Do you need help, Ma?"

"No, I said I got it." She laughed a little. "I need to be able to clean my kitchen, whether I've been drinking or not."

I put the leftover containers in the fridge and cut a small piece of sweet potato pie for myself.

I shouldn't, but I want it!

"I know *you* aren't eating pie this late at night!" Mom said. "What about the carbs? What about the fat content you're always worrying about? What about you turning into a balloon?" She laughed at her own joke.

"Don't make fun of me, Mom."

"Anaya! You could gain twenty pounds and still be underweight, girl. You need to stop worrying so much about fat content and concentrate on nutritional value and exercise. You're in good shape, Ny. Don't stress yourself out by counting calories and depriving yourself of my good cooking, 'cause it ain't necessary. Besides, you're too skinny."

Her smile made me love her a lot at that moment. She was so lighthearted and free. She really liked entertaining and feeding everybody. It made her happy. She picked up a bottle of water and drank long and hard.

"So, what did you think about Uncle Riley's girlfriend, Mom?"

She laughed so hard that she almost choked on her water.

"Girl, you're crazy! I don't wanna talk about Riley's girlfriend. That boy is sick in his head for bringing her here."

"What do you think of that voice?"

"I said I don't wanna talk about her. But Allen looked good, didn't he? Lost some weight, huh?"

"Yeah. Adam said he thinks Aunt Marie and Uncle Allen hate each other."

"That's not true. Did you tell him that's not true?"

"I didn't tell him anything. I don't know how they feel about each other, Mom!"

"Well, don't get in those kinds of conversations with kids if you can't handle it. You needed to reassure him that his parents don't hate each other, and that they love him and his sister a whole lot."

Ugh! You're turning from Fun Mom to Real Mom.

"What are you two still doing in the kitchen?"

It was Ava, coming in to mix one of her protein shakes.

Why do I get chewed out for my eating habits, and Ava doesn't?

"What kind is that, Ava?" Mom asked, blinking her eyes the way her sister did a couple of hours before.

"Wheat germ and honey, Mom."

Gross!

"That doesn't sound so tasty, sweetheart. Did you have some pie?"

"No, thank you."

As she poured the gook into the blender, I was sure I was going to puke up my pie any second. She finally sat down with her mud concoction.

"How are things going, Ava?" Mom asked.

I was quiet. Sometimes I felt that my sister was a stranger.

"Things are going good, Mom. We have a new minister at the church, and he wants to start an outreach effort, so we're working to get that off the ground."

"Oh, that sounds productive. Will you guys be going door to door, ministering to people?"

"No, not that kind of effort, Mom. We're reaching out to employees of capitalist companies that support and practice research efforts that are contrary to human morality."

Is she insane?

Mom's left eyebrow rose, which made me glad. Ava was over the top, and somebody needed to say something to her.

Ask her about the minister, Mom. Ask her about the church. Does she have to give blood samples to be a member? Do they all wear black Nikes?

"Ava," Mom asked, "will you be going to these people's workplaces?"

"We sure will." She smiled in an almost sinister way.

"Isn't that a bit radical?"

Mom must be starting with the easy questions. I'll just keep quiet and let her flow.

"We *have* to be radical, Mom, to awaken the sleeping spirits of those people who work for those awful corporations. Most of them have no idea what's going on, or what kind of company they work for."

I was about to say something, but Mom put her hand on mine, so I closed my mouth.

"Ava, you're supposed to be spreading God's word, aren't you? Why would you go to a business and talk to people about the company they work for? That has nothing to do with saving souls or leading people to God."

"It has *everything* to do with leading people to God, Mom. By exposing the cruel intentions and practices of those demon corporations, we're opening the eyes of their employees to see what kind of evil they work for."

Mom put her hand up to stop Ava from talking.

This is getting scary.

"Ava, you are not allowed to go to anybody's job and inform them about anything their employers are doing. If your church wants to do community outreach in the traditional way, that's fine. I have allowed you the freedom to express yourself, and you can protest everything under the sun. But I don't see you spreading the word of God, or even practicing the forgiveness and tolerance the Bible advocates. You are *forbidden* from participating in this outreach effort. Do you hear me, girl?"

"I *will* participate in this effort, Mother. I'm sorry if you don't agree."

"*What* did you say?"

Slap her, Mom! Slap her!

"I said, I *am* participating."

"Mom said you can't," I said. "Are you going to be disobedient? Doesn't the Bible speak about obeying your parents?"

"Anaya, your nefarious attempt to make me a villain with your dogmatic views of my Christian conduct is nothing but a trick of the enemy, and I recognize it. Good night."

Did she call me a dog?

I looked around to make sure she wouldn't hit her head on anything when Mom slapped the crap out of her. But my effort was in vain, because the longer I sat there, the more I realized there wasn't going to be any slapping going on. Mom was changing. Ava kissed Mom on the cheek and walked out of the room.

"Good night, Mom," I said, leaving the room shortly after Ava.

She's letting Ava turn into a fanatic.

FIVE

My workload at the faculty office was especially heavy because the application deadline for the master's programs was approaching. I don't know why the school chose a deadline so close to finals, because it caused twice as much work as normal. Despite the constant interruptions from the new office assistant, I managed to get through the day, albeit tired and grumpy.

Earlier that morning, Professor Alexander sent me an e-mail inviting me to lunch. I was surprised, but I accepted. Turning down the boss for lunch didn't exactly seem like a good idea, and even a short time away from work was appealing.

When lunchtime rolled around, he came out of his office, and we walked over to a tiny café near campus.

"Thanks for accepting my invitation," he said as we walked.

"Oh, thank *you*. But if you plan to fire me, you could have done that by e-mail," I said jokingly.

He laughed.

"I do not plan on firing you. You don't have to worry about that. You are one of the best workers our office has had since I've been here."

"You think so?" I asked as we went through the last crosswalk.

"Really," he confirmed. I relished the well-deserved compliment. I worked my butt off in that office.

When we got to the café, we sat in a booth near the window. I ordered a Caesar salad, and he ordered a hamburger.

"Have you ever been here?" he asked.

"No, I normally bring my lunch. I'm a starving student, you know," I said with a grin.

"Ah, a starving student with a sense of humor," he replied.

The conversation was seamless. We talked about the office, our goals, law school, and family. For the briefest time, I almost forgot he was my boss.

"Can I ask you a question?" he said.

My mouth was full of chicken and lettuce, so I nodded my head.

"How do you like working in the department?"

"Honestly?"

"Preferably, yes," he said.

I chewed fast and swallowed a huge bite of chicken. "I like it enough. The pay's decent but the work isn't all that interesting."

"Have you ever thought about working off campus?"

"No," I replied, wondering where this talk was leading.

"Why not?" he pressed.

"I like the flexibility, I guess. I can schedule work around my classes and not the other way around. I like that."

"What if you found a job with all the flexibility you needed, which paid you more than you make now, plus medical benefits?"

"Well, I would take that job into serious consideration," I said, narrowing my eyes. I chuckled, and he laughed a little, too.

There was a brief lull in the conversation, and I quietly concentrated on my salad. I opened my mouth to say something but thought better of it and continued eating.

"What are you thinking?" he asked.

"You really wanna know?" I countered.

"I asked, didn't I?"

I blurted out, "Why did you ask me to lunch?"

"Because you looked hungry," he laughed. "And by the way you are chomping down that salad, it seems as if I was right."

I giggled.

"Actually," he said, "I'm looking for a case clerk for my firm, and I think you'd be a good fit. You're a hard worker and I like that."

Huh?

"So, what do you say, Anaya?"

"Um, I don't know," I stammered, taken aback by his suggestion, which seemed out of the blue. I knew nothing about law and felt ill-equipped to be anybody's case clerk.

"If you need some time," he offered, "you can get back to me when you've thought it over."

I said tentatively, "It sounds good, Professor, but I've never worked in a law office."

"You have clerical experience, and you're organized. You'll pick everything up fast."

"I don't know," I said slowly.

"Just think about it, okay?" he pursued.

"Don't I need to apply and interview, or something?" I asked suspiciously.

"So this is your interview," he obliged. "Tell me about yourself."

"Well," I said lamely, "I like volleyball, clothes, and peanut M&Ms."

"Great!" he exclaimed facetiously. "You're hired."

We finished our lunch and headed back to campus.

"Thanks again for your time," he said as we approached our building. "I'll be in deposition all week," he explained, "so I'll only be on campus for my lectures. I do have a couple of assignments for you," he winked. "I'll e-mail you the instructions. I won't see you again until the Wednesday after next, unless you'll consider having lunch with me again on Friday."

"Can I get back to you?" I asked, wanting time to think more about his job offer.

He laughed, but I was serious.

"You're funny. Okay, you get back to me with your schedule."

"I'll send you an e-mail."

"You know what?" he said. "Why don't you take my cell number and just give me a call?"

The rest of the day went fast. Our wonderfully incompetent assistant had to leave early, so, ironically, I was able to get more done. I felt good about what I had accomplished that day and headed home.

When I got home, I saw Roscoe sitting in the den with the TV blasting, and I noticed that Ava had company in the dining room. I wasn't accustomed to Ava having company. It was a pleasant surprise . . . sort of.

"Hi, everybody," I said to Ava and her two friends.

Ava smiled at me from the head of the table.

"Hi, Ny. This is Camel and Noah from the church. Guys, this is my sister, Anaya."

What kind of name is "Camel"?

"I see beauty runs in the family," Camel said.

"Thank you," I said, unaccustomed to being flattered.

Ava smiled.

"What are you guys up to?" I asked.

"Just discussing one of the greatest gifts that God gave us," Noah said.

"Oh. Life?" I ventured.

"The Earth," Ava said dramatically.

Right.

"Nice meeting you guys," I said, trying to make a fast exit.

I walked into the den where Roscoe was sitting. I hadn't seen him take a drink, but I knew he'd been drinking. We'd been dealing with his alcoholism for as long as my memory allowed me to go. I have so many memories of ruined family outings and cleaning up puke. The history of his alcoholism ran deep. He almost lost his job a couple of times, and once he had to take a long leave of absence without pay. Mom had covered all the bills during that time, and I remember her being worried about losing the house.

"Hey, Ny-Ny!" he yelled out to me as I walked in.

His face was shiny, and his eyes were red. I had mixed feelings about him. Sometimes I felt sorry for him. Other times I was angry. I simply stopped wanting to be close to him because of all the pain he caused the family. There comes a time in your life with an alcoholic when you feel like enough is enough, and you don't want to keep giving to someone who isn't giving back.

"Hey," I replied.

"How you doing in school?" he asked cheerfully. He had on a black t-shirt and black jeans. He put his legs up on the ottoman and wiggled his bare toes.

Gross!

"School's fine." My head was feeling light.

"That's great. You always were good in school. I remember that when you were in kindergarten, they wanted to advance you to first grade. Your mama wasn't having it, though. She said she didn't wanna put that kind of pressure on you. Your mama always wanted what was best for you, Ny. I always felt there was somethin' special about you."

"Right," I said, as I quickly went up to my room.

I needed some time to myself, because I had agreed to go out to dinner with Carl. I knew that Carl was a nice guy and, to be honest, my love life needed a boost. I started getting ready for my date. I totally enjoy the process of getting dolled up, no matter where I'm going. I was excited about hanging out with a guy who thought I was cute. That's what youth is about, right?

I agreed to let Carl pick me up, but told him I'd meet him at his car.

When we got to the restaurant, I was in a better mood than I'd been in for a while. Carl was the perfect gentleman. He opened doors, let me order first, and complimented my outfit.

While we examined the menus, Carl turned on the charm.

"So," he grinned, "I'm happy you finally decided to go out with me."

"I'm glad, too," I said. "This place has a good wine list."

"I didn't think I was your type," he teased, his eyes flashing.

"Oh?" I countered. "And how would you know what my type is?"

"I don't know," he said, shaking his head. "I'm a little more . . . you know . . ."

"No, I don't know," I pressed, curious. "You are a little more what?"

"Never mind," he said, turning his face to scour the Mediterranean menu. "So how do you like living with your parents?" he inquired, changing the subject.

"It's okay sometimes. Lately I've been wanting to move. When I graduate, I'm going to get a place, I think." I hadn't really thought that plan out, but it sounded good.

"Yeah, me, too," he said, looking into my eyes. "I live at my mom's. Mostly to help her out. She is always drunk. She needs somebody around the house." He went back to looking at his menu.

"That's nice of you," I said. "Where's your dad?"

"Your guess is better than mine," he huffed. "Never met the dude. I hear I look like him, though."

"Oh," was all I could think of to say.

"After dinner, I'd like to go bowling," Carl said enthusiastically. "Is that cool with you?"

"I guess it has to be," I said with a smile.

He smiled back.

When the waitress came, I ordered a glass of wine. Carl ordered a soda.

"No drink for you?" I said playfully. "I won't take advantage of you."

"Nah, I don't drink. Watching my mom struggle made me decide I would never start drinking alcohol, and I never did. Probably never will."

"Are you seeing anybody?" I boldly asked.

"You," he said simply and sincerely. I couldn't help but notice how nice he looked in jeans, a red t-shirt, and a casual black jacket.

"Anybody else?" I asked again, just to make sure.

"There is nobody else," he said, totally serious. "I like you. And when I like somebody, that's the only somebody I want to see."

"What about you?" he inquired, clearly happy that I had made this question easy for him to ask.

"What about me?" I said, bashful.

"Anyone *special*?" he asked again.

"No," I replied.

"Ah, you failed the test!" he said, gesturing with his fork. "That's where you are supposed to tell me how special I am."

We both laughed.

My phone vibrated and instinctively I checked it. It was a text message from Professor Alexander. I had texted him earlier in the week to let him know I was still considering his offer. Now, he wanted to know if I had decided. According to the text, one of his partners had a niece who was recently unemployed, and his partner wanted to offer the job to her.

As I sat there staring at my phone, Carl gave me a funny look.

"Uh oh," he said in mock tragedy.

"What?"

"I just lost you to something else. What are you thinking about?" he asked. "Ny, are you here?"

"I do have something on my mind," I said, although I had no intention of telling him what it was. I did not feel ready yet to enter into such a complicated topic with Carl.

"Do you wanna talk about it?" he urged nicely.

"Not really," I brushed him off. "It's not important . . . Listen, I'm going to the restroom." I abruptly stood up and strode off.

When I got to the restroom, I called Professor Alexander from my cell phone. I don't know what made me feel that I needed to call him at that moment from the ladies' room, leaving Carl a bit abandoned. It was a ridiculous thing to do. But sometimes I act impulsively. I got his voicemail, rather than him, so I left a message. I told him I'd accept the job, and also that I'd go to lunch with him the following Friday.

"You look nice," I remembered to mention to Carl when I returned to the table.

"Thank you," he said. "I try."

After dinner, we went bowling. Carl was a good bowler; me, not so much. I kept getting gutter balls. After bowling, we went to the marina and walked. Predictably, Carl eventually stopped walking and turned to look at me.

"I like you," he said gently, holding my hands.

"I like you, too," I replied, looking into his eyes.

He leaned in and kissed me. I kissed him back, and it felt good.

"Wow!" he said. "It was even better than I thought."

"What?" I asked.

"Kissing you."

"Oh, so you've thought about kissing me?"

"Since the moment I saw you," he said and kissed me again.

It was a wonderful date. When I got home, I plopped down on my bed and saw an appointment postcard there from Judy. I had an appointment in a few days, and boy did I have some news for her.

SIX

The next day, I was sitting in my room just after work, contemplating getting my books together to go study back at the office. Suddenly, Sophie walked into my room. Surprised to see her, I sat up on my elbows and gawked at her.

"What's up?" she said. Her skin looked dry.

"Nothing. What's up with you? I've never seen anybody your complexion look ashy. Where are you coming from?"

Looks like you've been in a hole somewhere.

I got up and started hanging up some clothes that my mom had washed and put on my bed. I had told her that she didn't need to wash my clothes anymore, but she did it anyway. I made a mental note to thank her.

"I'm just tired," Sophie said.

She looked it, and so did her jeans.

"You're really breaking in those Blue Cults fast, aren't you?" I said.

"Where have you been?" she asked.

"Just working and school. You know my routine. The question is, where have *you* been?" I asked.

When she didn't answer, I thought perhaps that I had struck a nerve. But when I looked over at her, I saw that she hadn't answered because she'd fallen asleep.

While Sophie slept, I called Sophie's mom Carmen, but only got her answering machine. Getting in touch with her was like trying to reach the president of the United States. I had called her at least three times in the past couple of weeks. She could have sent me a return text or e-mail or something—but she hadn't.

She can't be that busy.

I tried Sophie's dad Terry, too, but it was the same thing. I had been calling them for weeks, but it seemed that they had both decided not to take my calls. The worst part of it was that I had left messages saying that I needed to talk to them about Sophie. You would think they would have called back immediately.

Leaving Sophie asleep in my bedroom, I walked downstairs to the kitchen, where Mom was sitting at the table, reading the newspaper. The first thing I noticed was that she seemed to be really concentrating. The second thing I noticed was her gray hair; she hadn't touched up her roots. That wasn't like Mom. She didn't play around with gray hair. The third thing I noticed was the dark circles under her eyes.

Roscoe was snoring in the living room. He only snored that loud when he had been drinking. There used to be a time when I would try and figure out what triggered his drinking. Each time I tried, I came up with plenty of reasons. Then one day, I realized they weren't reasons, they were excuses. As I looked at my mom, I couldn't help but think she had come to a similar conclusion. Sometimes enough truly is enough.

Is Mom really concentrating on the paper, or is she thinking about something else?

I sat down at the table next to her. She smelled like *Kors* by Michael Kors. Aunt Marie had told Mom that she shouldn't put perfume on her clothes but, as usual, Mom had ignored her.

As I sat down next to her, she looked up from the paper and took off her glasses.

It's so weird how much Mom and Aunt Marie still look alike, even after Aunt Marie's nose job.

"Where's Sophie?" she asked.

"Upstairs, sleeping. You saw her when she came in?"

"Yeah, I let her in. She gave me a hug and went straight upstairs to your room."

I didn't say anything because I didn't want to worry Mom about Sophie.

But her clairvoyance kicked in. "You're worried about her, aren't you?"

"Roscoe's drinking again," I said.

My response wasn't what she expected.

She sighed and put the palm of her hand on her forehead. "I know," she said.

So, what you gonna do?

"Is he gonna get help again?" I asked, intentionally adding the *again.*

"I don't know what he's gonna do."

She started to fiddle with the newspaper. At first, I thought she was going to start reading it. But then she got up from the table.

"Where are you going, Mom?"

"To bed. I'm not feeling well." She shuffled off to her room.

What? She always has her nose in everybody's business, so why is she letting Roscoe drink again without a fight? And why isn't she stopping Ava from congregating with that Jim Jones cult without snooping around even one service?

As I sat there, tapping my fingers, my head started to pound. I went up and checked on Sophie, who was still fast asleep. I tried calling Catie, but only got her machine. I hung up on it and called Carl.

"Hey, pretty girl," he said cheerfully.

"Hey yourself," I said.

"What are you up to?"

"Nothing, I think I'm just going to go and study," I said.

"So responsible. You want a little something to eat to fuel you?"

"Um, okay," I said.

"Let's meet at the sandwich place near campus. I promise not to keep you. I know you want to study."

That was the best offer I'd had all day. I grabbed my books and hurried off to meet him. Carl arrived smelling like he just stepped out of the shower. He looked a little worried.

"Are you okay?" I asked him.

"Yeah, it's just my sister," he said, letting his voice trail off.

"You want to talk about it?" I asked gently. I didn't want to pry, but I wanted to be there for him if he needed me.

"She's got four kids, no husband, and no money. She leans on me pretty heavily. Most of the time it's okay, but sometimes it drains me. Today I'm pretty drained."

"Oh," I said. "Is everything okay?"

"If she gets herself together, then everything will be fine. She thinks I'm her personal ATM. I don't want to talk about it anymore. I want to talk about how good you look today."

I blushed. Carl was nice. I had the feeling he liked me a little more than I liked him, though. After sandwiches and a fun, two-hour conversation with Carl, I went to the faculty office to study.

Someone was already in the office when I got there. I unpacked my things as quietly as I could, but then I heard footsteps.

"Hi, Anaya," a familiar voice called from the door.

"Hi."

Instinctively, I smoothed my hair down.

"Preparing for finals?" Professor Alexander asked, walking into the room.

"Yeah," I groaned, turning my cell off. I don't like distraction when I study.

"Well, I have to say, you are disciplined. Keep up the good work."

"Thanks. Working late again?"

"Yeah, I'm trying to get a few things taken care of before the end of the semester. Been busy at the firm, so I need to catch up here."

I smiled.

"I got your message," he said.

I sat down and smiled again. There was an awkward pause.

"Well," he said, "I'm gonna let you get your work done, and I'm gonna do the same." He started to walk out, but then he turned around. "Are you okay?"

"Oh, sure, I'm good. Just exams and . . . stuff."

My attempt to make light was weak.

"All right. Well, stay diligent and those A's will come," he predicted, a grin under his moustache.

"I was wondering if I made the right decision . . . to work in your office, I mean." I blurted out.

He walked back toward me.

"What are your concerns?"

My trepidations tumbled out. "I've never worked for a law firm before, and I don't know *anything* about the law."

"Those are fair concerns, but most of the work is administrative, and that's pretty much what you do here. Except in the law office, you'll get great pay and terrific benefits, and here on campus you get low pay and no benefits."

"I didn't quite think of it that way."

"Well, now you can."

"Thank you," I nodded.

"I was right," he said.

"About what?"

"That something was bothering you."

I smiled again, but I didn't say anything, and he went into his office.

I still hadn't given my resignation to the university. I knew that at the least, it was time to tell them that the assistant wasn't doing well, so I e-mailed Professor Klein, explaining that the new assistant didn't seem very interested in learning how to run the office.

After two hours of studying, I decided to call it a night. When I turned on my cell phone, I saw that Sophie had called me three times, twice from her cell and once from her house.

Aha! Sleeping Beauty decided to come out of her inebriated slumber.

On my way out, I peeked into Professor Alexander's office.

"Hey, Professor," I called. "I'm outta here."

He was packing his briefcase.

"You sound a little too happy about that," he said.

"Enough is enough," I said. "See you later."

"Anaya, can you do me a favor?"

"Sure."

"Call me Jeff."

We both smiled.

"Good night, Jeff," I said.

As soon as I got to my car, I called Sophie. "I'm on my way home," I explained. "Are you still there?"

"No, I came home," she said dryly.

"Oh," I said. "What are you doing?"

"Just sitting in my closet, trying to decide what to wear to the movies."

"The movies? Girl, it's the middle of the night. What movie are you planning to go to this late?"

"Oh," was all she said.

"I'll come to your house, then," I said.

"Where are you?" she asked in the same flat tone.

"I just told you, I'm on my way to your house, girl! Sophie, are you high?"

I knew she was going to flip out at that, but I couldn't hold it in.

"*What?*" she shrieked.

"Are you high?"

"No, dammit!" she yelled.

It was a challenge, but I kept her on the phone until I got to her house.

"I'll call you back in a few minutes," I said.

The Beats' kitchen door was unlocked. When I walked in, Irma, the housekeeper, was standing there in a bathrobe and a head scarf. I hadn't seen Irma in a long time. She had big brown eyes and smooth, dark, Nigerian skin.

Irma had been with the Beats for almost twenty years. She hugged me and offered me food, which I declined. I climbed the stairs to Sophie's room.

Sophie was still on the floor of her huge, walk-in closet, staring up at her clothes. When I came in, she looked up and smiled. Her hair was in a messy ponytail, and her mascara was smudged. Sophie's closet was the size of my entire bedroom. One wall was filled with shoes, another with jeans, a third with dresses and shirts, and the last with accessories, handbags, and photographs of herself with Catie and me. Her closet was the only organized thing in her life.

As I looked down at her, slumped on the floor, I thought, *How can someone with so much feel like they have so little?*

"Where's Carmen?" I asked.

"Probably getting Botox injections. Who knows?"

"Where's Terry?"

"He doesn't live here."

"What?" I asked in shock. "He moved out?"

She looked exasperated. "No," Sophie said. "He didn't move out, but because of work, he's never here. And all *she* does is drown in pilates and Botox."

I sat on the floor next to her. She was quiet for a few moments.

I thought for a moment about asking Mom to talk to Carmen, but then I reconsidered. I remembered that Carmen suspected everyone of fooling around with Terry, including the maid and even my mom. If I recalled correctly, my mom told me about a shouting match she and Carmen had one July 4th holiday. Carmen called Mom a "plump dinner maker and kid taxi." Not to be outdone, my mom had called Carmen a "wannabe."

I never told anybody, though, not even Sophie. She wouldn't have been able to handle it.

"Sophie," I asked, "how often do you get high?"

I spoke slowly because I knew this was a sensitive subject with her.

"Don't come at me like that, Anaya."

"I just asked you a simple question, girl. Why are you all mad?"

I got up and walked out of the closet.

She walked back in the room and stood directly in front of me.

"Do you wanna get something to eat?" I suggested, trying to distract her.

"No, I don't want anything to eat. I want *you* out of my house." Her eyes were a blazing red.

"Sophie, I'm sorry if I made you mad. But can't I care about you? Come to my house. Mom cooked lasagna. We can make strawberry Kool-Aid and watch *Dreamgirls*."

"I have plans tonight." That couldn't be true. And, if it were, she had no business going anywhere in her condition in the middle of the night. Maybe she was worse off than I thought.

"Okay, fine. How about we go to the kitchen and see what Irma cooked?" Sophie seemed to like the idea and followed me to the kitchen.

When we got downstairs, I was surprised to see Carmen standing there, talking to Irma. She looked so beautiful. With her designer jeans and short-cropped hair, she could easily have passed for Sophie's sister. I was so glad to see her that I almost forgot about her not returning my calls.

"Mija!" she said, grabbing me and hugging me hard. "How are you?"

The look of awe on her face made me think about what Sophie had said about Botox.

What exactly does Botox do, anyway?

"I'm good, Auntie," I said. "How are you?"

"I'm good," Carmen said. "Look at you! You look great."

"Thanks. So do you."

She glanced over at Sophie, who had been standing silently by the door.

"¡Hola, Sophie! ¿Cómo estás?"

Carmen only spoke Spanish to Sophie when she was irritated with her.

"I'm great, Mother. How are you?" Sophie said sarcastically.

Mother?

"I'm good, Sophie," Carmen said with her thick Cuban accent.

"Where's Daddy?" Sophie asked without looking directly at Carmen.

Didn't she just tell me he was never home?

"Your papa? He's in Florida. You know that."

Carmen moved closer to Sophie and studied her face.

"¿Qué pasa con sus ojos, Sofía?"

Sophie backed away, but Carmen walked up to her and grabbed Sophie's chin in her hand. From the corner of my eye, I could see Irma stiffen.

"What are you talking about?" Sophie said.

Carmen calmly repeated her question: *"¿Qué pasa con sus ojos?"*

"Nothing!" Sophie lied, raising her voice. "Okay? Don't be trying to act like you're worried about me and what I do. Nothing's wrong with my eyes. Just leave me the hell alone!"

Uh-oh!

Sophie backed away from Carmen.

It's about to go down.

"I just asked a question, *mija*. You look like you've seen a ghost."

"Well, I was thinking the same thing about you. Have you been getting injections again?"

"Sofía, don't talk to me like that!"

"Talk to you like *what*?"

"Like I'm one of your little friends."

"I can talk to you however I want."

"Come on, Sophie," I said. "Let's go upstairs."

"No, Ny," she insisted, putting up her hand. "I have to say this. I wouldn't talk to my friends like I talk to you, Mother, because I have more respect for my friends than I have for you."

Irma put her hand over her mouth.

"Ny has always been there for me," Sophie continued, "and she's just my friend. You're my mother, and I can't even get your attention for five minutes. You're always off to some spa appointment, or some stupid fashion show, or some charity something or other. What about your screwed-up marriage? Why don't you try to work on that? What about *me*?"

This is getting out of hand.

"Sofía Inez Mondragón Beat!" Carmen said firmly. "I have done everything I can do to raise you. I have given you everything. *Everything!* You are almost an adult. I should not have to run behind you, trying to figure out what you are doing and who you are doing it with. I made sure you went to the best schools. I made sure you were prepared for college. The rest is up to you." Carmen took a breath and then launched into her real feelings. "You want me sitting in this humongous house, waiting and hoping one day you will want to spend time with me? You and your father have taken me for granted for years, never thinking about me or wanting to spend time with me until it benefits you. Well, those days are over. Terry is never here, and neither are you. Now that

I have found some things to do that interest me and make me happy, you are mad?"

"What interests you? Getting your face frozen so that you look like a statue?"

"What does it matter to you what I do with my face?"

"Because you look like a freak. Why can't you be like Ny's mom? Why can't you cook and be like a real mom?"

"Don't you dare compare me to anyone else, Sofía Inez!" Carmen yelled. "Don't you *ever* do that!"

"Dad's only still married to you because he doesn't want to split his assets, you crazy bitch! All the Botox and working out in the world isn't gonna make him want you."

Carmen grabbed Sophie, and the two of them fell to the floor.

Carmen shrieked expletives in Spanish, Sophie threw insults at Carmen in English, and Irma and I were screaming for both of them to stop.

Sophie tried to pull Carmen's hair, but it was too short. Carmen had no problem grabbing a handful of Sophie's massive mane, however.

"Bitch!" Sophie screamed, scratching at Carmen's hand.

Irma and I pulled them apart. I put my arms tightly around Sophie, and Irma held Carmen.

"Sophie, stop!" I yelled. "That's enough!"

Deftly I pushed her out the kitchen door and down to my car.

I had seen Sophie and Carmen fight many times over the years, but tonight was by far the worst.

When we got to my house, it was late. Sophie crashed on my bed and slept as if nothing had happened.

I called to check on Carmen.

"Está bien," she said. "But I'm tired, Ny."

Then she launched into some Spanish, but I wasn't able to keep up with her. I knew she was talking about Sophie, so I let her vent.

"I gotta get some sleep, *mija*. Thank you for calling, and thank you for being a good friend to Sofía."

"Good night, Auntie Carmen," I said.

"I noticed you called me a few times. Was there something you wanted to talk about, *mija?*"

Um, yeah, about a month ago.

"No, it's fine, Auntie, we can talk about it another time. Just get some rest."

I wanted to talk to her about Sophie's drug problem, but not at that moment. Too much had happened, and I felt that all three of us were emotionally spent.

SEVEN

Professor Klein asked me three different times if I was sure about my resignation. It felt good to know that the office had valued my help. In a letter from his personal e-mail address, he wished me luck and told me to call if I ever needed anything. The other professors didn't show as much disappointment in my leaving, but they were all supportive and wished me well. I thought I might be sad about going, but I wasn't. I knew that it wasn't the type of work I wanted as a career. To leave them in as good hands as possible, I went over the office basics again with the new assistant and advised her to write it all down.

Over lunch I had an appointment with Judy. I thought about canceling it but decided to go and get a few things off of my chest. Judy was current on my new social life. She knew all about Carl and thought that it was a "step in the positive direction" for me to finally be dating again. She also said that my "aura" was different. I don't know if it is true or not, but I'm sure she would agree that our sessions were a heck of a lot more interesting than they used to be.

"How are things with Carl?" Judy asked me when I had settled down.

"He's not for me," I heard myself say.

"No? You have said such wonderful things about him."

"I know. But it's not enough. There's no spark, no butterflies," I said.

"Oh. You want spark and butterflies?"

"Yes," I said.

"Is there something wrong about him in particular?"

"No. I can't put my finger on it. I like spending time with him, and he's super nice. And I know he likes me. I just don't think he's the one." I looked away from her.

I didn't want to talk about Carl anymore, so I changed the subject to Sophie and Catie. I had no idea what to do about either one of them. Sophie was constantly missing in action and Catie showed no signs of giving up her lucrative career. The last time I tried to call her, she said she getting ready for "work" and she'd call me back.

"Sounds like they are going through a rough time. How does that make you feel?"

"Helpless."

We discussed some ways I could reach out to them without being overbearing and without stressing myself out. I left that appointment feeling heavier than I ever had before. Shortly after I left Judy's, Jeff called to ask if I wanted to take some of my things over to the legal office and get a "preview" of where I would be working. It seemed like a good idea, so I told him I would meet him there.

When I got to his office building, he was waiting expectantly for me on the street. My mood changed immediately.

"Hi," I said, walking up to him.

He smiled back. I was surprised when he gave me a hug. I hugged him back lightly.

"Have you been waiting long?" I asked.

"I don't know," he said, smiling again. "It's a little tricky getting inside, Anaya, so I just figured I would wait out here for you."

"Well, thanks," I said playfully. "Very thoughtful of you."

We both smiled as he took out his key.

"I'm excited about your coming to work here," he said, as he opened the door.

"So am I. A little nervous, but definitely excited."

He switched on a light and turned to face me.

"You look nice," he said shyly.

"Thanks. You look nice, too. I'm not used to seeing you in jeans."

"You like?" he asked, looking down at his pants.

"I do," I said.

"Well, since I meet your approval in my personal appearance, how about we look around the office a bit?"

I nodded.

Jeff's law firm occupied the whole ground floor of a six-story building. When we walked inside his office suite, it immediately had a homey feel to it. The modern gray and black furniture was pleasant, and there were photos of famous African Americans on all the walls, with potted ferns in the corners, and a large bouquet of bright yellow daffodils on the reception desk. Behind the desk, there were huge chrome block letters that read, "LAW OFFICES OF JEFFREY ALEXANDER."

Impressive.

"There are two other attorneys who practice here," he said. "There's a legal secretary and a receptionist, and now a case clerk—you."

I smiled.

"Things are busy around here. You'll be doing everything from court runs, to answering phones, to getting donuts for everybody."

I was going to ask him what a "court run" was, but I decided to hold that question for later. The work sounded similar to what I did in the faculty office, so I figured my transition would be fairly smooth.

"Where is everyone?" I asked.

"One of our attorneys just won a huge case," he explained, "so everyone is out celebrating."

I wanted to ask why he didn't join them, but I thought better of it.

He showed me the offices of his two associates, but he didn't take me inside any of them—we just peeked in.

"This one," he said, "is Taylor Covington's. She handles law briefs and motions. And this one is Morris Thomas's. He's our top litigator."

He did take me into his own office, which was very different from his office on campus. His degrees were hanging on the wall behind his desk, and two huge bookcases lined the side walls. One case was totally filled with books, and the other had books, awards, and photographs. His desk looked work-heavy but tidy.

"Nice office," I admired.

"Thanks."

My own workspace was an open cubicle just outside his office. *So much for catching up on Facebook during the day.*

When I got to my desk, there was a bag of peanut M&Ms sitting there. I turned to look at him.

"Welcome," he said with a warm smile.

"Thank you," I said, amazed that he'd remembered my weakness for M&Ms.

"I will give you some time to settle in. I've got a few phone calls to make," he said as he disappeared into his office.

I looked around the floor again. I made my way back to the kitchen, the copy room, and peeked into a couple of the offices for a second time.

When he came out, he said, "I apologize for taking so long. I thought I would be quick. Everyone should be back in about an hour, so you can stay around to meet them if you like, or wait until your official first day."

"I guess I can meet everybody tomorrow. On my official first day," I smiled.

"Sounds good to me," he said.

"Good."

"Are you nervous?"

"Yeah, a little. I don't think I've ever even been in a law office before. It never occurred to me that I would be working in one."

"Why not?"

"Why haven't I ever been in a law office?"

"No. Why didn't you ever think you would work in one?"

"I don't know . . . Maybe because lawyers have a bad reputation. Just kidding!"

"Yeah, I guess we do."

I let it go at that.

"I won't miss those phones from the office," I said. "Those people drove me crazy."

He smiled.

"You'll definitely be missed around there."

"You think so?"

"Oh, yeah. Especially by Professor Klein. I feel lucky that I still have you working for me."

"Thanks. That's nice of you to say."

"I mean it. Are you hungry? I'm sorry for taking up so much of your time. Let me feed you," he offered.

"Oh, no," I said. "You didn't take up my evening. This was fine. Some other time, though. Thanks. My mom's not feeling well, so I have to cook for the family tonight."

"Some other evening?"

"Um, yeah, that would be nice."

The next day was my actual first day at work. I arrived fifteen minutes early, but I didn't have to use the key Jeff had given me, because somebody had already unlocked the door. I walked past the empty reception desk. When I got to my own station, an older woman was standing there.

"You must be Anaya," she said with a warm smile. She was heavyset but well proportioned. Her big puffy hair had gray streaks, and her eyebrows were penciled in as black as they could be. Her flower-print dress, black blazer, and patent leather pumps made her look more like a librarian than a legal secretary. I suddenly felt underdressed.

"Yes," I said, "Anaya Goode."

"Jeff speaks very highly of you. We've all been waiting for you to get here. I'm Shirley Moore." She was still smiling.

I blushed.

What has he been saying about me to these people?

To change the subject, I asked, "How long have you been working here?"

"I was Jeff's secretary at a firm in San Francisco, and when he left to start this one, five years ago, he asked me to come with him, and I've been here ever since."

"Oh, okay," I replied, not knowing exactly what else to say.

"You want me to fix you some fruit?"

"Oh, no, I ate something already. Thank you."

"All right, just let me know. There's plenty for everybody. No sense in walking around hungry."

Just then, a pretty woman in an expensive-looking teal suit walked up to us.

"Good morning, Taylor," Shirley said.

The woman, who was about five-foot-eight, had long auburn hair. I tried to figure out her ethnicity. She didn't seem very happy to see me.

Give her a chance, Ny.

"Taylor," Shirley said, "this is Anaya Goode, the case clerk Jeff told us about."

I extended my hand, and she let me shake hers, which felt like a dead fish. Without saying another word, she walked into her office and shut the door behind her.

"It takes Taylor a little while to warm up," a male voice boomed behind me.

When I turned to face the man, he said, "I'm Morris Thomas. You must be Anaya. We've heard a lot of great things about you."

He extended a huge hand toward me.

"Nice to meet you, Mr. Thomas."

"Morris. Please call me Morris."

He made small talk for a little while, punctuating his comments with a loud laugh, and then told me how he had been working there ever since Jeff started the firm. Eventually, he excused himself and went to his office.

A few minutes later, a young woman in her early twenties walked up to my desk. She was stylish in an over-the-top kind of way, with long swooping bangs, huge hoop earrings, and dark red lipstick.

"Welcome, girl!" she said.

"Thanks."

"I'm Octavia, the receptionist. If you ever have any questions or concerns, come see me, okay?"

"Okay," I said, getting overwhelmed already trying to remember everyone's name.

By midday, I knew I was going to enjoy working at that firm. Aside from Taylor, I had a good feeling about everyone there. I also liked the aroma of coffee that lingered through the office all day because Shirley kept the machine cranked.

"We haven't given you much to do today," Shirley said. "The firm likes to break newbies in with a good impression before burying them in work." She laughed.

"It's okay," I said. "I was always busy at my last job. Makes the time go by faster."

"That's a good way to look at it."

By noon, Jeff hadn't come in yet, which was just as well, because I wanted to get used to the office without being distracted by his presence. I put a few pictures of Catie, Sophie, Andrew, Mom, and Roscoe on a shelf near my desk. I dusted and rearranged the drawers. I put out my personal rolodex, along with a small bear figurine that Andrew gave me on my sixteenth birthday. The words printed on its belly were *You are special.*

Around 11:30 a.m., Octavia, the receptionist, invited me to

lunch at a nearby Friday's. My first impulse was to decline, but I decided not to step on any toes, especially on my first day. When lunchtime rolled around at 1 p.m., she sent me an e-mail, asking me to meet her at her desk.

When we got outside, she pointed to her car at the curb and said, "I'll drive if you like." As I climbed in her car, she asked, "So, who was in the office when you got there this morning?"

"Shirley."

"Oh. Did she offer you something to eat?"

"Yes."

"That's Shirley for you. She prays for everybody and feeds everybody. She's cool."

"Yeah, she is. She showed me around the office today. She's really thorough."

When we got to the restaurant, we were seated immediately. Octavia ordered a root beer and glanced around as if she were waiting for somebody. Then she started talking. Without having to ask any questions about my new coworkers, I found out more information than I ever wanted to know. Octavia didn't hold anything back. I don't think the word *discretion* was a part of her vocabulary.

"Shirley's a Holy Roller, and her oldest son is gay. She doesn't know it, but the rest of the world does."

"Mmm," I replied. I didn't want to be rude, but I didn't want to pretend to be too interested, either. "What do you think you wanna eat?" I asked her.

"I don't know."

I pretended to study the menu, since I wasn't sure what to say.

"What's up with Taylor?" I finally asked.

Octavia rolled her eyes and took a deep breath.

"She's cool when you get to know her, but she gives a bad first impression. Like she needs to prove how much of a bitch she can be. She's got some issues with her looks, I guess." Octavia sipped her root beer as she pushed her long bangs out of her eyes. "Personally, I don't know why she's got a chip on her shoulder. She looks like Halle Berry, gets paid a bundle, and she's smart as a whip. I don't know why she's so insecure."

"Really?" I said. "Taylor seemed to me to be a lot of things, but insecure certainly wasn't one of them."

"Girl, yes! It's always gorgeous ones that have those stupid issues. I don't really know the entire story, so don't quote me. I just overheard something about the women in her Black lawyer group not inviting her to events, or something like that. I don't really know."

"Wait. Why is she in a Black lawyer group?"

"What do you mean?"

"I'm just wondering—is she part black?"

"The way she tells it, she's one hundred and ten percent black. And she's pretty proud of it, too. Have you been in her office yet?"

"No."

"Go in there, and check out the picture of her parents: midnight and dusk of dawn, girl. They are *dark!* I don't know how she turned out to be so light-skinned. It's a trip, huh?"

"I thought she was Latina."

"Everybody does."

"Is she rude to you, Octavia?"

"Nope. Taylor knows I'll light her ass up if she gets to acting a fool. She might be moody, but she ain't stupid. We had one altercation since I've been working there, and she hasn't given me a problem since. Like I said, she's a smart girl."

We both laughed.

"So, how do you know Jeff?" she asked.

I choked on my food and started coughing.

Couldn't you have handled the question better than that, dummy?

"What do you mean?" I asked.

"What do I *mean*? I mean, he's the one who hired you, right?"

"Yes. I worked for him in the faculty office at the University."

"He still teaches there?"

"Yeah," I said, surprised that she didn't know.

"Oh, I thought he would have given up that job by now. He doesn't have time. I don't know how his wife puts up with it."

All my radars were suddenly activated.

"Yeah," I said, trying not to sound too interested. "I guess he works a lot, huh?"

"Hell, yeah, he does. Works nights, weekends, all that."

"Wow," I said.

What else? What else?

"He's nice, though. You couldn't have picked a better boss if you tried. He must really like you, 'cause he never hires people without letting the other partners interview them first."

I didn't say anything.

"You must have made quite the impression on him at that faculty office, girlfriend." She winked at me.

"I guess."

"Sooo," Octavia whistled, "because I've given you the scoop on almost everybody else, let me give you the four-one-one on *moi*." She winked again. "I have a son, and I'm working my way through college. It's a slow process but, hey, slow and steady wins the race, right?"

"Sure," I nodded.

"Anyway, I'm a vegetarian and lifelong foster child. Never knew my parents or any of my natural relatives. I'm a survivor. Oh, and I'm single."

"Single seems to be the new epidemic," I said. I wondered what it was like not to have any relatives and why she was giving me full disclosure on her life.

"Are you single, too?"

I nodded.

"Why don't you have a boyfriend?"

I sighed. "I don't know. I haven't really put any time into a relationship, I guess. I have a friend, though."

"Oh, a friend. I have three of those." She winked again. "None are boyfriend or marriage material. Hell, one of 'em ain't even *friend* material, but I keep him around anyway. Why do we hang on to guys we know don't mean us any good? Why do we intentionally ignore the warning signs and just keep sticking in there?"

"*That* is the million-dollar question," I said, holding my glass up in a mock toast.

"I guess it is," she said. "Are you going to law school?"

"No."

"Really? That's interesting. Everybody else who's had your position left the firm to go to law school. Where do you live?"

"Maxwell Park, with my parents."

"I would never have guessed you lived over there. One of my girlfriends lives over there. I thought you were from Piedmont."

Piedmont?

"Why did you think I'm from Piedmont?" I asked, giving her the crazy eyebrow look she had been giving me.

"You just seem so . . . I don't know . . . mature and straight. Piedmont-ish."

I almost spit out my water.

Mature and straight? Piedmont-ish?

"That's not a bad thing or anything, Anaya," Octavia recovered fast. "You just seem different from other women I hang out with."

Thank God for the little things.

"We better get back to work," I said, looking at my watch. "Lunch was nice, Octavia. Thanks."

"Girl, no problem."

I didn't know what to make of Octavia just yet. I knew I'd keep her as a friend, though. She seemed to have a lot of valuable information. Information that could make this transition that much easier for me. I wasn't too big on the whole gossipy thing because we all know if someone gossips with you, they will gossip about you. I made a mental note to keep Miss Octavia at a safe, but friendly distance.

As soon as I got back to my desk, I ran into Taylor, who was walking out of Jeff's office, looking exasperated.

When Jeff saw me, he said, "Anaya, can you come in here, please?"

Taylor stared at me with a look that could have taken my head off.

I walked into Jeff's office and sat down. He was leaning back in his chair with his feet up on the desk.

"Hey, you," he said with a big smile. "I've been looking for you."

I felt awkward and shy, but tried to shake it off.

"Hey," I said.

"How's it going? Shirley told me you were catching on pretty fast. I knew you would." He seemed excited.

"It's been cool, actually. I haven't had much to do, though, so not much to catch on to yet."

"Good. Have you had lunch yet?" He asked this cheerfully.

He's never this relaxed on campus.

"Yeah, I just went out with Octavia."

"We will have to have lunch one day and catch up. I want to know what you think. What you really think." He sounded serious.

"We can have lunch whenever you want."

We both smiled.

Just then Taylor walked back in and handed Jeff something.

"Here you go," she said, standing next to his desk.

"Thanks," he said, immediately putting the document down and continuing his conversation with me.

"Good, I will have to put you on my—" Jeff stopped talking as Taylor continued to stand there, looking at me as if I owed her something.

"I'll get back to you," Jeff said to her.

Apparently, she had delayed hearing, because it took her a few extra seconds to get the clue and walk out. As she passed me, my eyes asked what her problem was, but my mouth stayed closed.

"Guess I'd better get back to work. I don't want to interrupt," I said, standing.

"You aren't an interruption," he said quietly.

I smiled.

"Talk to you later," I said and headed back to my desk.

When I got to my desk, Shirley was there to give me pointers on the firm's database software. But my mind drifted to what had happened in Jeff's office with Taylor.

What's her problem with me?

By the time Shirley had finished, I realized that I had only heard a fraction of what she said.

I hope I won't have to use this program anytime soon.

EIGHT

Working in the law firm was more demanding than in the faculty offices. I found myself behind, so I stayed late one evening to catch up. It wasn't unusual for others to work late, so when I heard someone else in the office, I wasn't alarmed. When I looked up, I saw that it was Jeff.

"You still here?" he asked.

"Yeah," I said. "Just finishing up these exhibits for Taylor."

"She's been keeping you busy, huh?"

"Yes, I have to find a way to balance my school work while she's in trial. It's a lot," I said.

"I remember when I was in high school, I was swamped with activities and homework. One semester, when grades came out, my GPA had dropped so low that my mom threatened to make me quit my other activities. I talked her out of it, though. It was a hard lesson, but I never took my studies for granted again. I always put them first. And you know what?"

"What?" I said, slightly rolling my eyes.

"You don't wanna hear this, do you?" he chuckled.

"Of course I do," I smirked playfully. "I wanna hear all about your study habits from thirty years ago. Please, tell me more." I gestured for him to come closer.

We both laughed.

"I'm only kidding," I said. "I know you're only trying to help."

There was a comfortable silence between us for a moment.

"Are you hungry?" he asked. "I'm on my way out. I know it's

late, but I haven't eaten anything all day. We can grab a bite at Skates, on the Berkeley Marina."

"Why are you always trying to feed me?" I asked.

"You always look hungry, that's why," he said jokingly. If it were anyone else, I would have probably taken the comment personally. Somehow I didn't get the feeling Jeff really thought I looked hungry.

"Okay," I said. "That's cool. I'll follow you there."

On the way, I sent Carl a text telling him that I'd call later. He had called me twice, and I hadn't called him back yet. When we got to Skates, I parked my car next to Jeff's.

As I eased out of the car, I smiled at the thought of something Aunt Marie had once said about men and cars.

"Share," Jeff said, having seen my smile.

"What?" I asked.

"Share your thought."

"Nah, it's nothing."

"You can't share your thought with me?"

Um . . . not this one.

"Okay," he countered. "How about we make a deal? You share your last thought, and I'll pay for dinner."

I laughed as we entered the restaurant. We were immediately shown to a table.

"Why is that funny?" he asked. "Oh, you already *thought* I was paying for dinner? See, that's just like a woman—she always expects the man will pick up the check."

I didn't respond.

"I'm only kidding, Anaya," he said with mock seriousness. "I have every intention of paying the bill."

That made both of us laugh, and as I sat with the menu, I felt myself becoming more comfortable.

"What are you having?" Jeff asked.

"I'm not very hungry," I said shyly. "Would you mind if I just got coffee?"

"I know you're not scared to eat in front of me. Girl, I won't watch you chew. Just order some food. You know you want some of these baby back ribs with Hawaiian barbecue sauce."

"Okay," I said. "I will have a chicken Caesar salad, though. I am not having ribs this time of night."

"Deal." He looked directly in my eyes. "Are you ready to tell me what you were laughing about earlier?"

"That was so long ago. Why are you so interested in what's going on in my head?"

"Honestly?" he asked.

"That's why I asked."

"You're an interesting person with interesting thoughts. Talking with you makes me think about things I haven't thought about in years. It's kind of nice," he said.

"That's fair enough. Can I ask you another question?"

"Please."

"How old are you?" I inquired.

"Thirty-seven," he said without hesitating. "Why? You think I'm old?"

"No," I responded.

When the waitress came around, Jeff ordered the Caesar salad for me, and fish for himself.

When she left, Jeff looked me squarely in the eye, and asked, "So, what do you think?"

"What do I think about *what*?" I asked.

"About *me!*"

I had hardly anticipated being asked that question. So I said carefully and slowly, "I think you're a nice person. I appreciate that you are taking a chance on me working in your firm. It means a lot."

He nodded.

"Well, I appreciate that you accepted the challenge," he said, leaning closer to me. "You made me very happy."

"Happy?" I asked, a bit startled.

"Yes," he said, looking steadily at me. "Happy."

The waitress brought our food. I didn't have much of an appetite, but I managed to get half of my food eaten. When I looked up, Jeff had finished his food.

"You have a big appetite," I said.

"Yeah," he said, looking down at his nearly empty plate. "I guess when I really like something, I just go for it."

"I will be sure to keep that bit of information in mind," I said, smiling.

"Please do."

I then asked him something I had wondered about for weeks. "How do you manage to work and have a personal life?"

He looked down quietly. I was almost afraid I had asked the question.

"I manage," he said simply, then focused on me. "What about you? What do you do for fun?"

"Fun? What's that?" I scoffed.

"Aw, come on, you are too young to be so serious. I know you have fun sometimes."

"Sometimes, but not much lately. There's a lot going on with my family, so I've been laying low on the fun."

"There's never too much going on to lay low on the fun. You gotta live. You can be there for your family, but remember to take care of you, too. That's important."

I hadn't thought of it that way. His advice was certainly more pointed than Judy's.

"Thanks," I said. "I will keep that in mind as well."

We talked for almost two hours. Jeff was funny and smart, and he knew a little bit about everything. I began to get sleepy.

"How do you know so much stuff?" I asked.

"I don't know. I'm a bit of a nerd, I guess. Always have been. I just like to learn and know stuff."

I smiled shyly. "Jeff?" I asked.

"Yes?"

"I've had a very long day. I really need to get home and get some rest."

He started to say something, but then he apparently thought better of it.

As we went out the front door, his hand brushed against mine for just a moment. When we got to my Honda, he took my hand in his.

"I had a nice time," he said.

"Me, too."

"We'll do it again soon?"

"Yeah," I said, biting my lower lip.

He gave me a gentle hug, and then he watched me get into my car and drive away.

I drove home in a blissful daze, thinking about our conversation. I kicked myself for missing opportunities to say something witty or cute. What was I getting into? I knew better than to ask my mom for advice, although I wished I could have talked to her about it. Better to stay quiet, I decided.

As the next few weeks flew by, I realized that I liked working in the law firm more than I ever had expected. The people-mix was anything but boring (the way I had thought it might be, with stuffy lawyers, ancient legal secretaries, and nerdy paralegals). Jeff's firm was fun. Everybody was friendly—well, almost everybody. Taylor still had a gavel stuck up her butt.

Carl and I dated when I made time. I could tell he still liked me, and I liked him, too. But I wasn't ready to be in a serious, full-time relationship with him, which is what I realized that he wanted. I kept promising him that I would hang out with him, but something always came up. Working in the firm consumed more time than I had expected, but admittedly, I could have made time for Carl—I just didn't. My biggest time-killer lately was Jeff. We talked on the phone at least once a week, and I wasn't sure what to make of it. Whenever we talked, we had such a good time. Plenty of laughter and good conversation. I was comfortable with him, and he made me feel like I could be myself. It was nice. I wasn't sure what to make of the fact that he hadn't tried to hit on me. Part of me was relieved, and the other part of me was offended. I was attractive enough for him to try something. Why hadn't he? Maybe he just needed a friend to talk to; hell, maybe we were distant relatives. I don't know. What I did know was that I enjoyed him, and I made sure to have time for him when he called.

One evening, while I was still at work, Carl called me.

"Hey," I said cheerfully.

"Hey. Have I offended you in some way?"

"No, what do you mean?" I said, even though I knew what he meant.

"I don't know what you are feeling anymore about us," Carl began. "When I call, you don't call me back. When I ask you out, you are always busy. I thought we were getting along just fine."

"We did get along fine. I mean, we do. I've been busy. I'm sorry. This new job is more than I thought it would be. It's not you, though, I promise."

"Okay," he said. "Are you learning a lot?"

"I am."

"And you like the people?"

"Yes, I really do," I said, smiling to myself.

"And this is Professor Alexander's firm, right?"

"Uh-huh."

"What made him decide to ask you to work there?"

Carl sure is being nosy.

"I don't know. He said I was a good assistant in the faculty offices, and he needed a clerk here."

"So he stole you from the university, huh?" Carl surmised.

"No, Carl. He didn't steal me. I came willingly," I said.

"He stole you," Carl said.

"Oh, stop it. I'm at work. I'll call you a little later," I said.

"Anaya?"

"Yes?"

"I miss you," he said sincerely.

"I miss you, too," I said quickly, to get off the phone. "Call you later, okay?"

"Okay."

Just as I hung up, I saw Jeff walk by.

"Hey, you!" I called cheerfully.

"Hey," he said slowly.

I got up and walked toward him. "Is everything all right?"

"Yeah," he nodded, but not convincingly. "Everything's fine."

"You sure?" I said, concerned about what was troubling him.

"I'm just tired," he responded. "I'm having some problems with the caterer for my parents' anniversary party, and I had a little issue on campus today. No big deal," he said with a rather forced smile. "I'll be fine."

"I was just on my way out," I said. "If you need to talk, I'll stay."

He thanked me, and I followed him to his office.

I sat down in one of the chairs that faced his desk.

He tilted his head to the side.

"How are things going?" he asked.

"Um . . . pretty good." I suddenly felt timid. I had thought we were going to talk about his problems, not about me.

"I'm happy it's working out for you, Ny. This is the second time

I've seen you here this late. Do you work this much overtime on a regular basis?"

"Sometimes. I want to finish an assignment I've been working on. Why? Am I not supposed to work late?"

"No, it's not a problem. But I'm worried about you walking in the parking lot when it's dark outside."

His tone was formal, like a supervisor, but his eyes weren't. There was a familiar, soft look in them.

"I'll be okay," I promised. "I have pepper spray in my purse, and I'm not afraid to use it."

I smiled, but he didn't.

"Please be careful. Let me know when you plan to work late. Maybe I can arrange to be here, or we can work something out."

"Okay," I nodded in agreement.

"I miss seeing you on campus," he said.

"I know. It's so weird not being there anymore," I said quietly.

"It's nice having you here, though," he quickly replied. He stood with his hands in his pockets. If I wasn't mistaken, he looked nervous about something.

"I haven't seen you much this week," I said.

"Yeah, there's a lot going on," he told me, but he looked away. "I've been busy," he offered vaguely.

"Okay," I said.

"I have an idea," he said in a lighter tone. "How about we make Fridays our lunch days?"

"Really?" I asked. "Every Friday?"

"Well, within reason," he laughed. "We obviously won't be able to make it every single Friday, but we can give it our best shot. How about that?"

I smiled. "Okay."

I was surprised when he walked over and gave me a hug. He felt warm and smelled like soap.

I knew that I was treading on tricky ground and that we

had begun to form more of a friendship rather than a working relationship. I considered backing off because I felt things for him that I had no business feeling. Our schedules were busy and often conflicted, so the majority of our time together entailed communicating over the telephone or e-mail. When I saw him at work, it was usually in passing. But even though we didn't spend much time together, he grew on me. I began to trust him and found myself wanting to share with him in a way I hadn't shared with anybody, ever. We talked about our dreams, our fears, and our mistakes. I should have known I was in trouble when I started talking to him about my family. I was a fiercely private person and hardly ever shared information about my family. This was something I hadn't even done with Carl. One night, Carl called and asked me to go out.

"I'm swamped with work and school," I told him.

"Wow, that must be one helluva position," he said with mock awe. "You ain't *never* got time."

"I know, I'm sorry," I apologized. "All my friends are out of the loop, too, I assure you. I believe things will settle down soon."

"Can you at least call every now and then?" he asked pointedly.

"Yeah," I agreed. "I mean, I *do* call you."

"No, you don't," he observed.

I didn't respond. I knew I wasn't making any sense. I didn't have a snowball's chance in hell of having a real relationship with Jeff. Why had I let my friendship with Jeff interfere with a potential relationship with Carl?

"I have to go to Arizona for a few days," he said suddenly.

I was immediately curious. "Oh?" I asked. "For what?"

"Mostly for pleasure. But one of my aunts has a house down there, and she wants me to check on the tenants. She thinks they're tearing the place up, and she won't be able to get there for a while. It's not a big deal, but I told her I'd go. A guy can always use a little getaway, you know."

"Oh," I said, realizing the other shoe was about to drop.

"Would you like to go with me?" he asked.

"Huh?" I asked stupidly.

He cleared his throat. "I figured if you wanted to go . . . I mean, if you wanted to hang out or had never been to Arizona before, then you might wanna go."

"When are you leaving?" I asked, intrigued.

"The day after tomorrow. I thought it would be nice to spend the time," he continued. "I know you like warm weather, and it seems like you could use a little vacation. We could visit my cousin Brian. He's interesting, an investment banker, and his wife's a teacher. Maybe we could even try to make it to the Grand Canyon, if you want. I mean, I know it's a pretty big deal. I just thought I'd ask. I understand if you don't want to."

"Sure," I said.

"I understand," he said. "I know it's short notice—Wait, what did you say?" he asked.

"I said I'd like to go to Arizona with you. I will have to request the time off from work, but it should be fine."

"Great!" Carl exclaimed. "Check with your job and let me know if you can do it. I'll take care of your ticket."

I could hear how giddy he was. A trip did sound like a good idea; I needed some time away from Jeff. However, even though it didn't make sense, I felt like I was betraying Jeff by going to Arizona with Carl.

Taylor approved my time off. I told my parents I would be away for a couple of days visiting friends.

My mom didn't even ask me what friends I was going to see. I thought it was unusual of her not to interrogate me about the trip. But she merely told me to be careful and to call when I landed in Arizona. I found it a bit strange, but I didn't push it. I hadn't told her about Carl yet, and I didn't want to try explaining why I was going on an overnight trip with a guy she hadn't met or even heard of before. I hadn't even told Sophie or Catie; I wasn't ready for their commentary yet.

Carl left early Thursday morning, and I left late Thursday night. That way I would only have to miss one day of work. That Thursday, I tried my hardest to avoid Jeff. I thought about telling him I would be out of town, but time got away from me. I didn't even see him that day. He was in meetings, and Taylor had me working on another project.

When Carl arrived at the airport to pick me up in the rental car, I got nervous. He got out of the car and put my bag in the back seat. He gave me a hug and opened the door for me.

I stared at his clothes. "Are you wearing pajamas?" I asked after he got in the car.

"These, my friend, are casual bottoms," he chuckled.

"They look like pajamas to me," I said suspiciously.

"Well, after I got in earlier, I showered and threw on some lounge clothes. Is that alright with you, *Mizz* Goode?"

"That's fine," I obliged.

The ride to the hotel was a little quiet. I started to get anxious about spending the weekend with Carl, especially because we were sharing a room. I knew he was a gentleman, so that gave me some comfort. The main thing was to get away from Jeff for a few days.

The hotel was nice; nothing fancy, but tastefully decorated. It smelled like lime, which made me relax. But when we got to our room, I got queasy again.

Carl sensed my anxiety. "Is this gonna be okay for you?" he said, concerned.

I nodded yes.

"I can get another room," he offered. "Are you uncomfortable? I should have asked whether or not you wanted separate rooms."

"No, it's okay. I didn't expect you to pay for two rooms."

I showered and got into my pajamas. When I came out, I sat down on the bed next to Carl.

"So, now what?"

"Now we chill," he said. "No agenda, no plan. We just hang out."

"Oh, okay," I said shyly. "Thank you for inviting me."

"Thank you for coming." He lifted my head and kissed me gently.

I kissed him back.

"Why are you making me chase you so hard?" he asked when the kiss ended.

"What do you mean?"

"I mean, why does it take an Act of Congress to get you to go out with me? I like you, Anaya. Give me a chance."

I am here giving you a chance, aren't I?

"Carl, I'm not ready for anything serious."

"I get that. I can understand that. Do you like spending time with me?"

"Of course I do. I've been busy lately and haven't had a lot of time to hang out," I said, feeling guilty as I spoke. That excuse wasn't technically a lie. But the truth was that I was too busy for Carl because I had been spending time with Jeff.

"When you like somebody, you are supposed to make time," Carl pointed out. "Food for thought, Miss Goode," he said with a short smile.

"Point taken," I said.

He nodded his head but didn't say anything. Instead, he kissed me again, a little harder this time. The kiss felt good. I didn't pull away. I kissed him back and found myself thinking about Jeff, who hadn't tried to kiss me at all. I tried to shake Jeff out of my mind. Carl and I cuddled and talked until we both fell asleep.

The next morning, we had a breakfast of trout and eggs at a bohemian place, and then we went to the mall. We held hands and laughed a lot. Carl bought me a t-shirt from the Armani Exchange store, and I got him a sweatshirt from Footlocker.

After we left the mall, we drove to his cousin's house through sunny desert terrain with hordes of tall cactus, all with their prickly arms out, reaching for me. I fell asleep on the way, but Carl woke me up with a small kiss on the lips.

"Wake up, Sleeping Beauty," he said sweetly.

I yawned. "I'm awake."

He kept peering over at me.

"What?" I squinted.

He grinned in happiness like a crazy man. "I like you, Anaya. That's all."

I quickly changed the subject. "So, who's going to be at the barbecue?"

"Cousin Brian said friends and family. They have a bunch of kids."

So I straightened up and prepared to meet everyone. As it turns out, their pug was the first friend I made at the barbecue. Next, I was approached by Brian's wife, who immediately asked me how I'd met Carl.

"School," I said. "We attend the same school . . . You have a nice home."

I didn't want to be obvious, but I didn't want to entertain a conversation about Carl. Relatives could be pushy about things like relationships.

"Well, when you have a house full of boys, it does take some work. But I'm the energetic type." She threw me a beautiful smile and got up to entertain her other guests.

The rest of the day was pleasant. Brian turned on some music, and Carl and I played dominoes with another couple. Carl was good at dominoes. He talked a lot, like Uncle Allen does when he plays. I enjoyed watching Carl slam the dominoes down on the table and talk trash to the other players.

At the end of the day, when we had returned to the hotel room, I told him, "I had a nice time."

"I'm glad," he nodded, his face suddenly serious. "I wanted

you to meet some of my family who weren't from the projects and didn't spend all day drinking or popping pills."

His words stung me. "Carl, I have never made any kind of comment or judgment about anybody in your family," I said firmly.

"You don't have to," he shrugged, striding across the room to face me.

"What's *that* supposed to mean?" I was getting upset.

"You don't think you're better than I am, Ny?"

"What?"

"You don't think you're better than I am?" he repeated.

"Carl, no," I said emphatically. "That's crazy. Where would I get off thinking like that? When I spend time with you, I spend time with *you*." I pointed to his heart, touching him gently. "I'm not thinking about your parents, or your sisters, or anybody else in your family. When I'm with you, I'm with you."

He looked over at me and blinked several times as if tears might come. After he was quiet for too long, I nudged him.

He looked at me oddly and said, "That's the first time you've ever expressed any kind of feeling for me."

"No, it's *not*," I protested.

"Yes, it *is*," he insisted.

"No, it's not."

"Yes, it is, Anaya."

Maybe he's right. It certainly wouldn't be the first time I've been accused of hiding my feelings.

"Look, I don't want to fight," he said. "I asked you here to show you a good time, and that's what I intend to do."

In silence, we re-dressed to go out on the town. I tried to recall all of our conversations and any comments I'd made about his family. I put it out of my mind for the sake of the trip, but it still bothered me.

We went to a club downtown. The music was good, and the atmosphere was nice. The best part was that Carl was a star on the dance floor, so we grooved the night away, taking a few breaks to drink a cocktail or two. As we danced, I felt him touching me in places he knew he shouldn't. At first, I pushed his hands away, but after a few apple martinis, I let his hands roam freely.

We kissed a few times as we danced, and on the way back to our room, we made out in the elevator of our hotel. The kisses were passionate, so when I stopped kissing him back, Carl noticed the change.

"Are you okay?" he asked.

"Is this elevator spinning?"

He laughed. "To you it probably is."

To keep my balance, I took off my stilettos.

When we got off the elevator, Carl helped me down the hallway, because now the entire fourteenth floor was whirling.

"Go slow!" I pleaded.

When he opened the door to the room, I staggered to the bed and collapsed in a fog. Somewhere out there, I could hear his voice.

"Do you want me to help you out of these?" he asked, tugging on my sleeve.

"Mmm."

I let him take off my jewelry and my dress, but I stopped him when he got to my panties. Even in my stupor, I was thinking about Jeff.

Carl started kissing me all over.

"We can't," I mumbled.

"Can't what?"

"Have sex."

"Who wants to have sex with *you*?" he asked breathlessly.

"*You* do."

"No, I don't," he explained. "You wanna have sex with me. I'm just trying to be nice," he said, still kissing me.

I remember laughing—at least, I think I laughed—and that's the last thing I remember. The next time I opened my eyes, daybreak was pouring in the windows, and I was lying next to Carl in one of his t-shirts.

He looks cute . . . Did we do it?

I tugged on his shoulder a couple of times, and he opened his eyes.

"What's up, Ny?"

"Did we . . .?"

"No," he said irritably and turned back over.

I was relieved.

"I suppose you're glad about that," he said with his back still to me.

"Carl, what's wrong?"

He sat up on his elbow and faced me.

"I've been busting my ass to show you how I feel about you. I asked you on this trip so you could see a different side of me, but all you do is push me away. If you didn't wanna be here, you shouldn't have come."

I had never seen him so hurt. I didn't know what to say.

"If you're not feeling me, Anaya, tell me. You aren't doing me any favors this way."

"Whoa! I never said I was gonna do you any favors. I came here because I wanted to. Are you mad because you didn't get any last night?"

"You're damn right, I'm mad! But don't get me wrong—I can get sex whenever I want."

"Then what's your problem?"

"*You're* my problem. I don't do games."

"Carl, I'm sorry if you feel like I'm playing games. Believe me, that's not my intention. I *do* like you."

"You like me, but not enough to be in a relationship with me, is that it?"

"I'm not ready for a relationship."

"With *me*, you mean."

I didn't argue. I didn't have the words or the strength. I wasn't giving Carl what he wanted, and I felt that probably I should stop seeing him. I knew I was stringing him along, and it was wrong. We flew back together that evening, and Carl dropped me off at home.

"Do you want me to carry your bag inside?" he asked.

"No, I can do it," I said. He gave me a quick kiss on the cheek.

"Thanks for coming," he said. He walked away before I could respond. He drove away and left me on the curb with my bag.

I had only missed one day of work, but when I returned to the office on Monday, Taylor acted as if I'd deserted her for a week. I had six e-mails from her and a stack of paper in my inbox. She was psycho. She had probably eaten the last case clerk.

I didn't see Jeff until later in the day, when he passed me in the hall.

"Welcome back," he said, but he kept walking without giving me a chance to reply.

What the hell?

I caught up on the work Taylor had for me, and I completed a small binder project for Jeff. Being busy was good. It helped me to focus on something other than Jeff's weird greeting.

The week went by slowly and quietly. Of course, I hadn't really expected to hear from Carl, and I hadn't called him either. But when I didn't hear from Jeff, I was confused. By noon on Friday, I must have checked my e-mail twenty times—but still no word from Jeff. I probably should have just called or e-mailed him like a sane person, but I didn't.

When two thirty rolled around on Friday afternoon, I grabbed my purse and headed to lunch. As I approached his door, Jeff stepped out of his office.

"Hey, Anaya. You going home for the day?"

"Going to grab a bite to eat."

"You're taking lunch kinda late, aren't you?"

"Yeah, I guess."

"Okay, have a nice lunch," he said as he walked into the conference room.

I wasn't really hungry, but I desperately needed to get out of the office. On the way to the sandwich place, I called Sophie and asked her to meet me there.

"Okay," she said. "See ya soon."

As I was getting out of my car, my cell phone rang.

"What did you decide to get for lunch?" Jeff asked.

I sighed.

"A sandwich. I'm meeting Sophie."

"Oh. What kind of sandwich are you gonna get?"

"I don't know. Did you want me to bring you one back?"

I was irritated.

"Uh, yeah, could you? I haven't eaten anything all day."

"Why not?"

"I haven't had lunch."

I didn't say anything.

"Anaya?"

"Yes?"

"Why didn't we go to lunch today?"

Is he kidding me?

"When I didn't hear from you," I said, "I figured you didn't wanna go. I was surprised, because we haven't been missing our Friday lunches."

"We did last week," he said quietly.

"I told you I couldn't make lunch last week. I went out of town."

"Yeah, I know that."

"So, what's the problem?"

"I don't know. I guess there isn't one."

"There must be," I said with growing frustration.

"There's no problem."

"What's wrong?"

"You can be really bossy sometimes, Ny."

"And you can be evasive sometimes, Mister Alexander. Now, tell me what's wrong."

"I don't know. I guess I don't like that you left last weekend and canceled our lunch date."

I wanted to scream piercingly through the phone, but I didn't.

"Maybe we should talk later when I get back from lunch," I said, and I hung up.

In the end, I had lunch by myself, because Sophie didn't show. I called her, but she didn't answer.

NINE

When I got home that evening, everybody was there. Mom was at the dinner table, Roscoe was sitting on his royal throne watching TV, and Ava was holed up in her bedroom.

"Hey, Mom, what are you up to?" I asked.

"Paying bills," she said, positioning her cheek closer so I could kiss it.

"Doesn't sound like much fun," I said.

"It isn't. I need to start looking for some new curtains for that living room. Those rags I have up there are so old."

Roscoe walked into the room.

"How's the new job coming?" he asked me. "We haven't heard much about it."

"Yeah," Mom chimed in. "You like it?"

"It's fine," I said. "I actually like it a lot."

They seemed pleased with that response.

"That's good," Roscoe said. "You thinking about being a lawyer?"

"No, that's not for me," I shrugged.

"Oh? Then why are you working in a law firm?" Mom asked.

Before I could answer, Roscoe changed the subject. "Anita, I'm hungry."

"There's food in the kitchen," Mom said, raising her eyebrows.

"Fix my plate," he crooned charmingly at her.

"What's wrong with *your* hands?" was Mom's response.

"Woman, serve me!" Roscoe joked.

Mom snickered and looked back at me.

"Ny," she said, with a playful eye to Roscoe, "make sure to check the mental health records of any man you plan to marry. Sometimes the symptoms increase gradually. Just be careful."

She and Roscoe laughed, and then she got up to get him a plate of food.

Octavia, the receptionist at work, and I were supposed to hang out that night.

I showered and then headed to her place. When I arrived, I double-checked the address she had given me. The luxury condos sported a sign that boasted three- and four-bedroom condos for sale starting at a quarter of a million dollars.

How can she afford to live here?

The doorman asked my name and the unit number I was going to visit. Octavia must have already called down, because the doorman pointed toward the elevator and told me to have a nice evening.

Her three-year-old son answered the door in cowboy boots with spurs and a huge cowboy hat. I smiled at him and extended my hand. He looked at my hand, expressionless, then looked back up at my face.

"What's your name?" I asked, bending down to his level.

Silence.

"I'm Anaya . . . your mom's friend."

He just stood there, staring at me.

"You stink!" he said.

I must have put on too much perfume.

"Ny?" Octavia called, coming to the door. "Come on inside. Boy, move and let her in." She chuckled at her son.

She was casually sexy in skinny jeans and a white, button-down shirt. As usual, she was wearing a lot of makeup—which she actually didn't need, because she was so pretty.

"Hey, Octavia," I greeted her.

"What's up, girl?" she replied.

"I'm good. This is a *nice* place," I said, looking around.

"Say hi to Anaya, Malik," she said to the mini-cowboy.

He pinched his nose and ran away, laughing.

"Well, make yourself at home while I finish getting ready. My cousin, Ebony, was gonna babysit for me. But she was supposed to be here fifteen minutes ago."

Octavia had a large, sunken living room that was perfect for children. There was a flat-panel TV on the wall in the corner of the room, and two red couches. The walls were adorned with pictures of Malik and one huge pencil sketch of SpongeBob, matted in a beautiful cherry wood frame. In another corner, there was a tent with a little table and chair set next to it. Near the TV, there was a bookcase full of DVDs and another bookcase full of books, coloring books, and puzzles. There was also a basket full of magazines: *Highlights, Jet,* and *Bay Area Parent.*

I was shocked.

And all this time, I thought she was a party girl.

I sat down on the larger of the red couches, which felt like it was filled with feathers.

Way too soft for me, but the kid probably loves it.

Malik came back into the living room, apparently for the sole purpose of ogling me, because that's all he did. I wasn't the greatest with kids, but I smiled at him, hoping he would speak first. He didn't. He just gawked.

"Hi," I tried again.

Still nothing.

"Is that your truck over there by the chair?"

"You stink!" he repeated.

He ran away again.

I lifted my arm and took a good whiff.

Octavia came in, her own perfume filling the room as she talked loudly on the phone. From what I could gather, the babysitting cousin had gotten caught up in some drama and was running late. Octavia shouted some expletives into the phone and hung up.

"Girl," she said, "I'm sorry. Ebony got into a fight with her boyfriend and is just now leaving the house. While we're waiting, would you like anything to drink, Ny? Wine? Vodka? Water? Apple juice?"

"No, thanks. You mind if I look at this?" I asked, pointing to a photo album under the coffee table.

"Go ahead," she said.

I like looking at other people's photo albums because you can get a feel for who they are and what they're like. In this case, Octavia had a lot of friends in her album. I expected to see club and picnic pictures, which were present. But what surprised me were the number of photos taken with her son—at Disneyland, in a park somewhere, and at the barber shop.

"Is this your mom?" I asked Octavia, pointing to a picture of a woman who looked a lot like her.

"Everybody says we look just alike," she said with a laugh.

Although I saw a lot of pictures of Malik—at soccer games and at his birthday parties, I didn't see any of him with his dad.

One of the pictures was of Morris, Taylor, and Octavia at an office party. As usual, Taylor looked gorgeous—but about as friendly as a barracuda. There was another one of Octavia and Morris at the same party.

Ebony finally showed up with tearstains on her face. Whatever happened with the boyfriend had made her pretty upset. She grabbed Malik and gave him a huge hug. It was obvious she had a good relationship with the boy. Malik talked more in the two minutes after Ebony arrived than he had in the entire time I had been there.

Just before we left, Octavia kissed her son and told Ebony not to let him eat cookies until after he ate the pizza she had ordered.

On the elevator, Octavia said, "She's a little dramatic, but she takes good care of my kid."

We had originally planned to take Octavia's car, but it was cluttered with fliers and bumper stickers for Malik's soccer fundraiser, so we ended up taking my Honda, which was fine with me.

We were a few minutes late for our dinner reservation, but we got seated right away in the crowded restaurant. I could see men looking at us, but I wasn't sure whether or not it made me uncomfortable. Sometimes it did, and sometimes it didn't.

Octavia was comfortable, though. I could see it all over her face. She looked around as if she were waiting for someone in particular. She stared back at each guy at the bar who looked at her.

In contrast, I avoided eye contact with all of them, and I looked around for a waitress. When one finally showed up, she handed us menus and said to Octavia, "That bald gentleman at the bar right behind me would like to buy you a drink."

"No, thank you," Octavia said, without looking at the man. "Just bring us water for now." When the waitress left, Octavia rolled her eyes. "I don't want anybody buying me a drink because they think it's cool to come over and talk. I ain't in the mood for that tonight. He can keep his lil' seven dollars."

We laughed.

"Octavia, you are crazy!"

"I know. That's how you have to be sometimes to stay sane. *You're* crazy, too. Gotta admit, though, you're much different than I thought you'd be."

"How did you think I'd be?"

"I thought you were one of those spoiled rich chicks full of herself, with the designer clothes and big trust fund. But you're real down to earth. Not at all what I expected when I first met you."

I laughed.

"What?" she asked, looking confused.

"Well, first of all, my parents are anything but rich. I work because I have to, not because I want to."

She looked genuinely surprised.

"So what do you do, spend all of your money on clothes? Because you got some nice stuff. Especially that black sweater jacket with the fur around the collar. I saw that in a magazine, and it cost more than my couch!"

"Girl, I would not and do not spend my money on expensive clothes. And no, I'm not rich, but my two best friends are, and they're very generous."

She looked at me over the top of her menu with a priceless expression on her face—a mixture of "Yeah, right!" and "Really?"

"Wait, hold up," she said. "You tellin' me you have friends who buy you that stuff?"

"Something like that. Sometimes they give me gifts. Sometimes they just give me things they don't want or that doesn't fit. And it all happens to be good stuff."

As she sat on this confession for a few seconds, her expression softened.

"So, I had you all wrong?"

"If you thought I was rich, yes. I'm striving for it, though," I chuckled. "Any other misconceptions?"

She raised an eyebrow. "No. Man, I wish I had a friend who gave me Gucci shoes. My punk-ass friends can't even pay for dinner half the time."

"The friends I have . . . Well, we've been friends for most of our lives, and we're close, like sisters."

"Oh, that's good. I guess I was definitely wrong about you."

"I guess I was wrong about you, too," I said.

"Well, do tell! What did you think about me when you first met me?" She leaned into the table.

Honestly?

"I kinda had you pegged for a party girl," I said. "I had no idea you were so into your kid. You seem like a really good mom. As a matter of fact, it's you who seems to be rollin' in the dough. That condo of yours is amazing."

She laughed uneasily.

"Life's a funny thing, girl," she said.

When the waitress came back, we ordered appetizer samplers and strawberry smoothies.

I was having fun out with Octavia. One thing I learned fast was that the girl did get a lot of attention from men.

Good grief, she's like a man magnet!

There was just something magnetic about her—especially her smile.

"What are you thinking about, girl?" she asked with mock attitude after I had been quiet for a while.

"Hanging out with you, Octavia, is not what I expected. Don't laugh, but in my entire life, I've only had two really good friends, so it's nice to hang out with somebody different."

"You thought that with me it was gonna be about partying and guys all the time?"

Yes.

"No," I lied.

"I do like to have fun," she admitted, "but that's not my life. My son is everything. I wanna show him something different than I saw as a kid. I grew up in a neighborhood where nobody wanted to be. I may have a rough exterior, but I'm a mother above everything else."

"So, are you still in touch with your kid's father?"

She looked me straight in the eye and revealed, "I get financial help." She said this slowly, as if she were trying to feel me out. Her eyes said something that I couldn't interpret. Then she dropped her gaze and stirred her drink.

"Well, that's good," I said. "Does he visit a lot? When I looked in your photo album, I didn't see any pictures of Malik with a man."

"Yeah," she said with a chuckle. "You saw him in my photo album. You see him every day at work, too."

"Huh?" I stammered, not understanding her meaning.

"Morris Thomas is Malik's dad," she said, biting into a buffalo wing.

My eyes must have looked like saucers.

I never would've guessed she was Morris's type.

"Girl," she said, "we hooked up after an office party a few years ago. It was stupid of us. Nothing ever really came of it. We're cool, though. He gives me money for Malik and used to spend some time with him. But since he got married last year, that stopped. I don't trip about it, though. I used to, but I can't make Morris do what he doesn't want to do."

"Do people at work know?"

"I'm sure they do. I haven't told anybody, but I'm sure they've all figured it out. Malik looks just like him," she said, stating the obvious.

She's right. So, that's why Morris's picture was in that album.

She changed the subject. "Shirley sure did look like a crayon last week," she said, "with the red suit, red shirt, red stockings, and red shoes. And Taylor—"

"I don't like Taylor," I disclosed, "and I don't think she likes me."

"Not many people like Taylor; but she's a good attorney, and that's why Jeff hired her."

The mention of his name gave me goose bumps. But since Octavia had brought up the subject, I decided to ask her a few questions.

"How do you like Jeff?" I inquired nonchalantly.

"He's fair," she offered. "The question is, how do *you* like him?"

"He's nice. And yeah, I guess he's fair."

"That's it?" she said, leaning toward me.

"Yeah."

"Now, that *can't* be true," she said with a wicked grin.

"What do you mean?"

"Just take care of yourself, Ny. That's all I gotta say. What seems like a good thing can turn around and bite you in the ass."

I let her words permeate. We ate dinner, gossiped, and had a drink. I dropped Octavia off at her luxury condo and headed home. Hanging out with her was different from going out with Catie and Sophie.

When I was ten minutes from home, my cell phone rang.

"Hey, you," Carl said.

"Hey, you, yourself."

"How have you been?"

I could feel his warm smile. I hadn't talked to him since the fight in Arizona, a week before, and I was glad to hear his voice.

"I'm hanging in there," I said. "Just working. How 'bout you?"

"I was just thinking I would give you a call and see how you were."

"What are you doing right now?" I asked him.

"Just chillin'. What's up with you?"

"Nothing. Just headed home. But I could be persuaded to make a detour."

"Is that right?"

"Hold on, Carl, my other line's ringing."

On the other line, I suddenly heard Jeff bark, "Where are you?"

"I'm getting on the freeway. Why? Where are you?"

"I'm at the office. I've been calling you all night," he said impatiently.

"I'm sorry. I didn't know. I was having drinks with Octavia, and I never checked my phone. Jeff, can you hold on for a second? I have somebody on my other line."

"No," he said brusquely. "You go ahead and get your other line. I'll talk to you later."

"Wait! I can hang up. Just give me a sec."

"Go ahead and talk. I have something to do anyway."

"Jeff, what's going on?"

"Nothing's going on. I just don't want to interrupt the other important late-night conversation you're having."

"What?"

"Look, just call me tomorrow or something, okay?"

"Jeff—"

"Anaya, I don't like to play games. I'll be honest with you, I am jealous. I know it doesn't make any sense, and I shouldn't be, but I am."

"Jeff, nothing's going on."

"Meet me," he said.

"What?"

"Meet me," he repeated.

"How? When? Where? It's late."

"Just meet me at the Starbucks parking lot. You know where. Ten minutes." He hung up.

In the meantime, I had completely forgotten about Carl on my other line. It was just as well, because he had hung up anyway.

When I got to Starbucks, I saw Jeff's car. I got out of my car and walked slowly toward his, twisting my hips for his viewing pleasure. When I climbed into his car, I was temporarily distracted by two turquoise boxes with bows on top, which were sitting on the back seat. Jeff was smiling.

"Hey," he said.

"Hey," I said back.

Even in the dimness of his car, I was certain that he felt exactly what I felt. So I ignored the doubts that lingered in my mind, erased the guilt, and embraced the feeling while I had it. I'd worry about the consequences tomorrow.

"I'm sorry I got upset," he said.

"It's okay," I soothed.

"No. It's not," he insisted.

Before I could respond, he kissed me. He put one hand on my thigh and the other one behind my neck. The pull was gentle but firm. The kiss was sensual, and I didn't want it ever to end.

"I'm sorry I shouldn't have done that," he said.

I caught my breath before speaking. "It's okay."

"Are you sure?"

"Yes," I said quietly. I had imagined kissing him so many times but I had no idea it would feel so good. He was soft and gentle and loving and I was going straight to hell. There was an awkward silence for a few moments.

"Are you going to open your gifts?"

"Yes."

Inside the larger box, there was a beautiful pink sweater. The smaller box contained a silver bangle.

"I love them, Jeff!" I gushed.

He couldn't stay long, so shortly after, I was back on the freeway heading home for the second time that evening.

I called Catie.

"Hello?" she drawled.

"Wow, I'm surprised you answered. You've gone so undercover, Homeland Security couldn't find you. Where have you been?" I asked.

"Shut up, Cow," was her retort.

"You shut up," I admonished her. "And call people back when they call you. I called you a few times last week."

"You know I'm a busy woman," she snickered, a bit wickedly. "What's up?"

I talked a little about work, and she mentioned some guy she was dating. It wasn't very often that Catie dated. It was hard for her to find men who were actually accepting of what she did for a living and Catie refused to lie about it. So, whenever she told me she was dating someone, I worried. You had to be a pretty unique individual to date a woman who slept with other men on a regular basis. I asked if she had talked to Sophie recently, and she said she hadn't.

"I'm worried about her," I said.

"Girl, please. Sophie's spoiled. She's just like one of those rich, spoiled hoes you see on TV. Got all that money and just be messin' up because she don't have anything else to do."

"Catie, that's not fair. You know Carmen and Terry don't give her any attention."

"Attention? Sophie's a grown-ass woman. Her days of needing attention are over. She better get a good therapist like you did and chalk her childhood losses up to the game. Nobody has time for all that nonsense. She needs to move the hell on."

"Catie, people deal with things differently. Maybe she's not the type to just leave her childhood in the past. Maybe she's acting out now because of what she missed back then."

"Well, if that's the case, she's stupid on top of everything else. Who has all that time to be wasting?" Leave it to Catie to dispense practical advice.

"So, who's the new guy?" I inquired politely.

"Just a guy. Armani," she answered cryptically.

"Armani? You're dating somebody named Armani?"

"Yes, I am. Dating is what people in our age group do. Try it sometime, Ny. When was the last time *you* had a date, Goode?"

Last night.

I had spent all this time trying to track Catie down to tell her about Jeff, and when I had the chance, I chickened out. Catie would understand. She knew all about men and relationships.

Tell her!

"I don't know. It's been a while," I lied.

"That's what I thought."

"Okay, so I'll live through you. Details, please."

"Not right now, I gotta go."

"Come on, Catie. We haven't talked in weeks. Just tell me about him."

"Later."

"Well, then, what are we gonna do about Sophie?"

"Sophie needs help. Until she admits that, there's nothing we can do."

I got off the phone feeling heavy. It didn't feel good to have Sophie running around out there with nobody to help her or love her. But Catie was right. All the concern I had didn't mean a thing if Sophie didn't want help.

TEN

The next day, I wore the silver bangle that Jeff had given me. I was walking on air despite myself, and I even arrived at work a little earlier than usual. My desk was exactly the way I left it on Friday, except for the king-size bag of peanut M&Ms sitting on top of my keyboard.

I smiled to myself.

"What are you smiling at?" I heard Jeff say.

When I turned around to thank him, he was already so close to me I bumped into him.

We stood face to face for only a few seconds, but it felt like forever. I needed to move, but I couldn't.

"I'm sorry," he finally said, stepping back a little. He looked embarrassed, almost shy.

Before I could respond, Shirley walked in, carrying two bags and a box of donuts. She put the donuts on the table near Jeff's office and walked over to my desk.

"Good morning, you two," she said, smiling.

"Good morning, Shirley," Jeff said cheerfully. "Looks like you have enough food there to feed the entire building."

"Well," she said, as she walked away toward the kitchen with her bags, "I bring enough to share, and everybody's welcome to whatever I have."

When she was gone, Jeff turned back to me. "I love you," he whispered.

"Please," I said, shaking my head. "Don't say that."

"I'm sorry," he said, looking down.

"Stop apologizing."

"I'm sorry for apologizing so much," he said tenderly.

"It's fine," I said. "I really need to get these summaries done. Can we talk about this later?"

"Okay," he said. "I understand." He walked slowly to his office.

I sighed and dropped down in my chair. I was the happiest woman in the world when I got to work this morning. How easily my euphoria had been replaced with disgrace. Reality bites. Being with Jeff made me feel beautiful, happy, and alive. Despite all that, the fact remained that Jeff was married. Not only was he married and my boss, but also I was totally out of my league. I stared at the M&Ms as if the answers to all of my problems were embedded on the packaging. When nothing surfaced, I took the completed deposition summaries to Taylor.

"Wow," she said. "That was fast. I didn't think you would get to them until next week. Can you do these, too?" she asked gratefully, handing me a huge stack of documents.

"Sure," I said.

The rest of the day was uneventful. Jeff hadn't tried to talk to me again. I may have hurt his feelings, or maybe he was just as confused and conflicted as I was.

When I got off work, I called Catie and told her I was on my way over there. I needed to talk to somebody or I was going to go crazy.

"On your way where?"

"On my way to your house."

"Um, girl, that's not really a good idea. I'm headed out."

"Well, I will catch you before you go, because I'm right around the corner." I hung up before she could respond.

After I got off the phone with Catie, I sent Sophie a text asking her to meet me at Catie's. I was pretty sure she wouldn't come, but I asked her anyway.

Catie greeted me at the door. "Ny!" she said loudly, giving me a big hug.

Why is she talking so loud? Good Lord, I hope she hasn't been snorting that stuff like Sophie.

"Hey you," I said, hugging her back.

"Come on in, girl," she said, leading me toward the living room.

"Catie, why are you talking so loud?" I asked, mystified.

Before she could respond, a dark-skinned guy walked into the room and stood next to her. She quickly introduced him as Armani, and he walked back into Catie's room, closing the door behind him. Before I could begin my interrogation, Catie started to explain. It turned out that she'd started seeing him a week ago. But she was now tired of him, and she wasn't sure he had anywhere else to go. Apparently, he managed to pull the wool over Catie's well-trained eyes and misrepresented himself with a rented BMW and stories of his successful music management company. The problem with lies is that eventually, the truth comes out.

I wasn't surprised at his being a phony, but I certainly was surprised at Catie. She was normally able to spot an impersonator several miles away.

As Catie finished telling me about the mooching music manager, Sophie called my cell.

"Hello?" I said. "Yes, I'm here, Sophie. You have Antoine with you? How did *you* guys get together? Oh, okay. See you soon. Bye."

Catie raised an eyebrow as high as it could go.

"I asked her to meet me here. She said she was on her way. She has Antoine with her."

"Wait," Catie said, holding her hand up and shaking her head from side to side.

"*You* invited Sophie to my house? And she's coming here with some dude I don't even know?"

"Yes, I invited her here, and Antoine isn't some dude. You remember him. His mom used to date my Uncle Riley," I reminded her.

"Yes, I remember that hoodlum," she snipped.

When we were kids, Antoine had a huge crush on Catie. I think she had a crush on him, too, but she wouldn't admit it. Whenever he came to our house with his mom, Catie didn't let him out of her sight. Sophie and I always thought they would make a good couple, but it never happened. We hadn't seen Antoine in a long time. I texted him occasionally, but we hadn't hung out in ages. I couldn't figure out how he and Sophie ended up hooking up.

"Antoine's not a hoodlum, and you know it. He works for the city's transportation department, and he makes good money."

"Whatever. He's a hoodlum to me."

I looked at a text from Sophie on my phone. "Sophie and Antoine are here," I informed Catie. "Can you let them up, please? And be nice?"

She hesitated.

"Why are you acting like that?" I argued. "You used to think Antoine was cute when we were kids," I reminded her.

"No I didn't! And even if I did, I'm not a kid anymore. I'm a fully grown woman now, and I don't get down with the thuggish, ruggish bone," she said. "Besides, Sophie hasn't returned my calls in weeks," she said, sounding more like an adolescent than a fully grown woman.

I gave her a look. "She hasn't called me back either, but she's still our friend."

"Tell them to drive into the garage," she relented. "I'll call the doorman."

When Antoine and Sophie walked through the elevator, Catie rolled her eyes and plopped down on the couch. Sometimes she was such a toddler.

"Hello to you, too," Sophie said sarcastically to Catie.

She and Antoine both gave me a hug.

"Bitch, please," Catie admonished Sophie. "Ny and I both have been calling you for weeks. Don't come up in here talking crazy to me."

Antoine then said to Catie, "Well, you haven't been calling me. So do *I* get a hug?"

I hadn't seen Antoine in a while, but time had certainly been good to him. He was still tall and well built, but he had matured in ways I couldn't put my finger on. It didn't hurt that his biceps boldly crept from beneath his All Saints tee and his Seven for All Mankind jeans hung just right on his slim waist. He was looking good, and there was no denying that. I shot a glance over at Catie, who was apparently thinking the same thing by the look on her face. I fought the urge to tell her to close her mouth. It was too late, anyway.

She got up slowly and hugged Antoine. She tried to hug him quickly and let go, but he held on to her. Sophie and I exchanged glances.

"What are you two doing together?" I asked Sophie and Antoine after he let Catie go and sat down on the couch.

"Oh, I ran into Antoine at the car dealership. I put my car in the shop and was going to get a courtesy rental when I ran into him. We went to lunch, and then you called and told me to come over here. And here we are."

"It's been so long," I said to Antoine. "You're looking good, too. Isn't he looking good, Catie?"

"Huh, what?" Catie asked, still apparently in awe of Antoine.

"I was just telling Antoine how good he looks. Wouldn't you agree?"

"Oh, yeah. You look nice," Catie said, going to the kitchen. "Can I get anybody anything?"

"No thank you, but maybe you should get yourself a glass of ice water," Sophie said teasingly.

Catie shot her a dirty look.

We sat around and talked for about thirty minutes, when Armani emerged from Catie's bedroom. He had a backpack and a video game console, and he left on the elevator without a word. Catie sighed in relief.

Sophie and Antoine looked at Armani, then Catie, then me. Their amazement and curiosity were apparent. Neither Catie nor I had mentioned the fact that Catie had a man in her bedroom.

"Sophie, you look a little tired," Catie said to Sophie, who did actually appear thin and very tired. It was an obvious deflection.

Sophie wasn't buying into it. "Please don't sit there and act like a man didn't just walk out of your bedroom," Sophie exclaimed. "Who the hell was that?"

Defeated, Catie recapped her story about Armani. I was surprised that she was so candid in front of Antoine since she had given him such a hard time. Antoine didn't seem to mind, though.

"You guys want something to drink?" Catie offered, trying to change the subject again.

"You have any chocolate?" Sophie asked.

"No, but I have some soap," Catie replied. "You also look like you need a bath."

Sophie didn't say anything. She wandered into the kitchen.

Catie didn't hide that she had little sympathy for Sophie's drug problem. Catie believed that Sophie was spoiled, bored, and selfish.

"You *did* have chocolate, you liar!" Sophie said, coming back into the living room and sliding back down on the couch.

Jeff called my cell, and, excusing myself, I went on the balcony to talk to him.

"Where are you?" he asked possessively.

Surely, he could have thought of a nicer way to greet me.

"I'm at my friend Catie's house. You remember, I've told you about my friend, Catie?"

"We need to talk," he said.

"I'm listening," I said, admiring the view from Catie's balcony.

"When would be a good time for you?"

"I don't know. I have other things on my mind right now, and I can't make room for this."

Why did I say that, when he's the only thing on my mind?

"Oh, you don't have time for our issues?" he demanded.

"Our issues?" I realized that I was about to be brutally honest, but I kept going. "I fell in love with you for who you are, despite all of the nonsense that comes with it. I've opened myself up to you in almost every way possible. I've made myself available to you when you need me. You sleep with someone else every night, not me. Stupidly, I put up with that. I feel as if I'm sacrificing my soul for this relationship. In fact, I know I'm sacrificing my soul for this relationship. Do you even realize that?" I stomped my foot in frustration.

There was a long silence. Finally, he simply said he was sorry. I heard the apology, but I didn't know what to say.

"Anaya?"

"Yes?"

"Are you sure you don't want to see me?"

I really wasn't sure about anything, but I said firmly, "I'm tired of my heart being broken every time we get off the phone, because I know you're going home to *her*. I'm overwhelmed with guilt whenever you tell me about your life that doesn't involve me in any way. I'm pretty sure I deserve better."

"I love you, Anaya."

My heart began pounding, and I started sweating.

"I love you," he repeated.

"I can't do this anymore, Jeff."

"Did you hear what I just said?"

"I heard you, but I just can't do it anymore."

"I don't want to talk you into anything," he said. "I know your mind is set. It is so hard to let you go. How am I supposed to do that? You know I love you, Anaya. I blame myself for letting things go too far. I know this is not the kind of thing you're happy with, and I know you struggle with it. I'm so sorry I'm doing this to you, but I can't let you go. I feel like you belong to me."

His possessiveness felt stifling. I explained, "But I *don't* belong to you, Jeff, and I never will."

"I know," he agreed reluctantly.

"Why do you love me?" I coolly asked him.

"Why are you asking?" he said, puzzled.

"I want to know."

Jeff put his best case forward. "I love you because your heart and your feelings for me are so strong. You want me for who I am, not for what I can do for you or give to you. I love you because when you smile, my day is brighter. I love you because you're the most intelligent woman I've ever had the pleasure of kissing. You're the most beautiful and sweetest woman I've ever known."

Although he said these complimentary, compelling things, something just didn't make sense to me. Why would he be so enamored of a mere college student, with limited life experience, who still lives at home with her parents? What did he want from me? Not believing him gave me strength.

"What are you thinking?" he asked.

"I'm just wondering what you see in me that you don't see in her." I knew he didn't want me to ask, but it was a reasonable question.

He sighed. "Are you asking me if you're better than she is?"

"I'm asking what you want from me and why."

Jeff's feelings tumbled out, and those feelings centered on himself. "I enjoy you, Ny. I enjoy your passion for life. I'm totally and completely in love with the way you love me. Nobody has ever loved me the way you do. Nobody, ever. In the middle of everything else that life has to offer, when you find someone who loves you that way, it feels good. It feels *damn* good."

He paused, and I nervously drummed my fingers on the balcony railing, waiting to hear the rest.

"I don't know what I want from you," he continued vaguely. "I don't have a logical answer for that. Whatever time you want to give me, I'll take it. You're a beautiful, smart woman. You could date anyone you want but you choose to spend your time with me, and you choose to love me. Sometimes when I think about you, I'm overwhelmed that you even chose me. I'm older, with a family and serious obligations. You're young and beautiful, with your whole life ahead of you—"

"Wait," I interrupted. "Are you telling me you are insecure about my feelings for you, Jeff?"

"Maybe a little insecure. You might wake up one day and decide I'm not worth it. Decide that we are not worth it."

"Why do you think I love you?" I asked.

"I know this might sound overconfident," he said, "but I think I'm the best thing that has ever happened in your life, as far as men go. I think you love me because I know what you want, and I know what you need. We share the same determination in trying to be the best we can, and you like that. I also think you trust me more than you're willing to admit."

"But I don't trust you, and I don't feel that I chose you. You chose me," I blurted out.

"Why don't you trust me?" he asked.

"Because you're married, Jeff. How can I trust a man who cheats on his wife?"

"How can I trust a woman who falls in love with that man, Anaya? This is not about our circumstances. It's more than that. It's about friendship and the feelings we have for each other. I didn't come looking for you or this relationship. I don't have time for all of this drama and confusion. Do you think I wanted this to happen? I didn't. But it happened. And now I can't stand the thought of being without you. I love and trust you for who you are, and for what you are to me, regardless of our circumstances."

I felt worn out and said, "I need to go. My friends are waiting."

"Please, don't," he pleaded. "We really need to finish this."

"I have to," I wearily explained.

"Anaya?"

"Yes?"

"Please," he begged.

"I can't, Jeff. I can't do this anymore, and I can't talk about it anymore. It's too much."

"Why do I feel like you're punishing me for loving you?" he asked.

"I'm not punishing you, Jeff." I blinked my eyes to hold back the tears. "I'm probably hurting more than you are. Sometimes I can deal with it, and sometimes I can't. Lately, it's been getting harder for me."

"Tell me what you want me to do," he said.

After a long pause, I said, "I want you to go home. Go be with your family."

"Sweetie, please don't do this."

"I can't, Jeff," I said. I hung the phone up just when Sophie opened the patio door.

"Who was that?" she asked.

"Who was who?" I replied, nonchalantly.

"Who was who?" she repeated. "Who was that on the phone?"

"Oh, no one," I said.

"Since when do you need so much privacy to talk to no one?" Catie asked from over Sophie's shoulder.

"No, it was nothing. Just someone asking something," I stammered, walking back in the apartment.

I am a horrible liar.

"Right," Catie said. "You want to watch a movie with us?"

"No. I hate to jet out, but I have an appointment," I said, relieved to be telling the truth.

Catie eyeballed me suspiciously.

"You are up to something," she said, narrowing her eyes at me.

"I'm not," I said, kissing her and Sophie on the cheek. "I will call you guys later."

I looked at Antoine, who was still sitting on the couch.

"You staying?" I asked him.

"Yes, I'm gonna wait until Sophie's car is ready and drop her off at the dealership," he said.

"Okay, see you later. Tell your mom I said hello." I kissed him on the cheek and raced out to get to my appointment with Judy.

On the way to see Judy, I called Mom. She told me that Sophie's mom had asked her out to lunch. I couldn't wait to see how that meeting turned out. She also told me she was having a "get together" with a couple of our relatives and Aunt Marie. I knew better than that. They were going to try and ambush poor Aunt Marie, to tell her what to do about the situation with her daughter Amber. Amber decided she was going to rebel against anything and everything. She was acting out in school and giving Aunt Marie a hard time. Aunt Marie called mom to confide in her and mom told other members of the family. I didn't think that was such a nice thing to do, but that was my family. They were always in each other's business.

I knew that Aunt Marie would be better off without our family giving her advice, but I would never say that to Mom.

I was more relieved to talk to Judy than I had ever been. I didn't waste a moment.

"I'm in love with a married man," I said.

She was a trained professional, and I was thoroughly impressed that her only reaction was a mere raised eyebrow. "When did this happen?" she asked.

"Over time. I thought we were just friends. I mean, that's what I kept telling myself. But I love him. I hate myself for it, because it's wrong."

"Why do you hate yourself?"

Didn't I just tell her why?

"Because it's wrong. I know I can do better. I deserve better. I don't know why I even let things get this far."

"Do you think he loves you?"

"Yeah," I said, looking down. "I do."

"Are you sure about that?"

"I think so."

If he loved me, he would be with me, right? He wouldn't still be married to his wife. Is that the point she's trying to make? No, she's not trying to make any points. She's trying to help.

"What are you going to do?" she asked.

I can't believe I pay for this.

"I don't know," was the only response I could muster.

"What do you want to do?" she persisted.

I shrugged. "I don't know that, either."

"When do you think would be a good time to figure it out?"

"Anytime soon."

Checkmate.

She raised her eyebrow again.

"Why are you so hard on yourself?" she asked.

"It's not right," I said.

"Who says?" she asked.

"What do you mean?"

"I need for you to think about that," she said.

She suddenly made me sick, with her loose morals and poor taste in fashion. Why couldn't she just tell me what to do and what to think? Isn't that what she was paid for? The session drained me by forcing me to think about the truth. I was ashamed of myself.

When I got home, I saw that Aunt Deb, Aunt Marie, and Uncle Riley were sitting in the living room.

"Where's Mom?" I asked.

"She's in the kitchen finishing the appetizers," Aunt Deb said.

While we waited for Mom to come out of the kitchen, Uncle Riley talked about the Lakers, and whether or not it was safe again to bet on them.

"Wait until next Tuesday," Aunt Deb advised him.

"Next Tuesday? Why?" he asked with a frown.

"Because Mercury's in retrograde, that's why," Aunt Deb explained, as if the retrograde of Mercury was common knowledge. "You're not supposed to meddle in finance when Mercury's in retrograde. Wait until next Tuesday."

"Aw, come on," Uncle Riley scoffed with a smirk.

"Okay," Aunt Deb smiled mysteriously. "I'm just trying to tell you what's right. You don't have to listen to me, but you should listen to the stars. They never lie."

Mom came out of the kitchen, and everybody started eating the finger foods she had prepared.

"So, Marie," Deb started, "Anita tells me things aren't going well at home."

I almost choked on the celery stick I was eating. She didn't waste any time.

Aunt Marie chewed on her miniature sandwich slowly.

"It's nothing to be ashamed of," Aunt Deb continued. "We all have family problems. The key is to make sure you talk about it and get a little help."

I looked over at Aunt Marie and saw in her face that she was not interested in their advice. I think Mom sensed it as well, because she changed the subject.

"Enough about that. Did everybody choose possible dates for the family reunion?" Mom asked.

"I don't want to do it in the summer," Aunt Deb said. "The energy in summer is too condensed for a family reunion."

"Too condensed?" Uncle Riley asked. "What the hell does that mean?"

We all laughed.

"It means, we should wait until fall," Aunt Deb said.

"You wait until fall, Deb, and we will have our reunion this summer," Mom said, laughing.

"I'm in," Uncle Riley said. "You cooking, Anita?"

"Is Anita's food *all* you ever think about?" Aunt Marie asked.

I had had enough, so I went upstairs and took a shower. As I passed Ava's room, I observed that she was sitting on the floor with a bunch of pamphlets around her.

That girl never, ever cleans her room.

"Ava, why don't you clean your room?"

"It doesn't need it."

Looking at her face, you would think she really believed that. But there was no way a sane person could look at that room and think it didn't need cleaning.

"Um, yes, it does, Ava."

"No, it doesn't. It just needs a little organizing, and I haven't had time to do it. I'm busy with this project."

She was always talking about working on some project. You would think she was a part of the president's administration, with all her busy-ness.

"Oh," I said.

I went in my room and closed the door.

Is it me, or is everybody in this house nuts?

ELEVEN

Taylor's case was going to trial in two weeks, and she was frantic. She was e-mailing assignments to me with instructions that had two or three exclamation marks after every sentence. Taylor was one e-mail away from my limit.

"Taylor gets nervous when she goes to trial," Shirley told me. "It'll pass, trust me."

Maybe when I'm your age, Shirley, I'll be ripe with patience, too.

One morning Taylor came to the office with coffee in hand, swept past my desk like an arctic breeze, and shut her office door behind her.

I called Jeff from my desk phone. It probably would have made more sense to just walk in his office, but I didn't want to.

"Hey," he said.

"Just wanted to say hi," I said.

Just then, Taylor walked up to my desk.

"Anaya, get these responses copied and delivered to Sandra at Pearl and O'Connor."

"I'll call you back," I said to Jeff, and hung up.

"Today!" she snapped, then quickly disappeared into her office.

Lord, I prayed. *Give me the patience to deal with this demon spirit named Taylor so that I don't do something rash.*

A few minutes later, she appeared at my desk. "Are you feeling all right, Anaya?" she asked in a tone that shocked me. It sounded like a cross between compassion and irritation.

I'm betting on irritation.

Eyes don't lie, though. When I looked up, her face expressed true concern.

"I'm fine, thanks," I said, astonished. "I'll get this to Sandra before noon. Is that okay?"

"That's fine. Anytime today works, actually. She's been bugging me about them. I should have told her to come and get them, because she lost them, but I didn't think that would be very professional. Sometimes you have to bear with difficult personalities. You know what I mean?"

I looked up at her with what I hoped was a smile.

"Can you come in my office for a minute?" she asked.

I wasn't comfortable being alone with Satan's spawn, but I went anyway. When I followed her into the office, she closed the door behind us.

"Have a seat, Anaya," she said, pointing to a large leather chair in front of her desk.

I sat down. She pulled up a chair next to mine and looked directly at me. She was one of those anatomically blessed people who always look good. As I studied her pale skin and straight hair, I found it hard to believe that she was black. When Octavia first told me, I thought she was lying. As I sat there looking into her light-brown eyes, I still had my doubts. Out of the blue, she started talking about her childhood, looking away from me.

"My father was controlling and verbally abusive, and my mother was weak." She seemed to be talking to herself. I considered that she needed me only as an ear, and that she wasn't asking for anything back.

"I knew I was going to college, because I didn't want to depend on a man like my mom did." She still wasn't looking at me.

"When I was in college, everybody thought I was a model. No one gave me credit for being smart."

But you're a beautiful, successful lawyer—so I'm having a hard time sympathizing with you.

"Most guys assume I'm a gold digger. I make six figures, so I don't need anybody else's money."

I wasn't sure why she was telling me this. Did she suspect something was going wrong between me and Jeff?

"So, I'm sorry I've been a bitch to you. You're the best case clerk we've ever had. Jeff was right. You *are* the bomb."

Jeff said I was the bomb?

I was afraid that Taylor had something up the sleeve of her Chanel pantsuit, so I decided to be guardedly nice. By the time she was finished with her little monologue, I felt like facing the day.

Jeff and I hadn't had a serious conversation since the day I was at Catie's. We had shared a few text messages and made plans to get together, but nothing came of it. I was missing him and decided to pop in his office.

As I walked in, he looked up.

"Hello again," he said in a formal tone.

"We still need to finish our talk," I said.

"You know, I'm sure we do, but I have a telephone conference in about ten minutes, and I need to dial-in soon. Can we do it another time?"

Did he say another time? No, he couldn't have said that. Agree and walk out. Or agree, toss his computer through the window, and knock everything off the desk.

I tried to pull it together.

"Will another time work for you?" he asked. Both his expression and his tone were impatient.

"Never mind. We don't need to talk. In fact, we don't *ever* have to talk again. How 'bout *that*?" I spun on my heels and stormed out. I wish like hell I could have slammed the door, but I'm not that crazy. I went to my desk, grabbed my purse, and left. In my heart, I knew that I didn't have the game or the emotional control to deal with this.

My toes hurt from walking away so fast. I bit my bottom lip as hard as I could without drawing blood.

How did I grow up to be so stupid?

"Anaya, wait!" he called, irritated.

The cool outside breeze made me shiver. I wanted to get to my car and get away from him. I was embarrassed that I could already feel tears forming, because I didn't want anyone to see me crying. I couldn't find my keys, so I kept rummaging through my purse with one hand.

Not even looking at him, I said, "Go back to your stupid conference call and your perfect life."

Damn me for being so emotional! Where are my keys?

"Anaya!"

But I didn't answer and just kept rummaging.

"Can you please look at me?" he demanded.

"What?" I looked at him for two seconds and started walking.

"Anaya, what's going on?" he yelled after me. He finally caught up.

"You tell *me* what's going on, Jeff. You didn't bother to call me last night, you didn't say hello to me this morning, and when I come into your office to try to talk to you, you just dismiss me like I'm a nobody!"

He looked miserable, but I tried to concentrate on the sidewalk ahead. "Didn't I ask you not to treat me this way, Jeff?"

I was panting by now, so I slowed my pace and lowered my voice, which had gotten way too loud. We both looked around to see if anyone had been listening.

"Anaya, I'm sorry, okay? I don't always do things the right way, but I wouldn't ever do anything to hurt you. Please believe that." He looked defeated, and I almost felt sorry for him.

"Go back and make your call," I huffed.

"I've already told Shirley to reschedule. I needed to come and see about you . . . about us. This is not a game to me. What's going on with you?"

"I don't know." I shook my head.

I finally stopped walking.

"What do you want from me?" he asked.

"I don't know," I lied.

Yes, I do.

He questioned me again. "What do you want, Anaya?"

"I don't know!" I repeated, louder.

Yes, I do!

"What do you want?" he asked a third time.

I want you to help me pick out my first new car. I want you to encourage me when I'm feeling down, and remind me when I'm being too silly. I want to fall asleep in your arms and wake up to your bad breath. I want to fight with you and make up before going to bed. I want to take vacations with you and have my picture on your desk. I want you for myself.

"I don't want anything from you, Jeff," I said mechanically. "I've been hurting and didn't know how to express it."

"Since when don't you know how to express anger?" He smiled.

We both laughed at the same time. When I looked in his eyes, every ill feeling I had disappeared. I wanted to hold him, and I knew he wanted to hold me. But we couldn't.

"Hey, guys!" Octavia called out, driving up alongside us.

"Hi," I said, trying to recover.

"Hello, Octavia," Jeff said.

Octavia parked her car and walked quickly over to us. I was uncomfortable, but Jeff seemed to be relaxed.

How does he do that?

"I had a dentist appointment," she said. "They gave me two fillings, and my lips feel huge. Am I drooling?"

"No," he answered, laughing a little.

"Well, I gotta go. I'm already late. I was supposed to be in fifteen minutes ago. Who's covering the phones?"

"I'm not sure," Jeff answered, looking a little worried.

It was a little weird for the receptionist to comfortably tell her boss she's fifteen minutes late and has no idea who's covering the phones.

"Okay. I'll see y'all later."

She smiled and rushed toward the office.

"Wanna go to lunch?" Jeff asked.

"It's not lunchtime yet."

"In Chicago, it is."

"Are you asking me to go to Chicago?"

"No, I'm asking you to get something to eat with me."

"I'll pass on lunch," I replied.

He just stood there, looking at me, making me melt on the spot. "No, you won't," he said. He moved closer to me.

"No, really," I insisted. "I have some things I need to do for Taylor, and she needs them done today. I can't spend all day hanging out with you."

"But you were on your way out. How are you working?"

All I could think of to say was, "Be quiet!"

"You're too serious for somebody so young. But if you really want to get some work done, then go ahead."

He stepped back as if he were going to let me pass, but as soon as I got closer, he blocked my way. As he stood there, looking into my eyes, I almost forgot how mad he had just made me.

"I'm sorry," I said. "I really do need to get back."

"I understand. Can we get together later?"

"I would like that." I headed back toward the office.

"Wait," he said. "When?"

"I'll let you know," I said coyly.

Back at my desk, I started going through e-mails. About twenty minutes later, Jeff came in. He looked over at me, smiled, and disappeared in his office. I still felt guilty that he had missed his conference call.

While I was still going through e-mails, Catie called.

"I miss you," she said.

"Miss you, too, Catie. Where have you been?"

"With my man, girl. He's fine as wine and twice as mellow. This chick is happy right now." Catie went from not being able to find men who approved of her lifestyle to having two different boyfriends in less than a month.

"This isn't that phony Armani again, is it?"

"Hell *and* no!" she giggled.

"Who is it?"

"Tell you later. We need to get together. Dinner tonight?"

"Yes, and don't flake on me. I need to talk to you."

"What happened?"

"You're so impatient. Nothing happened. I just wanna catch up. We never talk anymore."

"Okay, I'm game."

"Don't flake," I warned her again.

"I won't," she said, and hung up.

A few hours later, I had finished my assignments and was ready for the work day to be over. I sent Jeff an e-mail that I was leaving. He wrote back, saying that he'd call me later. The day had left me emotionally drained.

On my way home, I called Catie.

"What's up?" she said.

"Can we do dinner another time? I'm tired tonight."

"Oh, so who's flaking now?" she said and hung up.

When I got home, the house was empty. I went to my room and got in bed. I thought about Jeff and a recent conversation we had had about my getting my own place. He thought it would be nice for me to have a private place where we could hang out. I didn't have the nerve to tell him that I wasn't going to get an apartment just so that I could make our affair more convenient for him. Instead, I had brushed the idea off with a half-truth and told him that my family needed me.

As I stared at the ceiling, I contemplated the mess I was in. The more time I spent with Jeff, the more I cared about him. On the other hand, I hurt now more than ever. Our relationship wasn't going anywhere, and it was clear to me that I needed to get out. I couldn't keep up with the back and forth. It was so played out.

At about 1 a.m., Jeff called. "Hey, sweetie. I'm headed home now."

"Wow," I said. "You worked late."

"I know. Nights like this, I wish you had your own place."

"I bet you do."

"Then I could come cuddle with you."

"Oh. And then you could call your wife and tell her you'll be late?"

Did I say that out loud?

"Anaya, what's wrong with you?" Jeff asked.

Guess I did.

"Nothing," I lied.

"No, there's definitely something going on with you. Please talk to me."

I'm tired of hiding, weary of lying, and fed-up with pretending.

"I don't have anything to say, Jeff. Really. It's been a long day for both of us. Let's just get some rest and talk tomorrow."

"Anaya?"

"Yes?"

"I do love you, you know," he said.

"Okay. Talk to you tomorrow," I said wearily.

I knew my response was cold. But I didn't feel very good about us.

I must have fallen asleep right after that, because the next thing I knew, my cell was ringing and sunlight was beaming in the room. I sat up to answer it.

"Hey, sweetie!" It was Jeff again.

Give me strength, Lord!

"Hi," I said, sinking back down in my pillow, trying to sound cool.

"Are you dressed?" he asked.

"For what?"

"For driving up to Sonoma. Get up and take a shower."

Sometimes I liked it when he took charge, and sometimes it got on my nerves. On that day, it got on my nerves.

"I have plans today, Jeff," I lied. Lying had become my new pastime, and I didn't like it.

"No, you don't. Get dressed. Come on."

"I can't," I answered with a heavy sigh.

"I'm on my way, sweetie. Just get dressed, and I'll pick you up in thirty minutes. Come on, baby, it's a beautiful morning. I did a lot of rearranging of my schedule to get this morning open."

His voice was patient, as if he were talking to some psycho on the edge of a bridge.

"I said I can't." I insisted so fervently that I even shocked myself.

I can't believe I'm turning him down.

I didn't know which way was up, because he had become such a huge part of my life and such a huge part of me.

"Ny?"

"No, Jeff, really. Catie called me, and we have plans today. You know, I haven't seen her in a long time." And yet another lie.

"How can you have plans with Catie, when we've already made plans?"

"We haven't made any plans. You made plans."

Where's your family on this beautiful day, Jeff?

"I can't see you now," I said. "Maybe we can get together later."

"I won't be available later."

Good!

"Okay. Well, then, call me tomorrow."

He was quiet for longer than I knew how to handle, but I kept quiet, too. I let him think about whatever it was that vexed him— probably that he couldn't control me. I concentrated on not giving in. I was growing more logical about the situation, but my heart still loved him desperately. Eventually, he agreed to call me the next day, and he hung up.

I called Catie. She was sleeping, but she sounded happy to hear my voice.

"Get up," I said, "and meet me at the gym."

Forty-five minutes later, I was winding down on the treadmill when Catie finally bounced in, wearing purple velour sweats and a clingy purple tank top. Who worked out in velour? I smiled at her. When she got on the machine next to me, I noticed a huge red mark on her neck.

"Mind your business," she said, before I could say anything.

"You freak. What have you been doing?"

"The question is, what have *you* been doing? Every time I call you, I get your voicemail. Every time I stop by your house, you aren't home, and nobody knows where you are. For a while, I thought you were trying to avoid me. Where the hell have you been? And don't say you been studying. Nobody studies *that* much."

I wanted to laugh, but I couldn't. My best friend was right next to me, and I was so ashamed of myself that I couldn't even tell her what was happening in my life. I looked at her while she talked. She was okay with who she was; if people didn't like it, she didn't care. I was jealous of that. Because even in her lifestyle choices, I felt like she was in a more respectable position than I was. I knew I couldn't tell her, because she wouldn't see my situation with Jeff as a problem. She would see it as an advantage.

"Girl, it's my new job," I said, trying to laugh. "They keep me busy. What's up with you?"

"Not much. I really want to go shopping. You wanna come? My treat." She sang out the word *treat*.

"Where are you gonna shop?"

"Ungrateful little wench. If I was going to Goodwill, what do *you* care? I'm offering to treat you." She put her hands on her hips and raised her eyebrows.

I looked at her with pursed lips.

"Stop doing your lips like that," she said. "It makes you look like Cicely Tyson."

"I just asked a question."

"And I just gave you an answer. I ain't gonna beg to spend money on you, foolish girl. Now are you in or not?"

I laughed as we headed to the lockers to change.

I hadn't realized how much I had missed being around Catie. She could be abrasive, but she was still my best friend. I felt guilty that I hadn't told her about Carl *or* Jeff.

We drove to the city in Catie's BMW. Her driving scared me because she usually drove too fast. It didn't matter if she was in a hurry or not. She drove fast on general principle. She rolled through stop signs, tailgated, and honked her horn impatiently at other drivers. Most times, riding with her was like being in a high-speed chase.

By the time we had parked, we were still in one piece. We walked over to Barneys to shop. We had fun trying on clothes and laughing at each other. Catie and I could fit into some of the same things, but our shapes were completely different—hers tall and thin, mine petite and curvy.

"Try these on," she said, handing me a pair of coated Hudson jeans.

As we made our way toward the dressing room, Catie got

the usual open stares, and not only from men. She was always mistaken for a celebrity because of her striking beauty and super stylish way of dressing.

In the dressing room, I liked how the jeans made me look taller. When I went out to get Catie's opinion, she was looking at a Judith Leiber clutch. Before I could ask her anything, a man walked up to her.

"Do I know you from somewhere?" he asked.

"Possibly," Catie replied, still eyeing the clutch and not looking up at him.

"I'm certain I know you from somewhere," the guy said.

"Well, then, maybe you do." Turning to me, she said, "I love them. They make you look taller."

"That's what I thought, too," I said.

"What's your name?" the guy persisted.

"If you knew me, you'd know my name," Catie said with exasperation, finally facing him. Guys approached her for all kinds of reasons, all the time. She didn't seem to have much patience that particular day.

"I guess you're right," he said.

Catie looked him dead in the eye and said, "Okay, since you don't know my name, it must mean you don't know me. So get the hell out of my face and let my friend and me enjoy our shopping." She looked at me and winked.

The man turned beet red and walked away.

"Catie, you didn't have to be so mean."

"*Me?* He's the one coming up, acting like he knows me. You like this clutch?"

"It's okay. How much is it?"

"Six hundred and fifty dollars."

"No."

"Neither do I. You hungry?"

"Yes."

"Me, too."

Before leaving, Catie picked up a couple of scarves, and I got two shirts and a sweater.

Lunch was fun. We ate at a little café near Barneys. I continued to feel guilty about not telling her about Jeff and Carl. But I figured I'd get to that later. I didn't want to ruin the trip with my issues.

"It was good seeing you, girl," she said, as we drove back across the Bay Bridge.

"I had a good time," I said. "We can't let such a long time go by without hanging out."

"I concur," she said with a chuckle.

After Catie dropped me off at my car, I drove to Aunt Marie and Uncle Allen's house. I hadn't talked to Aunt Marie since the family meeting that had been a failure. I wanted to see how she was coping. The last time I asked, Mom didn't have any news on Amber, so I hoped the matter had calmed down some. I called Amber last week and tried talking to her. As suspected, she blamed her parents for everything and said she wouldn't respect them until they respected her. I had no intention of sharing that bit of information with mom; she would come over and deal with Amber herself if she heard that.

When I pulled up in front of Aunt Marie's house, I looked at her impressive front yard, which had always been immaculate and beautiful. I noticed that Aunt Marie's car wasn't there, but Uncle Allen's truck was. I went up to the door and rang the bell.

When Uncle Allen answered, he was wearing sweats and an Oakland Raiders t-shirt. He needed a shave and a haircut, but he still looked handsome.

Uncle Allen was a good provider. Whatever Aunt Marie and the kids wanted, he gave it to them if he could. Mom thought it had backfired on him now, and that was why Amber was acting out.

"How you doing, Ny-Ny?" Uncle Allen said, giving me a bear hug.

"I'm good. How about you?"

"Ah, doing okay."

He rubbed the stubble on his face and looked blankly at me in a way that made me uncomfortable.

"Your aunt just ran to the post office," he said. "Should be back any minute. Would you like anything to eat or drink?"

"No, I'm okay, thanks. Is Amber here, or Adam?"

"Adam's at basketball practice. Amber's up in her room."

"Okay, I'll go and say hi."

I walked through the entryway, which was completely empty except for a huge black-and-white print of Amber when she was a toddler. There was something dramatic and beautiful about it. There was a baby grand piano in the living room, which Mom always thought was unnecessary, but it fit right in with the rest of the décor. No one in the house played piano, so Mom said it was just for show, like everything else in Marie's life. I didn't care whether it was for show or not; Aunt Marie had a beautiful home.

I ran up the circular staircase to Amber's room. She was sitting yogi-style on her bed, thumbing through a magazine while listening to the radio. When she saw me, she got up and gave me a hug.

"Hi, Anaya. What are you doing here?"

"Just came by to say hi. What are you up to?"

"Nothing . . . Grounded." Her eyes and her voice fell. "My parents treat me like a little kid. I have a boyfriend, and my parents hate him. They don't let me do anything."

I looked around the room. Amber's walk-in closet was full of shoes, clothes, and purses. On her bed was her iPhone, which was sitting next to her MacBook.

She looked away, clearly irritated.

"Your parents are the only ones you get. They treat you as if they love you. You have to respect them."

"I *do* respect them," she said quietly.

"You need to show it," I smiled.

"Hey, Ny-Ny!" Aunt Marie said, walking into the bedroom.

"Hey, Auntie," I said.

"How are you doing? Come on down into the living room."

I looked over at Amber. She was pretending to be engrossed in her magazine, as if Aunt Marie and I weren't even there.

Aunt Marie looked gaunt. She had lost weight.

Probably from stressing over Amber.

She offered me everything under the sun, but I refused it all. I wasn't hungry. I wanted to talk to her, but she seemed too distracted. I would probably have to catch her when no one else was home.

TWELVE

I left Aunt Marie's and came home to Roscoe sleeping in front of the television. Mom and Ava were gone, so I had no one to talk to or distract me. I put on some gym clothes and attempted to exercise and hopefully work up a sweat, but that didn't quite work out. My attempts to call both Sophie and Catie were also colossal failures, as I got voicemail for both of them. After roaming anxiously around the house, I decided to put my gym clothes and sneakers to use. The air was crisp but not too cold. As I got to the end of the block, I stopped to play with Scooter, the cocker spaniel that belonged to old Ms. Grier. She was the resident grumpy lady, so I was naturally shocked when she walked over to me. I was really taken aback when she actually spoke to me.

"Hello there," she said, not sounding unfriendly in the least.

"Hi, Ms. Grier. How are you?"

"I'm good. Y'all doing all right down there?"

"Yes, we're doing fine, Ms. Grier."

"That's good. Y'all miss Andrew, huh?"

"Yes, Ms. Grier. We miss him a lot," I said, not surprised by her comment. Andrew had been gone for a long time, but in Ms. Grier's mind, everything had happened recently.

"Yeah, he was a sweet boy. Nothing like these other knuckleheads running 'round here. When he would see me picking up in the yard, he would come right up and help me. Never asked any questions. Just helped me pick up. Never asked for any money, either." She winked at me.

"Yeah, that was Andrew. He always wanted to help."

"Sweet boy he was. Shame what happened to him."

"Yeah."

"So, when's your daddy gonna paint that fence? Makes the neighborhood look a mess!"

"Have a good day," I said, walking away.

"It looks a mess," she said to my back.

I kept walking.

When I had warmed up enough, I began to jog, and it felt good. I started to run a little faster. It was a challenge for me, but I needed it. I ran fast, but my mind ran faster. I thought about Jeff's last message: "Hey, it's me. I'm heading out of town for a day or two. It's my anniversary. That's why I was pushing so hard to see you earlier. I wanted to tell you in person. I'll call you as soon I get back."

I felt the ground pound against the bottom of my feet. It hurt, but I didn't stop. Instead, I ran faster and harder. I ran until my thighs felt like they were on fire. I could barely breathe, but I kept running. I was trying to run from *me*, but I kept catching up with myself.

Sweat poured, and I could feel the dampness all the way down to my socks. I had no purse, no money, not even any identification. If something happened to me, nobody would even know who I was.

My attempt at forcing myself to think I could run any farther was futile; soon, I was walking.

I turned to look when I heard a car honking behind me. If I had the energy, I would have jumped for joy to see Irma driving slowly next to me. She asked if I needed a ride, and breathlessly I asked if she could take me back to Aunt Marie's house. I wasn't sure what led me back to Aunt Marie's house, especially since I had just been there earlier that afternoon. I didn't want to overextend my welcome, but I desperately needed to talk to someone. Before I got out of the car, Irma confided that Sophie was not home much, except to sleep.

When we got to Aunt Marie's house, I thanked Irma for dropping me off.

"See you later," she said.

When I knocked on Aunt Marie's door, I knew she was going to be surprised to see me back so soon.

"Anaya? Hi, sweetheart."

She looked puzzled but stood back to let me in. Then she threw a look out to the street.

"How did you get here?" she asked, looking confused.

"I ran part of the way, and Irma brought me the rest of the way."

"Who?"

"Sophie's housekeeper."

I followed Aunt Marie to her huge gourmet kitchen with stainless-steel appliances. Despite the grandiosity, she had Chinese takeout on the stove. The house was quiet—totally different from my house, with Ava's radio blasting, Roscoe's TV screaming, and Mom tossing complaints from the kitchen or the dining room. I noticed how different Aunt Marie's kitchen was from ours. There were no family pictures on the refrigerator and no sticky notes or flyers announcing events. I didn't see a cookie jar or any empty water bottles set to the side for recycling.

"There's Chinese if you're hungry," she said, smiling sincerely.

No matter what Mom said about Aunt Marie being a phony, she had always been sweet and genuine to me, and I liked her a lot.

"No, thanks," I said. "I'm not hungry."

I sat down at the kitchen table and stared at the mahogany hardwood floor. Aunt Marie sat down across from me.

"Where is everybody?" I asked.

"Oh, Allen took the kids and some friends skating. They'll be back in a couple of hours."

"Why didn't you go?" I asked.

"Girl, your auntie been wearing stilettos too long. Bad feet." Then, without warning, she asked me gently, "You wanna talk about something, sweetie?"

I tried, but I couldn't speak. The lump in my throat had already formed, and my eyes were brimming with tears. I nodded and waited until I could get the words out. She sat there, patiently waiting for me. I swallowed a couple of times, wiped my eyes and my nose with the back of my hand, and began to spill out everything about Jeff.

I told her how I met him, how the friendship began, how we let it evolve, and how I was heartbroken and conflicted. When I got to the end of my story, I felt relieved. I still had a heavy heart, but I didn't feel so alone. I could breathe again.

Aunt Marie hadn't said a word the whole time, and her face offered no clue to what she was thinking. When I stopped talking, she went to the fridge and pulled out a bottle of mineral water.

"Wow," she said at last. "That's a heavy load for such a young lady to be carrying around."

She walked back to the table, sat down, and grabbed my hands, which were crusted with tears and snot.

"Anaya, don't feel bad for falling in love, and please don't condemn yourself for making a mistake. We all make mistakes. But we also learn from them. As I listened to you talking just now, I realized that you're a woman now, and you have a woman's feelings. What you have done is classic. You have bitten the forbidden fruit by falling in love with a married man. It's similar to falling in love with the wrong man, but with . . . special circumstances."

I nodded, which was about all I could do.

"Love's a funny thing," she continued. "If you aren't careful with your feelings and how you wear them, love will sneak up on you. Is that what happened?" she asked.

I nodded again.

"I'm not condoning it in any way, because it's wrong."

"I know," I said.

"But I understand your heart," she said tenderly. "I'm certain you don't mean to hurt anybody. What you need to do now is the hardest part, but it's also the most relieving. Whether you think he's going to leave her or not, whether you think he loves you or not, you need to stop now."

Knowing what I had to do ripped at my heart. My head ached. I started crying all over again. A fresh flow of tears broke, and with it, a fresh flow of pain.

We talked, Aunt Marie ate Chinese food, and we talked some more. She told me a story about when she was sixteen. Something similar had happened to her with a football player. He wasn't married, but he had a steady girlfriend. According to Marie, it came to the same thing.

"Women need to stick together," she said. "If he's got a woman, he's off-limits."

I agreed with her. I wouldn't want somebody running up on my man, if I had one, and I wouldn't want anybody doing that to my mom or aunt, either. I knew Aunt Marie was right, but how was I going to break up with Jeff?

"Where is he now?" she asked.

I almost started to cry again. "He went away with his wife and kids for the weekend."

Her eyebrows shot up, and for a minute she looked exactly like Mom. Then she opened her mouth, but no words came out. Finally, she said, "How do you know that?"

"He told me."

"He *told* you?"

"Yes."

"That's honest."

"What do you mean?"

"Does he normally tell you when he's going away with her, or if he's going to do something special with her?"

I nodded.

"What else does he talk about to you?"

"We talk about everything: school, my dreams, my sadness about Andrew. He talks about work, his future, his family, his in-laws. Why are you asking?"

"Does it bother you when he talks about his family? I mean, do you get jealous, or does he worry about your getting jealous?"

"I guess sometimes I do," I admitted. "But no more than he does when I go out with my friends. When we do get time together, it's good. I look forward to being with him, and he likes being with me. That's why it will hurt so much not to be together, because we're happy when we are."

She was quiet for a few seconds.

"What, Auntie?"

"I guess I wasn't expecting him to tell you that kind of stuff. Or expect that you two had real conversations about life."

She paused as if she were deep in thought.

I started realizing that throughout this ordeal, I had come to understand myself so much better. At the least, I now knew about love. So although I was embarrassed for ending up in a predictable mess, I was also grateful for the lesson.

"I'm never going to find another like him," I mourned.

"No, you won't. You'll find somebody better than him. Somebody available. Don't sell yourself short. He can't give you what you need. And he's got kids. You don't even want kids."

She was certainly right about that. In all of my fantasies about Jeff and I being together, I never included his children. They just weren't on my mind the way he was. I sighed so loudly that Aunt Marie literally jumped.

"It's okay," she said, putting her hand on my knee. "I know it hurts. But in time, things will be much better."

She pulled out two wine glasses and poured a glass of red for each of us.

In my mind's eye, I had let Jeff go. I imagined him playing on a beach with his wife, or feeding her strawberries, or looking at pictures of their children.

I sighed again and shook my head hard. This time Aunt Marie poured herself another glass of wine. My glass was still full. I never did finish it, but Aunt Marie took care of the rest of the bottle for both of us.

By now, I was tired of talking.

"Would you mind if I took a shower?" I asked.

"You go right ahead," she offered.

The hot water was soothing. I cried like a baby.

Which anniversary is this? Are they drinking and kissing? Is he thinking about me? God, give me strength to leave Jeff.

Aunt Marie let me borrow a sweat suit and a pair of her flip-flops. I couldn't have put my feet back into my tennis shoes if I had wanted to; the bottoms of my feet still seemed like they were pounding against the pavement. I felt strong and sure, so I decided to do something right away.

"Aunt Marie, can I borrow your car?"

"The Beamer?"

Aunt Marie's 850 rode like a dream. I drove carefully, because the last thing I needed was to pay for Aunt Marie's car to get fixed. I parked in front of Jeff's firm and sat there for a little while. It would only take me fifteen minutes to pack up all my stuff and get out. My stomach danced, but I ignored it. I was focused. Jeff had given me keys to the office when I first started working there. I never used them, but I had kept them on my key ring. I opened the top and bottom locks, but the one at the very bottom, near the floor, was already open. Jeff would be pissed if he knew that someone had left that last one unlocked.

I walked inside, locking the door behind me.

The office was dark, but I knew the place well and could get around blindfolded. When I saw that the light was on in the copy room and heard a noise coming from the back of the office, I put my hand on my pepper spray and squeezed my toes together so Aunt Marie's flip-flops wouldn't make a sound as I walked. It wasn't unusual for the attorneys to work late. I had parked in front on the street, so I didn't know if anyone had parked in the garage. I thought about calling Jeff, but then I remembered why I was there in the first place. He was off in La-La Land with his darling wife. If I hadn't been so scared at that moment, I would have puked. I walked slowly to the copy room entrance and stood there in disbelief.

"Anaya!" Jeff said, startled, looking up at me.

I didn't respond immediately, because if I had, I would have uttered a string of expletives.

I whirled around on Aunt Marie's flip-flops so fast that I hurt the inside of my big toe. As I rushed away, tears were streaming full-force down my face.

Jeff caught up with me and grabbed my wrist. I used every ounce of strength I had to break free. My breathing was fierce, and my glare was icy. But he wouldn't let go. I kept twisting and turning, but his grip was too strong. I used my other hand to try to push his hand away, but that didn't work, either. I tried pushing his face, but he still didn't let go. Instead, he grabbed my other hand by the wrist. I was panting and sweating.

"Anaya!"

"What?" I screamed.

I stopped fighting.

"What?" I yelled again.

"I know what you must be thinking, and I'm sorry."

I glared at him. "No, you don't know what I'm thinking. You don't need to know, either."

"Let me explain," he pleaded.

Neither of us said anything for a moment. I was mad, but I

wanted to hear what he had to say, every single bit of it. Why had he lied about the anniversary trip?

His eyes sought my understanding, but his grip was still tight. I started to panic that maybe I didn't want to hear what he had to say, after all. I just wanted to get away.

"Why did you lie?" I beseeched. "Am I so hard to talk to? Am I so unreasonable? Or am I just stupid? You probably feel like you can tell stupid little me any old stupid lie."

I'm outta here, I decided. I tried once more to get free from his grip.

"Anaya, please!" he entreated.

He finally released me. I folded my arms across my chest.

This better be good.

"Go!" I said.

"What?"

"Talk!"

He hadn't shaved, and his eyes were red. He looked pathetic and didn't seem to know where to start.

Finally, he said, "This thing between us has been driving me crazy. I can't think straight. I can't concentrate on work. I can't even make love to my wife anymore. All I think about is you, all the time, every day."

He saw that I was still waiting for an explanation, so he said, "I'm sorry I lied to you about this weekend. I needed time to clear my head. She and I have been fighting like crazy, and it's taking a toll. I'm in love with you, but I don't know what the hell to do because I have a family . . . and a baby expected."

Goosebumps formed all over my body. *A baby? Well, then, there must have been sex somewhere along the way.*

"I needed time alone," he continued. "I'm sorry I lied to you. You don't deserve that."

"Wait," I halted him. "She's pregnant?"

He looked broken and haggard. Until this moment, I had thought I was agonizing all by myself. I didn't realize he had been struggling, too. A single tear rolled down the side of his face as he nodded yes.

Damn!

"That's why I tried so hard to see you earlier. I wanted to tell you."

I tried to walk away, but I couldn't because he moved closer to me and took me in his arms. I hugged him back and could feel the intense emotions between us. He kissed my neck and cheek. As I wiped away his tears, I let my feelings carry me away.

Don't let him fool you, I heard Sophie say in my mind.

Three months ago— three *days* ago—I would have been afraid of what was happening, but tonight I welcomed it. I *wanted* it. Nothing mattered except this moment. As I stood there in his arms, I felt closer to him than I ever had been before. I had wanted this embrace for so long.

The flesh is weak. Don't succumb. I turned my head to the left to block out Ava's voice in my mind.

Jeff looked at me, turned my head back to him, raised my chin, and kissed me, softly and slowly.

Might as well follow your heart, 'cause if you don't, it's gonna follow you. I ignored the Roscoeism in my mind, and I kissed Jeff back.

Your love signs are in sync! I hear you, Aunt Deb.

Put your back into it, bitch! Quiet, Catie!

I arched my back as his hands searched my body. I felt myself letting go. I shook my head slowly to clear my thoughts. Jeff stopped kissing me. He caressed my cheek and searched deep into my eyes. When I kissed him again, I listened to my heart, listened to my body, and acted on the passion that was building between me and the man I loved so dearly.

I heard my keys drop to the floor as he found his way to me through Aunt Marie's jacket. I never wanted anything so badly in my life. He moved with intensity, showing all the desire he had for me. My heart raced with physical need. I adored this man, and at that moment, there was no one else in the world but the two of us.

"Jeff," I moaned breathlessly.

"I love you, little lady," he whispered.

My mind and body exploded at the same time. I was emotionally and physically exhausted.

We lay on the floor of the copy room, looking at each other, surrounded by stacked-up reams of paper. I was the first to look away.

After all this time, I choose this day to let go of the last shred of self-respect and morality that I have in me. Terrific.

I sat up. We were both uncomfortably quiet for the first time since we started seeing each other. I looked down at the floor, because I knew he was looking at me. I didn't want to face him.

I dressed quickly and grabbed my keys. I don't think he expected me to run away, but that's what I did. As I ran to the door, I heard him fumbling to put his pants on.

"Hold on! Please!"

I didn't slow down, and I didn't say anything. Once outside, I jumped in the Beamer and sped off.

He called my phone six times as I headed to Aunt Marie's. When I got there, she didn't ask any questions. She gave me a big hug and told me to stay as long as I needed. I called Mom, told her where I was, and said I would be home the next day. She was curious, but she let it pass.

I cried throughout the night, prodded by replaying everything over in my mind: how he mentioned the baby, how we ended up on the floor.

He lied about the anniversary trip to protect me. Another damn kid? Making love in the copy room—Why did I let that happen? Now he's all over me, mentally and physically.

I turned my phone off because I got tired of hearing it ring. My body felt numb, my head hurt from thinking too much, and the soreness between my legs was a constant reminder of what had happened. I couldn't fix it, and I didn't want to. I was the other woman, and I felt every bit of it.

Aunt Marie checked on me a couple of times. But mostly she just left me alone, which was exactly what I wanted.

The next day, she brought me home. As we walked through the front door, she yelled cheerfully to no one in particular, "Hey, everybody!"

Ava came down from her room. "Hi, Aunt Marie," she said, giving her a hug. Then to me, Ava said with concern, "Where have you been? Mom was looking for you. You haven't been answering your cell."

"I'm okay," I said quickly and headed upstairs.

When I got to my room, I called Shirley and told her I wouldn't be in because I was sick. I knew I couldn't go back to the office *that* day, and I did, indeed, feel ill.

When I finally got my bearings, I started making some changes. First, I called Professor Klein to find out if he knew of any open positions. He said that a teaching assistant was needed for the extension campus down in the valley, about a forty-five-minute drive from my parents' house. He told me the salary and that housing came with the job. I reminded him that after psychology, teaching was my second choice of profession. Then I went online and applied for the job.

I also went to see Judy.

"Are you okay?" she asked as soon as I sat down.

"No," I admitted.

"Okay. Tell me what's going on."

"I'm making bad decisions. I know I should have broken it off with him a long time ago. But instead, I deepened it by making it physical."

"Why didn't you break it off?"

"Because I love him."

"And that stops you from breaking it off?"

I cannot believe I pay you for this.

"I love him," I repeated.

"What do you want?" she asked.

"I don't know."

"Do you want to marry him?"

"I don't know."

"Do you want to spend the rest of your life with him, without being married to him?"

I didn't answer.

"Do you know what you want from Jeff?"

If I did, I wouldn't be torturing myself sitting here with you, would I?

Irritated with myself, I started to fixate on her brown corduroy jacket, brown loafers, and bright red lipstick. *So unattractive. Next time, I'm gonna ask if I can lie on that couch over there, so I don't have to look at you.*

"If I knew what I wanted, I wouldn't be here."

"Explore it, rather than get frustrated. What do you want? What would make you happy?"

If you wore nude-colored lipstick . . . that would be a pretty nice start.

"If there were peace on Earth," I said, exasperated. Then I slumped far down in my seat like an angry fifth grader.

Judy closed her notebook. "You can't hide behind other people's happiness," she advised me. "Establish your own desires. Figure out what you want. Get an idea of what will make you truly happy."

"I don't know how to do that. I'm so used to doing things for other people, that I don't know how to do things for myself," I admitted.

"Well, knowing is half the battle. Let's come up with some ways you can start doing things for yourself. One thing we've been talking about for as long as I've been seeing you is living at home. I know that bothers you. Why don't you start there, and explore your feelings about that. Figure out why you really won't move out. Develop some pros and cons, and when you come back next time, we can talk about them. How does that sound?"

"It sounds hard."

"It doesn't have to be," she said with a smile.

On my way home, I thought hard about the assignment Judy had given me.

For the next three days, I focused on myself and my family. I helped Mom plant new flowers in the backyard. I went to the gym more than usual. I even watched sports on TV with Roscoe a few times. I didn't leave the house, nor did I answer my cell. I wasn't ready to deal with the world beyond the walls of home. I just couldn't do it.

Jeff called my cell every day. I didn't take his calls, and I instantly deleted his messages without listening to them. I didn't want to hear anything, and I didn't want to read anything. I couldn't deal with it. It had only been a few days since I'd last seen him, but it felt like weeks.

One day, out of the blue, Professor Klein called me back and asked if I could do a phone interview right then and there. I was unprepared, but I agreed, not wanting to interfere with any potential job opportunities. I was in a temporary slump, but I needed a job. There was no denying that. Soon after my phone interview, I was offered the teaching assistant job.

When I finally began reaching out to the real world again, I called Octavia. I asked her to pack my things from my desk and bring them to me.

"What's happened?" she asked, curious.

"Let's just say I have an emergency in my family. Tell everyone that, will you, please? Has anyone asked any questions?"

"Only Jeff. He seems concerned. Why don't you at least call him? He did hire you. You don't wanna burn any bridges."

Oh, Octavia, if you only knew.

My feelings changed from day to day, but that particular day I felt that Jeff really loved me, and that I needed to see him. That last time we were together, I felt passion from him that he could not have faked.

I spent the next few weeks trying to finish the last of my final exams. I couldn't remember a single question on any of them, and I prayed that I had passed. My mind was foggy, and focus was far from within my reach. I did the best I could. I thought about Jeff every single day, but I still resisted the urge to call him.

I don't care what Aunt Marie says, or anybody else says. Maybe it's not right, and maybe both of us should have known better.

A few weeks after finals, I attended my graduation ceremony. Jeff was the keynote speaker. I saw him from a distance after the ceremony, but I didn't make eye contact. I knew he wouldn't approach me in front of my parents. I received well wishes from other staff members from the faculty offices. Life was so simple when I worked there. It's amazing what one harmless decision can do to your entire life.

After the ceremony, I went directly home to find half of my family in the backyard, munching on the appetizers Mom had made the night before. Aunt Deb had let everyone in. The university had given the graduates only four tickets per family, so I had given mine to Mom, Roscoe, Ava, and Aunt Marie. Mom hurried to the kitchen as soon as we walked in.

"I hope Deb didn't mess anything up," she said.

Aunt Marie and I followed her to the kitchen. When I walked through the door, Aunt Deb rushed up and gave me a big hug.

"Oh, Ny," she said, "your lunar cycle's in high gear. You're approaching your new moon, and I'm so proud of you!"

She hugged me hard. I loved Aunt Deb, but sometimes I had no idea what she was talking about.

"Hush with all that cosmic nonsense," Mom told Deb, as she looked in her pots and put on her apron. "Did you stir the greens like I asked?"

"Yes, I did," Aunt Deb said, and then turned back to me. "You're gonna be very successful. The stars are all lined up for you, sweetie."

"Well, she comes from a line of successful people," Aunt Marie said.

"Merle," Mom said, deliberately changing the subject, "can you peel those potatoes for me?"

"Peel potatoes? I'm not peeling any potatoes in this dress. I'll get Amber in here to do that."

"What, you too good to peel potatoes, Merle?" Mom shot back.

"In this dress, absolutely, I am," Aunt Marie smirked.

"You're not too good to eat 'em, though," Mom pointed out.

Aunt Marie spun around and walked out of the kitchen.

I'm outta here before Mom asks me to peel the potatoes.

As I headed to the backyard, I passed Amber, who was on her way in. She smiled at me and gave me a big hug.

"Congratulations," she offered.

"Thank you," I replied.

"Diva!" Catie called, walking over to me. As she gave me a hug, she handed me a little gift bag.

"Thanks, Catie," I smiled.

"I'm proud of you," she gushed. "You always were the brain of the group. And I was always the beauty."

I hugged her again just as Sophie came up to us.

"Well, it's about time," she chided me.

"I'm so happy to see you," I said in her ear as I hugged her tightly. She squeezed me back.

"I wouldn't miss this for the world," she said.

I looked around and saw that Uncle Riley, Miss Troy, Uncle Allen, and some other people were all smiling in my direction. One by one, they came up, said a few sweet words, and pressed a gift or a card into my hands.

It was nice to see everyone, especially Catie and Sophie.

"So, what are you gonna do now?" Sophie asked me, picking up a finger sandwich from the table as we sat down and talked.

"I'm not really sure yet," I said, knowing that wasn't entirely the truth.

"Well, that's fine," Uncle Riley said. "You'll figure it out soon enough."

"Yes, she will," Roscoe added. "And if she doesn't, she has time to think about it. It's not what you do with your talents, but the time you use developing them. You have to crawl before you walk."

Everyone looked totally confused.

"I'll probably substitute teach for a little while, Uncle Riley," I explained. "I like working with kids, and there's no long-term commitment."

"Be selective about which school you choose," Miss Troy boomed in her scary baritone. "Some of those schools are rough, and those kids will disrespect you."

From the corner of my eye, I could see Sophie giving Troy a funny look before picking up another sandwich.

"If they don't listen," Catie advised, "just clock them bad kids in the head."

Everybody laughed.

"Nah, don't do that," Uncle Riley said. "Then we'll have to be bailing you out of jail."

"I can't picture Ny in jail," Troy said.

"Neither can I," said Catie.

"No," Roscoe piped in, sitting up in his seat, as if he needed to provide wise words for the occasion. "She won't be in no jail. She has strong values. They won't allow her to get into trouble. See, there are choices and consequences in life. And when you make certain choices, there are consequences to pay. And when you pay, the price ain't cheap. You have to be strong in your judgment, strong in your faith, and strong in your steps."

Roscoe sat back in his seat as if he had just delivered the Sermon on the Mount.

Catie opened her mouth to say something, paused, and then closed it. There were simply no words.

At that moment, Mom came out, followed by Aunt Deb.

"The food is about ready," Mom announced. "But before y'all eat, I just wanna take a minute to tell Anaya how proud I am of her."

She walked over and stood next to me. Everyone looked on.

"Anaya, you have turned out to be a beautiful young woman, and I couldn't be a prouder mama. You have grown so much, and this phase of your life is over. There's a whole world out there, waiting for you to make your mark, and I know you'll do just that. You always inspire me to do better, to think a little bit different, and to try and grow. I love that about you. You don't just go with the flow, you use your own mind and your own instincts. I learn things from you every day. I know you are moving on and will be leaving us soon, and I will miss you more than you can ever possibly know. We are all so proud of you, and I know Andrew is celebrating right along with us. Roscoe and I can't be with you every step of the way, but we hope to make your journey a little bit easier."

I wiped tears from my eyes as she pulled out an envelope from her apron pocket and handed it to me.

I looked at the envelope and then back at her. She nodded for me to open it.

I looked around the yard quickly. Everyone looked as curious as I was.

When I opened the envelope, in it there was a cashier's check for twenty-five thousand dollars.

"Mom!" I gasped.

"What is it?" Ava asked.

I gave my mom a big hug.

"Thank you! How did you—?"

"We hope it helps," she said, hugging me long and hard.

I held on to her for dear life.

"What is it?" Ava repeated.

"Yeah," Catie prompted. "What is it?"

I looked at Mom. She wiped her face and gave me a look that said it was okay to tell them.

"A check for twenty-five thousand dollars!"

"Damn, bitch!" Catie said loudly.

Everyone turned to look at her. She quickly covered her mouth with her hands.

"Sorry," she said, sitting down.

Mom and Aunt Marie gave her a dirty look.

"Sorry!" she said again, sinking down lower in her seat.

After that, we all ate and talked late into the night. Some of my classmates dropped in, and we hung out.

Antoine also came by. He said sincerely, "I wanted to come through and offer my congrats. Mom couldn't make it, but she told me to give you this." He handed me a card.

"Thank you," I said. "Tell your mom I said thank you, too."

Catie and Sophie came over and hugged him. I eyeballed Catie, thinking she was going to say something stupid again.

"That was nice of you, Antoine," she said, giving him a small smile.

Huh?

Antoine smiled back.

Huh?

He spoke to Uncle Riley and to my parents, and then he said goodbye. I saw him talking to Catie by the door before he left. I made a mental note to ask Catie what that was all about.

By the time everyone was finally gone, I was exhausted.

When I got to my room that night, I looked at my phone. I purposely hadn't come in to check it all evening.

Jeff had sent me a text message. I decided to read this one:

YOU LOOKED BEAUTIFUL TODAY. CONGRATULATIONS ON YOUR ACCOMPLISHMENT. PLEASE ACCEPT MY CALLS. WE NEED TO TALK.

The next day, I changed my cell number. I was emotionally drained, and I couldn't tolerate a conversation with Jeff. My family still had no idea about Jeff, and I felt bad about not telling them. It was too late, though, to tell them now. I especially didn't want to tell Mom. She hadn't been herself lately. I was worried about her. She said she was going through "the change." I wasn't so sure that this was just menopause, though.

THIRTEEN

Catie and Sophie were already seated when I met them for dinner at one of our favorite restaurants. I finally had told them about my new job, and we had decided to get together for a little farewell dinner. Before I even had a chance to hang my purse on the back of my chair, Catie started in on me.

"So, what are you running from?" she asked pointedly.

I opened my mouth to speak, but she put her hand in the air to stop me.

"The *truth*," she emphasized.

There were varying versions of the truth. There was the truth-truth, the half-truth, or the partial-truth. Lately, I'd been giving only snippet-truths, so I decided to tell my two deserving best friends the complete truth. I opened my mouth to speak, and tears welled up in my eyes.

"Wow," Catie said, motioning for our waitress. "Here we go with the tears."

"Three lemon drops," she told the waitress.

"Two," Sophie corrected her. "And one lemonade."

"Right," Catie said. "*Two* lemon drops, and one lemonade for my sober acquaintance here."

Through my tears, I looked at Sophie and smiled, relieved. She was trying to stay sober, and I was proud of her.

Both Catie and I had finished our lemon drops by the time I finished telling them about Jeff. Sophie looked intrigued, but I couldn't read Catie. Her cheeks were red, and her eyebrows kept wrinkling up.

"What does all of this have to do with you leaving?" she asked impatiently.

"She's in love with him," Sophie said, assessing me with a calm and knowing look.

Catie, shocked, said, "Is that true?"

I nodded yes.

"So then why in the world are you moving a hundred miles away?" she asked, incredulous.

"It's not a hundred miles," I rolled my eyes.

She didn't reply.

"It's too much," I explained. "I love him, so I don't want to be around. I don't want to bump into him or have the urge to go and see him. I need to get away and start over."

"Start over?" Catie's voice rose. "Start over and do what? You find a man you love. A good man, who loves you, who has a good job. This makes you want to leave and start over? That's some backward-ass shit."

"What do you mean?" I asked sincerely.

"I mean, you naïve little twit, that you love him and he loves you. What's wrong with that? Why are you fighting it?"

"Because he's married, with a family," Sophie interjected. "That seems like a reasonable cause to me."

"Shut the hell up, Sophie. Marriage doesn't mean anything. People get married and divorced all the time. Ny didn't cause his marriage to break up. He and his wife caused their marriage to break up. Ny just came and picked up the pieces," Catie said, signaling the waitress again.

"You are evil," Sophie said. "She cannot date a married man. That's wrong. You know that's wrong, Ny, don't you?"

"Yes," I said dumbly.

"Then leave him alone," Sophie said, buttering a piece of bread.

"Well," Catie said, looking genuinely confused, "be stupid if you want to. And good luck finding another man you love this much. That kind of love isn't just stored around. It's hard to find."

"He's married!" Sophie said again, a little too loudly. I looked around, but no one seemed to have heard her.

"And?" Catie asked.

"She's not that kind of girl, Catie," Sophie replied. "You already know that. She likes this guy, and the fact that she has to share him hurts her. If she doesn't leave now, she's gonna keep going back to him, and it's *never* gonna be over."

"Why have you been keeping this from us?" Catie hissed at me. "Better yet, how have you been keeping this from us? You're a sneaky little liar."

"Because she's been so busy trying to make sure *we're* okay," Sophie said. "She hasn't had time for herself."

"We haven't been having issues every single day of the week," Catie insisted. "She's had time to tell us what's going on. Ny's a sneaky little thing."

"Catie," Sophie said, "it's not easy for a woman to confess she fell in love with someone's husband. That's unacceptable. Also, there's the fact that she saw it coming. Something she probably doesn't want to admit."

Catie frowned. "Who cares that he's married?" she said. "He obviously loves you. Be with him."

"And then what, Catie?" Sophie argued. "If he did it to his current wife, why wouldn't he do it to Ny when he meets somebody else? Then what? She will end up like my mom, spending her days and nights waiting for him to come home. No one deserves to live like that. You're doing the right thing, Ny."

"You need to be quiet, So-*fee*-a," Catie said. "All of a sudden you're a damn life counselor? Life's hard and short. If she loves this man, and this man can take care of her, I repeat: What's the problem?"

"It's over now," I said. "He's married. He has a wife and a life that doesn't include me. There's no place for me."

"Have you seen her?" Sophie asked with a mouthful of bread. "What does she look like?"

"She's pretty," I said.

"You think *every* damned body is pretty," Catie snapped. "If you stay with him, he'll leave her. He loves you, girl. Just give him time. Divorce is a big step. He don't wanna give that woman half of everything he has and then support her for the next fifteen years."

"You don't want him to leave his wife," Sophie said. "Because then he'll do the same thing to you one day. Plus, you said he has kids. You hate kids." Sophie picked up another piece of bread.

"You gonna blow up like a little piglet, if you keep eating that bread," Catie said.

"I don't hate kids," I said.

"Yes, you do," they said in unison.

"That's not true. Well, maybe it is." I sighed heavily. "You think he would bring his kids with him if we got together?"

We all laughed.

"Silly girl!" Catie said.

"Ny, you have your whole life ahead of you, girl," said Sophie. "You're beautiful and smart, and there's someone out there who'll give you what you deserve. You don't wanna raise some other woman's kids."

"Yeah, they probably look like her, too," Catie said. "I know you don't want little people running around your house who look like the ex-wife. It'll ruin your mood." She laughed.

"Seriously," Sophie said, "It's hard right now, but you're doing the right thing. You know that, don't you?"

"I do. I miss him so much, though." I wiped away a tear.

"You know what you need?" Catie advised. "A different

atmosphere. It's dead in here. I know where we can go. A friend of mine's having a get-together tonight." She looked over at Sophie. "And don't worry, there'll be bread there."

Sophie shrugged.

On the way to the party, I thought about the conversation with my friends. I should have talked to them about Jeff a long time ago. Things might not have gotten so bad if I had opened up to them. But that was probably why I didn't tell anybody—I didn't want anybody to talk me out of it.

When we arrived at the house having the party, the street was dimly lit, and there were only a few cars parked outside.

"What kind of bootleg party is this?" Sophie asked when Catie turned the engine off.

"Oh hush. Like you have something better to do? Come on."

We walked up a few cobblestone steps. I struggled to balance in my four-inch sandals.

"Diva!" the hostess hollered when she opened the door.

"Hey!" Catie greeted her.

London was a friend of Catie's from Fresno. She was very over the top, wearing all red with hair that hung down to her waist. Her lips were extra shiny, her makeup was piled on flawlessly, and her contacts were blue. She told us to make ourselves comfortable.

"I love that gloss," Catie cooed to her.

"Nars, baby. It's fabulous. Just like *moi*." London blew a kiss in the air and disappeared into another room. I looked around the beautiful foyer that led to a spacious den.

"Wow," I whispered to Catie. "Is this London's house?"

"No, it's her boyfriend's," she whispered back.

"Wow, does she live here?"

"I don't know," Catie groaned, exasperated, as we followed London farther into the house.

"What does her boyfriend do for a living?" I whispered to Catie.

"If you don't shut the hell up with your nosy tourist questions, I'm gonna cut you," Catie cautioned through clenched teeth.

Sophie laughed.

London led us to a game room where there were at least twenty other people. Catie grabbed a drink immediately. There was a huge TV, pinball, and a video game. A pool table was featured in the center of the room. A couple of people were playing, while others sat around talking. Light music played in the background.

London brought a plate of appetizers into the room and sat near her boyfriend, Reggie.

When Sophie took three breaded chicken wings and put them on a plate, Catie laughed.

"Alright chubby-kins. You are gonna regret eating so much."

"London looks cute," Sophie said, ignoring Catie's insult. "I haven't seen her in a long time."

The three of us sat on a small, circular couch, the color of a tangerine. We talked, ate, and drank wine. Sophie stuck with water.

"All I wanna know," a girl said to no one in particular in the room, "is how you go to a zoo to look at animals and don't come out alive." She was referring to a recent tiger attack.

"Tigers are savage beasts," London quipped. "You can't take a wild animal and lock him up for too long. He's bound to attack somebody. Ain't that right, Boo?"

Reggie smiled. He was very handsome.

"Tigers aren't savage by nature," Catie asserted, working on her second drink since we had been at the party, and her fourth drink of the night.

I nudged her. When Catie drank too much, she had a tendency to become an expert on everything. Sophie gave me a knowing look, and I nudged Catie again.

"Damn!" Catie said, nudging me back a lot harder than I had nudged her. "That hurts!"

I ignored her.

"The radio said they were taunting the tiger," another girl pointed out. "Even so, you would think that the zoo would make tiger cages more foolproof."

Reggie chimed in, "All I know is, I won't be taunting any tigers in the near future, and I offer that valuable piece of advice to all you lovely ladies. Now, I'm gonna go away to attend to business and let you all have your ladies' night."

"Okay, Boo," London said.

He kissed her and went out of the room. When he was gone, she started to act like a teenager.

"Oooh, weee, that boy is *good* to me! Y'all hear me?"

"Yeah, girl," Catie said, holding up her drink.

"Does what I want, when I want him to. Gives me what I need, when I need it." London snapped her fingers and did a two-step. She was so dramatic.

"Well, looks like you got a good one this time," Catie said. "What more could a girl ask for?"

One of the guests, Melinda, replied, "How about a house key?"

"Shut the hell up!" London warned.

But Melinda kept going. "You practically live here already."

Catie asked, incredulous, "You don't have a key to this place?"

London admitted, "Not yet. But I will soon, baby."

She said this with a snap of her fingers.

"Well, that means you haven't been doing what I showed you," Catie said, standing up.

"I don't want to chase him off. They get scared when they think you're a pro."

"Whatever. I bet if you do it tonight, you'll have a key tomorrow."

Feeling tipsy, Catie sat back down.

"Men like it when you try new stuff," Melinda said. "It keeps 'em guessing. Keeps the spice alive."

"But you don't wanna be too risqué," another guest said. "Some men don't like all that."

"Um, what men have you been dealing with, darling?" London asked. "They all like a little freak nasty. Don't let them fool you."

"Well, my ex told me he respected me," the woman said, "and didn't like a lot of freaky stuff."

"What were you trying to do?" Sophie asked.

"Let's just say I wanted to use some toys. He didn't wanna use any. He also didn't like oral sex, either way."

"Those must have been some off-the-hook toys," I said.

"Girl," London said, "the next time you see him, he's gonna be wearing a glitter headband and some skinny jeans. All men like oral sex. *All* of 'em."

"You might be right," the woman said, gulping down her drink.

"That's one thing about men," Melinda said. "They're so sneaky. What have they got against telling the truth?"

"Don't start a man-bashing session here," London said. "I have a good man, and he tells Miss London the truth at all costs. So cut that out, right now!"

"I hear that, London," I said. "Stand up for your man."

We all laughed.

We spent the rest of the night like a gaggle of hens, drinking. London turned up the music, and we danced as best we could on our drunken legs. Sophie was the only sober one, but she didn't dance any better than the rest of us. It was the most fun I had had in a long time.

Having fun like that made me wonder why I was leaving in the first place. I had enough support to stay. But I knew that my trouble wasn't only about Jeff. Leaving was about gaining independence. I wanted to live on my own and find out what I wanted in life. I was almost twenty-five and had never lived alone. It was time.

Does Jeff think of me as much as I think about him? Admittedly, I'd mull on staying every now and then. But when my heart started to ache, and that stupid lump started to form again in my throat, I knew I needed to move on.

Somewhere around 3 a.m., we left the party. My house was the first stop.

"Ny, I love you," Catie said.

"I love you, too," I said, hugging her from the back seat.

"Call us if you need anything," Sophie said. "And visit."

"Don't forget the Seafood Festival, either," Catie said. "You promised to go."

"I will. I love you guys so much." I hugged them again.

"Catie!" Sophie exclaimed. "Are you crying?"

"Hell, no, girl! I got allergies," Catie said, wiping her nose with the back of her hand. "Take me home. Call me tomorrow, Ny."

"I love you guys," I said before getting out of the car.

We hugged in the street like I was being deployed to war.

It was after 3:30 a.m. when I threw myself down on my bed. I thought about calling Jeff, then I thought about getting undressed. But I fell asleep before I could do either one.

FOURTEEN

"What are you gonna do with all of these?" Ava asked, walking into my bedroom and seeing clothes all over the floor. It was the day before I was to leave for the new job, and I had attempted to clean out my closet.

I walked over and gave Ava a bear hug. She must have been shocked, because a couple of seconds passed before she returned my embrace.

"What's wrong?" she asked.

I didn't answer. I couldn't, without crying. All I could do was hold her.

"Are you sad about leaving? It's not that far away. Mom said you'll only be there about three months, right?"

"Yeah, for the summer," I finally managed to say, releasing her from my ninja hold.

"It'll be good for you. Besides, you never got to get away for college. Been sticking around here with us. It's time."

I hugged her again and felt bad about the times I told people she was autistic or adopted.

"You see anything you want?" I said, motioning to the mound of clothes on my floor.

"Where do you get all this stuff?" she asked. "There's probably fifty pairs of jeans in here."

Forty-six.

"Mostly Catie and Sophie," I said.

"They *still* buy you clothes?"

"Mmm-hmm," I answered. "Is that weird?"

"It's not weird. I think it's a blessing you have friends like that. God has been good to you." She began to rummage through the piles.

"Ava?"

"Yes?"

"Does God forgive any sin?"

She paused and looked at me.

"Yes, he does. Any sin. God is forgiving, loving, and merciful."

I felt a rush of ease and guilt at the same time.

"How are things going at school and at church?" I asked, trying to change the subject. Although I'd told Sophie and Catie about Jeff, I wasn't ready to tell anyone else.

"You are trying to change the subject, just like Mom does, but I won't pry. I love school. I'm thinking of stepping down as president of the Christian Club, because it takes up so much of my time, and I don't want to quit choir or drama club."

I opened my mouth but quickly shut it. How ridiculous would I sound, telling my sister that I didn't know she was involved in any of those other things? What was wrong with me?

"Why aren't we closer?" I asked her.

"You've always had Sophie and Catie," she mused. "I could never compete. You wanted to hang out with them, and when I tried hanging out with you guys, you wouldn't let me. When you started eighth grade, it was like I'd become invisible. Everything was 'You're too young,' or 'You don't get it,' or 'Never mind.' Whenever they came over, you just shut your door, and shut me out."

I listened to her explain how I had closed her out of my world.

"I was terrible," I said.

"Oh, stop it. You thought you were protecting me."

For the next hour, Ava and I sat on the floor, first folding clothes and then looking through my old photo album.

"Do you remember that time Andrew shaved his eyebrows off?" she asked.

"Yes! And tried to cover it up with that baseball cap?"

We both laughed at the memory of his face with no eyebrows.

It was my time to ask Ava about church. For whatever reason, mom was letting her strange behavior slide, but I couldn't do it. Whether we were close or not, I needed to know that my sister was okay.

"Can I ask you a question, Ava?"

"Of course."

"Your church. Is it a real church like in a building or is it in somebody's house?"

"It's in a building," she said and went on describing the various programs the church sponsored, including a food bank and computer training programs. I had never heard of a cult that offered computer training.

"Is it a cult, Ava?"

"A cult?!" She was obviously taken aback.

"But the protests and the radical statements, what was that about?"

"My vigilante nature kicked in. What can I say? The church didn't sponsor those protests, it was a few of us students that got together to protest," she laughed at the misunderstanding but I didn't. I felt bad. Not just for the question about the cult, but for not knowing my sister. Not knowing her interests or talent and for not taking the time to get to know her. I spent too much time and energy worrying about Catie and Sophie and trying to support them that I had sacrificed a relationship with Ava.

That night, I lay in bed and asked God to forgive me for my sins. I asked God to say hi to Andrew for me. Then I thanked Him for giving me back my little sister, and I cried myself to sleep.

The next day, I packed up to leave. My parents were going to follow me down to campus and help me settle in.

"I'm sorry I can't go with you," Ava said. "I have two rehearsals tonight."

"I know. I understand."

"You'll be fine," she said, kissing me on the forehead. "Call me."

She was wearing one of the shirts I had given her.

I got in my car and watched my mom fuss at Roscoe as they got in his truck.

When we pulled out of the driveway, I heard Mom say in a loud voice, "Good Lord, you need a tune-up! How in the world do you drive this thing?"

My new job would be at the extension campus, which was an hour and a half round-trip from my parent's house. According to Professor Klein, I'd have plenty of autonomy, because regular professors couldn't make it to the campus as much due to other commitments. I would be supervising student research assignments and giving lectures. In the past few months I'd gone from an administrative assistant, to a legal clerk, and now a teacher's assistant.

Look out world, I'm moving up!

I appreciated the campus housing. I wouldn't have to pay rent, and I'd get the privacy I needed.

During the drive, I replayed that last night with Jeff over in my head. As learning experiences go, this had certainly been a hard one. I started wondering what other ones were ahead.

The university extension was in a small, hot town that reeked of cow dung. My parents and I pulled up to the apartment complex. We passed a waterfall, a small playground, and a swimming pool before we reached my apartment.

"It's safe here," Mom said once we entered my new home. "Even though it is on the ground floor. I'm glad a lot of families live here."

The furniture was simple, but clean and fairly modern.

After I unpacked and settled in, we had lunch before my parents prepared for the drive back. I started to feel a little anxiety, but I didn't dare show it.

Mom shouldn't have to worry about me while I'm down here. I don't want her trying to come and stay with me for weekends because she thinks I need her.

"Get to know the older lady upstairs," she advised. "She seems like a good person."

"Okay, Mom."

"Socialize with your coworkers, so you won't be all alone."

"Okay, Mom."

"And call—"

She started to cry.

"Oh, Nita," Roscoe said. "Cut it out. The girl is damn near thirty. It's *time*."

"She is *not* almost thirty," Mom said.

"I certainly am not!" I agreed.

We all laughed.

"I'll call you, Mom. Don't cry. I'll be fine."

"I know," she sniffled. "I know."

She kissed me on the cheek and headed out the door.

Roscoe hugged me quickly.

"I'm proud of you. You're making your mark on this world."

After they left, I walked to campus to take some of my things to my new office.

The campus was new, so all of the buildings were modern, and the grounds were impeccably clean. When I walked into the classroom, I immediately started shivering. My first assignment was to find the air conditioner and turn that sucker down. Although the classroom was small, it did have a side office for me, which I liked. I sat down and re-read Professor Morgan's instructions. I wanted to be sure I was totally prepared for the students.

I thought about Jeff. I missed him. I actually missed everyone already.

I didn't try to stop the tears from falling. I pulled myself together and headed back through the extension buildings, toward my apartment. I enjoyed the warmth outside.

My thoughts were interrupted by the sound of rolling wheels. I turned to see a big guy rolling a wagon full of books. He was six feet tall and easily three hundred pounds. When he approached me, I could see his eyes were a startling grey, and his skin was the color of barely creamed coffee.

"Hey!" he said cheerfully.

"Hi," I said, trying to sound pleasant.

"Are you a student here?" he asked.

"No, I'm the new teaching assistant, Anaya Goode."

I extended my hand, and he shook it heartily.

"I'm Travis Dale, the teaching assistant for the dean of the English department. You have your room set up?"

"Sort of," I said.

"Do you need help with anything? This is my third summer working here, so I know my way around."

"Actually, could you help me turn down the air conditioner in my classroom? It's freezing in there."

He chuckled.

"Ah yes, I know that problem well. You have a minute? I can show you now."

We headed back to my class. Not only did Travis help me find the air conditioner switch, he also helped me get my syllabus copied and set up an alternative mailbox for students to drop off assignments after hours.

"You live on campus, too?" I asked him.

"No, I live at home," he said, "just across the hills and cows from here."

We laughed. He was right. There wasn't much else that separated the communities.

"I live on the better side of the hill, though," he advised.

"Oh? What's better about your side?" I asked, curious.

"Because on my side, there's a grocery store, a bowling alley, and a coffee shop."

We laughed again.

The campus livened up after the first week. And so did my friendship with Travis. It was terrific to have met a friend so soon. He was funny, honest, and smart. His degree was in English and psychology. He didn't know what he wanted to do with his degree, but he had worked as a teaching assistant for the past few summers because he liked teaching.

One day we talked about his career plans. "My parents told me to take my time," he told me, "and figure out what I really want to study before rushing into grad school."

"What a good deal for you, if you like living at home. I used to be glad that I lived at home, but now I wonder if I haven't been too sheltered all my life. I've spent so much of my time giving and doing for my family and friends."

He nodded. "The idea is to realize you can't fix everyone else."

"Yes," I agreed.

"So when will you let me make dinner for you?" he asked.

"We've eaten at every fast-food restaurant in town," I said. "So I'll take you up on your invitation." I didn't want to offend him by turning him down too many times. We had started to spend a lot of time together, so it made sense that I would meet his family, because they were close to the campus, and I lived alone.

Travis and his teenaged sister lived with their parents in a beautiful home. His dad was an architect, and his mom was a nurse. Hanging out with the family was just the therapy I needed. I ate good food, laughed, and felt comfortable. They were warm people, and I immediately felt at ease with them.

Soon, I was going to their house several times a week. Travis's room had its own bath and was like a little apartment in the back of the house. He had a huge bed, a walk-in closet, a small refrigerator, and an air hockey table in the middle of the room. We played air hockey a couple of times, but we spent most of our time listening to CDs and talking.

Travis was a talker. Good grief, he loved talking. He was filled with "what ifs?" and "how comes?" His questions made me think about things that I probably never would have thought about. I started to realize that Jeff was not the only man who could hold an interesting conversation. Travis was also a great listener. I never rambled with him, because he always had a question, or nodded his head, or looked me directly in the eye. He would have made a good therapist—a heap better than the one I was seeing. But his keen observation could be both good and bad.

"Tell me what your issue is," he asked me one midsummer evening, after a game of air hockey.

"What do you mean?" I replied.

"I mean, what the hell is wrong with you? Who broke your heart?"

I laughed. "It's that obvious?" My first impulse was to brush him off and leave it there. But instead, I told him everything. He listened carefully, without interrupting me or asking a lot of questions. Then he gave me general advice on love and how to deal with the consequences of our actions. He was nonjudgmental and open. Travis was just who I needed to restore my faith in men as a worthwhile species.

At about two in the morning, I fell asleep at the foot of his bed. It was the first peaceful night's sleep I'd had since leaving home.

My class met on Mondays and Wednesdays. I enjoyed teaching. In so many different ways, it fit me well. Summer classes are packed with a lot of material, so I didn't have much time to let my mind drift. I still thought about Jeff, but my thoughts were mostly occupied with the students and class preparation.

One night, Travis and I were grading papers, working on the floor of my living room, sitting on cushions in front of the coffee table. He suddenly confronted me about my love life.

"So what are you gonna do?" Travis asked while he took a break.

I looked over at him and frowned.

"Anaya!" he called again.

"What?"

"Are you daydreaming about him again? I asked you, What are you gonna do?"

"About what?"

"About *what*?" he said, mocking me. "You know about what. You still love him."

I do still love him, but I don't feel like talking about it.

"What are you talking about?"

"This morning I saw a teaching assistant from the mass communications department ask you to lunch. You turned him down."

"So? He wasn't my type. I don't have to go to lunch with somebody just because he asks me. I'm not desperate."

"I didn't say you were desperate. You are lonely. Yet you won't even give anybody the time of day. What about the guy from the pizza parlor on Friday night? You told him you had a boyfriend."

"He looked like a frog."

"You need to keep it real with yourself, before you have any chance of keeping it real with anybody else."

"I love him even more now than I ever have." I was surprised to hear myself say that. But, for once, I didn't feel a lump in my throat, and I didn't tear up.

Am I healing?

"Do you think he loves his wife?"

"Yep."

"Do you think he loves you?"

"Yep."

"I think you should call him."

"Nope."

I got up and headed straight for the shower. Sometimes it amazed me how much I was becoming like my mom—just cutting off a conversation when I didn't want to talk about something.

When I got out of the shower, Travis was gone. On my computer monitor, he had left a note that simply said, "Call him."

I wish it were that simple, Travis. How do you call somebody after pulling a disappearing act, and say, "Hey"?

That night, I dreamed that Jeff was in the hospital, and I had just delivered a baby—who looked exactly like him, mustache and all. The nurse who came to take the baby away was Travis. He kept looking at the baby and shaking his head, saying, "This is not that man's baby." Jeff kissed me on the cheek. When Travis brought the baby back to me, it was Chinese. Jeff flew into a rage and started cursing that the baby wasn't his. "A damn Asian, Anaya?" I woke up, dripping in sweat. The dream freaked me out.

Ava called me and reminded me that Roscoe's birthday that year landed on a three-day weekend in the middle of the semester. I packed some stuff and hit the road. I was homesick. Living alone had some advantages, but I wasn't used to the quiet and the routine. I was used to living at home, where people stopped by unannounced, and there was always good food in the fridge. Travis invited me to stay with his family for the break, but I told him there was no way I could miss Roscoe's party. Plus, I had promised Catie and Sophie I would go to the Seafood Festival with them that weekend.

When I got home, the first thing I noticed was the smell of gumbo. I walked into the kitchen and kissed Mom on the cheek.

"You lost a little weight, girl," she said. "I guess you're happy about that."

"I know, Mom. It's been ninety-five degrees almost every

day down there. The only thing I can do is drink water and eat popsicles."

"Well, you're home now, and it's only sixty-seven degrees today, so grab a bowl. You better not be out there dieting in that heat."

As I fixed myself a bowl of gumbo, I thought, *I'm a size two, and I like it that way.*

The gumbo was good—so good that I had three bowls before the company arrived. That's how I knew Mom missed me. She never let us eat before she served food to company.

"I'm gonna fix you some things to take back with you," she promised, as she watched me down the third bowl. "You're already too thin. What do you wanna do? Blow away?"

I sighed and shrugged.

"You heard about Mister MVP?" Mom asked, referring to the hoop star in trouble with the law.

"Yes, I can't believe it," I said. I didn't normally get into Mom's celebrity gossip conversations, but I wanted the full experience of being home.

"Just trying to bring another black man down," Mom said. "Happens every day."

I was *so* not in the mood for a "holding the black man down" conversation.

"Where's Aunt Marie?" I asked, changing the subject.

Mom shot me a sideways glance.

"Girl, you know Miss Prissy is always late, trying to make her diva entrance."

"Oh. Who else is coming over?"

"Aunt Deb and Uncle Riley," Mom said. "Plus whoever he's dating this week."

"What happened to Miss Troy?"

"Who?"

"Mom!"

"I don't know. I guess he's still dating her."

"Where's Roscoe?"

"He's next door, putting on Miss Baby's screen door. You know her sons don't help her out much over there."

"Oh, yeah. Where's Ava?"

She paused.

"Ava . . . she's with her boyfriend." She said this very slowly and with a huge grin on her face. "They'll be here for dinner."

"Well, I guess she's human."

I heard someone come through the front door.

"Is that my Ny in there?"

I grinned and walked out to greet Roscoe. He was sweet when he wasn't drinking. Reminded me of Andrew.

"Hey, Roscoe," I said, hugging him tight.

"You look good, girl. You must like it out there in the boondocks."

"It's okay for work, but I wouldn't wanna live there."

I followed him to the den and sat down in front of the TV with him. I told him about the apartment and my student teaching assignment. He listened intently to every word and asked a lot of questions about everything under the sun, from what the job was like to whether I had found out if I had timed sprinklers at my apartment complex. After a while, he started flicking through the channels.

"So, what's been up around here?" I asked.

"Ah, nothin' much. I think your sister got herself a boyfriend. And I think your mom's finally ready to clean out Andrew's room. I don't know if it's time, but you know how she is, once she gets somethin' in her head."

"Do you think she's ready for that?"

"I don't know. She says she is. I told her we need to ride out there and see about you. We haven't been out there but once since you moved."

"I know."

He reached over to pat my knee and rested the remote on a basketball game.

"I heard about your boy," I said, referring to the disgraced basketball star.

"Yeah. That's a shame. When the party's over, it's over. And there ain't no rehiring of the DJ."

"You think he deserved it?" I asked, just for fun.

"Sometimes people deserve things, and sometimes they reserve things. In this case, he reserved good judgment . . . And there you have it."

Good ol' Roscoe.

Just as I stood up to kiss him on the forehead, Aunt Marie came in with her family.

"Hey, there!" Aunt Marie called, walking in the den. She looked good, in a tan pantsuit and black flats. After patting Roscoe on the shoulder, she gave me a tight hug and a kiss on the cheek.

"Hey, Auntie."

Uncle Allen walked in, with Adam and Amber right behind him. Both Allen and Adam hugged me, but Amber, looking sullen, sat down in the chair near the entryway, fidgeting with her fingernails.

"Hi, Amber," I called.

"Hi," she said listlessly.

"How you doing?" Uncle Allen asked me.

I caught him up on my new job, and then he and Adam started watching the game with Roscoe. Uncle Riley turned up with Troy.

I walked back to the kitchen with Aunt Marie. Aunt Deb called a half hour before brunch to say that she couldn't make it. That pissed Mom off. She was big on punctuality and courtesy. For the first time that day, I realized how good Mom looked. She had lost weight! I was so busy trying to defend my own weight loss, that I hadn't recognized hers. Then I noticed something else.

"Mom, you're wearing jeans!"

She smiled.

"Yes, I am. I was wondering when you were gonna say something."

"You look great, Mom. Are you dieting?"

"No," both she and Aunt Marie said in unison.

"I'm not dieting, girl. I'm eating right, and I'm exercising. It's not *what* you eat, it's *how* you eat. I walk the lake with Miss Thing here three times a week."

She nodded in Aunt Marie's direction.

"Sometimes, four times a week," Aunt Marie added.

"Go, Mom! I'm happy for you."

"I'm happy, too. I was walking to the laundry room the other day, and I caught your daddy looking at me, girl." She giggled.

Aunt Marie rolled her eyes as she nibbled on a celery stick.

"Merle, don't touch my vegetable tray. I have food already set out on the dining room table. That's the food you can eat. Anything in the kitchen is still being prepared and is off-limits."

She tried to swat at her hand, but Aunt Marie was too quick.

"Hush, Anita!"

Marie picked up another celery stick. Mom swatted but missed again.

How do they manage to walk together three or four times a week?

Brunch turned out nice. Mom doted over Ava and her handsome boyfriend, Stanley, but I understood her joy at Ava's finally acting like a normal teenager. Aunt Marie tried to downplay it some, and Ava seemed downright irritated by Mom's doting.

We got to know Stanley a lot better. He seemed smart. And most importantly, he loved God. He smiled at Ava a lot, and each time she responded with a nod. She was wearing a yellow shirt and a light-blue denim skirt. It was the first time I had seen her in a light color since third grade. I didn't think she would ever in her lifetime wear anything but black. Once, during dinner, she and Stanley slightly disagreed about the nutritional value of asparagus. It was cute.

Aunt Marie and Uncle Allen barely spoke to each other; they had no problem letting the world know when they were feuding. In contrast, Mom and Roscoe fought like cats and dogs at home and then pretended in public to be best friends. During brunch, Uncle Allen asked Aunt Marie to pass him the salt, and she completely ignored him. When he asked her again, she continued to ignore him. I loved Aunt Marie, but sometimes she acted like a teenager. Uncle Allen got up, walked around Aunt Marie, grabbed the shaker, plopped back down in his seat, and sprinkled the salt on his macaroni and cheese.

After this little scene, Roscoe and Troy got into a discussion about car engines. No one joined that conversation. When brunch was finished, everyone went to the living room to watch Tyler Perry's new movie. But I went up to my room to change into cooler clothes. I had promised Catie and Sophie that I would go with them to the Seafood Festival, and I knew how hot it could get in the South Bay. I didn't really want to go, but I didn't want to flake out, either. The three of us had made a deal to start spending more time together.

If they wanna walk around a hot, crowded marina with tent-cooked food, who am I to spoil the fun?

On the ride down to the marina in Catie's car, we listened to old songs on Catie's iPod and talked about old boyfriends, old rivalries, and old fashions. It felt good to catch up. Every song Catie played reminded us of someone or something. When she played our favorite Aaliyah song, we all smiled. It reminded me of Justin. For Sophie, I knew it brought back memories of Andrew. And for Catie . . .

"Big Bear!" I screamed over the music, and we all laughed.

Catie looked back at me through her rearview mirror with a huge grin on her face.

"Girl, I loved me some Big Bear. He had those deep dimples and those long eyelashes."

"Yeah, and that rashy neck," Sophie said.

"He had eczema," Catie said. "Be quiet, Sophie."

We all laughed again.

"Um, you be quiet, Miss Ny," Catie said, "with your down-low boyfriend, Justin."

"Justin wasn't gay," I said, defending him once again.

We continued to laugh and dance in our seats during certain songs.

"What's up with the married man?" Catie asked.

"Haven't talked to him."

Sophie looked back at me and smiled.

"I'm okay," I said.

"No, you're not," Catie said. "But we'll talk about it later."

The parking lot at the festival was full, so we had to walk four blocks to the marina. Then it took us fifteen minutes to get through the entrance line. There was a five-dollar charge and a hand stamp at the gate.

Sophie was talkative, and that made the day a lot of fun. Sometimes, when she was moody, it impacted our moods, too. She talked about a new group that Terry had decided to manage.

"He finally dipped his hand into managing, after toying with it for all these years," she said.

I watched her talk about her dad, noticing how cute she looked in her cropped Joe's Jeans, striped halter, and flip-flops. She wore the simplest things, but she was always so stylish. I had to work hard to look cute, and I almost never accomplished Sophie's "no fuss" look.

Catie was overly sexy, as usual, in a white tank dress without a bra, white tie-up sandals, and huge diamond studs in her ears. One could say she was overdressed for the occasion, but she either didn't think so or didn't care.

I was casual, in some Paige cut-off denim shorts, a clingy tank, and gladiator sandals. We ignored the whistles and ridiculous lines from guys standing around. You would think, after all these generations of dating and courting, men would have figured out more interesting ways to approach women.

I pretended to ignore it, Catie was flattered, and Sophie was truly oblivious.

"Must be nice to be unaffected by the animalistic wiles of the male species," Catie said to Sophie.

"I'm not unaffected," Sophie replied. "Just because I don't always date men doesn't mean I don't go through the same things you guys do."

"I guess that's true," Catie said.

"I wish people could be themselves from the beginning," I said.

"You mean instead of letting you date their well-behaved 'representative' for six months?" Catie laughed.

"Yeah. When you meet them, they're all good. Then, in six months—"

"You find out they drink too much," Sophie said.

"Or have bad credit," Catie said.

"Or already have kids and a wife and pretend to love you," I said.

They both stopped walking and looked at me.

"Ny, are you sure you're okay?" Catie asked.

"Sure," I said. "Really, I am."

They continued to look at me.

"You'll find somebody," Sophie said in a soothing tone.

"I know," I said. "And he'll be honest and sweet."

"And single," Sophie added with a chuckle.

"Yeah," I said. "And single."

"And don't forget fine," Catie said. "He's gotta be fine. Just like that fine candy bar over there." She looked across from us. "Ooh, he's cute!"

"Careful, Catie," I said.

"I know, but why does he have to look so *good*?"

"He doesn't," Sophie said.

"We're here to eat and have fun together," I said. "Not find boyfriends."

"Speak for yourself," Catie said with a sly smile.

There were a lot of vendor booths at the festival. Some had food, and some had clothes or jewelry. There was a stage in the middle of the grounds where a bunch of preteen girls tap-danced to old songs. The music was loud, and the atmosphere was positive. We went from booth to booth, trying to figure out what to eat. A couple of places claimed to have real Louisiana gumbo, but I didn't try them, because only my Mom made the best.

Sophie and I stood in line at a frozen lemonade stand while Catie chatted on her cell.

Sophie pulled out her wallet and asked me if I wanted regular or strawberry lemonade. I told her strawberry, and I turned to ask Catie which kind she wanted. But when I looked over, she was busy talking to some guy. I can't say I know Catie's "type" of man, but the one she was talking to certainly couldn't have been it. He was tall and sickly thin, probably in his mid-twenties—cute, but in a sinister, sneaky-looking kind of way. His greasy hair was slicked back, and his Hawaiian print shirt was unbuttoned—no doubt to show off the hair on his chest. He wore faded navy blue pants and loafers without socks. I couldn't understand why Catie was all smiles, but she was, and it looked like they were exchanging phone numbers. I turned to nudge Sophie, but she was already eyeing them.

"Is she kidding?" she asked me.

"It looks like she's getting her Mack on." I laughed.

"With Tony Montana? Look at his shoes."

Sophie handed me my frozen lemonade and then gave Catie one. Catie took a sip, smiled at us, and then introduced her new friend.

"Hey, guys, this is Tony."

Sophie almost spit out her lemonade, and I couldn't control my smile.

Putting her hand on her hip, Catie just glared at the two of us. I stopped laughing and extended my hand.

"I'm Anaya. Nice to meet you."

He took my hand in his, and I immediately wished he hadn't, because he was so sweaty.

"Anaya," he said, repeating my name with a Spanish accent. "A beautiful name for an even more beautiful lady. The pleasure is all mines."

Mines? Well, maybe his Spanish grammar is better.

Catie smiled, so I guessed she wasn't irritated with us anymore.

Sophie raised an eyebrow, sipped her lemonade, and mumbled through her straw, "Wuzzup, dude? I'm Sophie."

Tony's annoyance with Sophie was obvious, but he managed a smile anyway.

"The pleasure is mines, Sophie."

Catie and Tony said their goodbyes, while Sophie and I walked over to a nearby booth.

"Anaya!"

I turned to see familiar beautiful eyes and perfect teeth.

"Hey, Carl!" I said pleasantly.

I felt Catie move close to me. I wanted to kick her and leave a sandal print on her white dress.

She's so nosy.

Carl gave me a long hug. It felt good.

"Hey, how are you?" I said, moving back from him a little.

"I'm good. Missing you, though. Where have you been? You just disappeared off the face of the Earth."

He grabbed my hand and looked me up and down.

"I've been around," I said, blushing. Catie was in my peripheral, staring at us.

I couldn't stop thinking how good he looked.

I knew Catie and Sophie were eating up every single word. I hadn't mentioned Carl to them before.

"So," he asked, "how do you like working at the law firm?"

I shifted my feet. "I don't work there anymore."

"Oh. Did you find a therapist gig?"

"Not exactly. I've been teaching a summer school course at the university extension."

"Wow. That's good. Different from what you wanted to do, though."

Catie cleared her throat.

"Um, Carl, these are my friends, Catie and Sophie."

"Nice to meet you, ladies," he said politely.

Catie and Sophie said hello.

He turned his attention back to me. "I tried calling you a couple of times. Did you change your number?"

"I did. Take my new one." I gave him my new number, and we talked for a few more minutes. He was still the same Carl, and I was genuinely happy to see him. Only good thoughts came to me.

"Listen," he said, "I need to catch up with my boys. I just wanted to come over and say hello to the prettiest girl out here. I'll call you, okay?" He hugged me hard.

Still smells good.

"Okay," I said.

"Nice meeting you guys," he said again to Catie and Sophie.

"You, too," they said together.

"Bitch, who was that?" Catie demanded the second Carl was out of earshot.

"*Mentirosa*, you told me you were not seeing anybody," Sophie added.

"Didn't you just see me give him my number? How can I be seeing someone if he doesn't have my number?"

Sophie gave me a funny look but didn't say anything else.

Catie got close to my face and laughed. "You know what? You are officially a sneaky little liar! How many *more* men are gonna come running out of the woodwork? All I have to say is, if you aren't interested in that fine hunk, there's something wrong with you."

Sophie satirized Catie and said, "Well, Catie, if *you're* interested in that weird Spanish dude, then there's something wrong with you."

Catie pointed at me. "Don't be over there trying to get quiet," she said to me, licking her lips. "We didn't forget about you and that beautiful Hershey bar that just walked away from us." She could make a baptism sound erotic.

"What? We used to work together on campus."

"Used to work together on campus? Bitch, please! The look is all over his lovesick little face. What did you do to that boy? Did you do that trick I taught you?"

I didn't want to talk to them about Carl, or what we had together, or why we stopped seeing each other. At that point, I didn't even remember what had happened. He just kind of faded out of the picture, because he liked me more than I could reciprocate. I had allowed Jeff to consume me.

If I can just manage to get through the rest of this afternoon without any more questions, I'll be grateful.

We circled the festival three more times, and when we ran into Tony again, Catie gave him a big hug, as if they had known each other for years. He was with his friends this time. They looked like they had been getting phone numbers and drinking beer all afternoon.

One of his friends, a chubby guy with a mouthful of gold teeth, looked at Sophie hungrily. She turned to me and said she would meet us at the car. I wanted to follow her, but I didn't feel comfortable leaving Catie alone with the degenerates. When she finally broke free from Tony's pawing, sweaty hands, we headed toward the car.

"He's so cute," she said to me breathlessly. "I'm glad we came."

"Enough, Catie!" I grumbled, and walked ahead of her.

FIFTEEN

A week after the seafood festival, Sophie went missing. Ava, whom I recently had talked to more than I ever have in my life, called and asked me if I had heard from Sophie. I hadn't heard from her and when I called and asked Catie, she hadn't heard from her either. I didn't drive home because there wasn't anything I could do. I left Sophie messages and sent her texts—all to no avail. I didn't expect that Carmen knew where she was, but I called her anyway. She didn't seem as worried as one would think she would be given her daughter was missing.

When things settled down that night, I sat in my apartment and reflected over the past few months. Things had moved blindingly fast—my job transition, the relationship with Jeff, Sophie's addiction, and my mom who was turning into a stranger right before my very eyes. I picked up my phone and considered calling Jeff. I needed so badly to hear his voice and hear him tell me that everything was going to be okay. I had made a huge mistake by falling in love with him and I wondered if I had made another mistake by cutting things off the way I did. I picked up my laptop and began writing him an e-mail. I didn't know if he'd ever see the e-mail but it didn't matter—I just needed to release and get some things off of my chest, things that I knew he needed to hear.

Catie called me while I was writing and we made a deal that when Sophie came home, we were going to do all we could to support her.

The next day, Catie called and told me that Sophie was home with Carmen. She still hadn't returned any of my calls or texts but that was fine with me. As long as she was home and safe, nothing else mattered. I drove home that weekend to see her at Carmen's house. Carmen was casual in sweatpants and she looked a lot more worried than she had sounded on the phone a day or so ago.

She led me up to Sophie's room and gave us some time alone. Sofie looked awful. It hurt my heart to see my friend so frail and unhealthy. She walked over to me without a word and hugged me. We both started crying.

"I'm sorry, Ny," she said in between sobs. "I'm so sorry I let you down."

"Shhhh. Don't apologize. I am here for you and I love you. We are going to get through this," I said holding her even tighter.

I thought about her as a little girl. She had been so carefree and happy as a child. She was a beautiful soul. What in the world had happened to my friend? How could something like this happen to such a good person? She wasn't raised that way. It made me think of a lecture in one of my classes. The teacher had explained to the class that bad drugs happen to good people and there's no way to definitely say who will get addicted and who will not.

Sophie finally stopped crying and sat at the foot of her bed. Her red eyes had dark circles around them. She started talking. She told me that after we got off of the phone the other night, she had called her dad. He didn't answer her call and she said she felt like she was losing it and she needed something to make the pain go away.

We cried twice more by the time Catie arrived and then the three of us cried some more. Sophie needed help and we were going to make sure she got it.

With mom's guidance, and not Carmen's, we found a rehabilitation center for Sophie. The day she was supposed to enter, she changed her mind, claiming she could beat her addiction on her own. We rescheduled for the next day and she backed out again. On the third try, she checked in. We communicated with Carmen the entire time and she knew exactly what was going on. She didn't bother to come when we dropped Sophie off and she didn't call to see how the drop off went. The lack of concern both hurt and angered me. Sophie was her only child, how could she really be so heartless that she didn't care to be there when her child went to rehab?

Sophie wasn't allowed to communicate for the first seven days of the program. During her first few days in the program, Catie and I met halfway for dinner some nights which was nice. It gave me a chance to talk to her about some of the things I was going through and, in turn, she cut her "dates" down to weekends only. She said she had enough and wanted to get out of the lifestyle.

On the eighth day of being in the program, Sophie called me. She didn't sound great, but I knew she was getting the help she needed.

"Family Day," she announced, "is when family members come and attend a group meeting. We're gonna have one in a couple weeks."

"That sounds good," I said, unsure if she was inviting me or wanted me to invite myself.

"It is. They had one since I've been here, but I didn't participate. I think I want to participate this time."

"Great, Sophie! Is Carmen coming?"

She was quiet for a moment. "No. She hasn't been up here yet. I haven't invited her."

"Oh. Do you want me to come up for Family Day?" I asked.

"I'm not sure. I'll let you know."

After that conversation, Sophie called me every other day or so. She was only allowed to use the phone for a few minutes each time. I was happy to be supportive, but I wanted her to talk to her parents, too. I put the Family Day date in my calendar, noting that it was after the semester ended. I was actually looking forward to the end of the semester. I missed home. I loved my new teaching job, but I missed home, too. I had too many emotional things going on to be so far away from my family and friends. Sometimes a girl just needs to be around someone familiar.

Jeff still ran through my mind far too much. When I was working, exercising—even during my sleep. Sometimes I woke up in the middle of the night with an ache in my heart and an empty feeling in my stomach.

I kept praying for a breakthrough, something to take the pain away. Even a mild numbing of the pain would do.

One of the last things I had to do as a teaching assistant was to grade the final research assignments, which I did in my office. Several of the students had done terrific work, and I was engrossed in reading when my phone rang.

"I'm worried about Mom," Ava started.

"What about?" I asked.

"She's not herself."

"What do you mean?" I asked.

Ava provided examples. "She sleeps all the time. She hasn't been cooking. In the past couple of weeks, she's been to the doctor three times."

"What were the appointments for?" I wondered.

"She won't say. Something about making sure everything works properly. But I don't believe that."

"She seemed fine when I was home," I pointed out.

"Yeah," Ava argued, "but you were only here for a couple of days. I'm telling you, she's not herself."

Mom hadn't mentioned anything to me about feeling ill.

"Okay," I promised, "let me think about it, and I'll call you back."

"All right," Ava said reluctantly.

"Don't worry. She'll be fine. Have you talked to Roscoe?"

"I mentioned it to him, but he doesn't see anything wrong," Ava said.

I reassured her again that everything would be fine, and then I hung up.

There was a knock on my office door. I was happy to look up and see Travis.

"Hey, you!" he said with a big smile. "What are you up to?"

"I was grading papers."

Travis made his way inside and sat down.

"Why are you so happy?" I asked.

He smiled again.

"Wait!" I remembered. "This was the day you met up with Faye, isn't it? How did it go?"

"A gentleman doesn't tell," he said, still grinning.

"You had better tell me," I said firmly.

"She wants me to ride down to Southern California with her, to meet her parents," he said triumphantly.

"Her parents? You guys have only been out twice," I reminded him.

"Hey. When you got it, you got it. And apparently I have it, because she wants me to meet her parents."

"Wow!" I exclaimed. I had to admit that Travis did "have it." For the right woman, he was a catch.

"So, now all I have to do is lose seventy pounds before we go," he joked.

"When are you guys going?" I asked.

"In two weeks," he replied.

I laughed.

"It's not funny," he said.

"You look fine, Travis."

Travis and I chatted for another hour before he left. He was in such a good mood that I didn't want to burden him about my phone call from Ava, even though it was still heavy on my mind. As soon as he left, I got in my car. I hadn't planned to go home, but the conversation with Ava worried me.

So I drove home, not knowing what I would find there. When I walked in the house, I went to the kitchen, but Mom wasn't there. I knew she was home, because I had seen her car in the driveway. I went to her room and found her lying in bed, watching TV, which was something I hadn't seen her do since I was a kid. Her skin was pale, and her eyes were puffy.

"Hey," I greeted her.

She managed a wan smile. "Hey," she said as enthusiastically as she could. She sat up and hugged me. "You hungry?"

I nodded.

She got out of bed. "You keeping that apartment clean?" she asked as she put on her robe.

"Of course."

"Are those kids respecting you?"

"Some of them are older than I am, Mom. They're very respectful, though."

She smiled. "I guess I forgot about that."

When we got down to the kitchen, she sat at the table for a minute, and then she got up to fix me a plate.

"Mom, are you okay?" I asked.

"Yeah. I've just been a little tired lately, but I'm fine."

"Are you sure?"

"Yes, I'm sure. I'm just going through the change." She placed a bowl of spaghetti in front of me and sat down. "Wait a minute . . . What are you doing up here on a weekday?"

"I got in my car, started driving, and ended up here," I laughed.

"Uh-oh! What's wrong? When you start driving, something's always wrong."

"Nothing serious, Mom. I have a few things to consider, that's all."

"Okay. You have to go to work tomorrow?"

"Yeah. I'm leaving in a few minutes. I wanna make sure you're okay." My hands grasped hers for a moment. Her skin felt fragile and cool.

"I'm fine," she shrugged. "Don't worry about me. You eat this food and get back on the road before it gets too late."

She stayed in the kitchen with me while I ate. When it was time for me to go, she hugged me tightly and went back upstairs.

Roscoe was asleep in his chair with the TV blasting. I kissed him on the cheek, which woke him up.

"Hey, I thought I heard your voice," he said. "What are you doing here?"

"Just came to check on everybody," I explained.

"Aw," he said, "everybody's fine."

"Yeah?" I said. "Is Mom okay? She looks tired."

"Well, it's funny you should say that. I've been thinking the same thing."

"Has she been going to work?"

"Yeah, she's been going to work. Comes home and goes straight to bed, though. Same way she did when Andrew died."

"We need to get her to the doctor, Roscoe."

"Well, she's already been going to the doctor, apparently. She won't tell me what's going on, though. Marie came over and talked to her, too."

"How did that go?" I asked.

"Your mama put her out," he laughed. "That didn't stop Marie, though. She comes by here and calls every day. Said she won't stop until Anita goes to the doctor. Marie thinks Anita needs some hormone supplements or something. I don't know about all that woman stuff."

"Okay, keep me posted," I said.

He got up and hugged me.

"I will," he said. "But don't worry about us. You just do your work. You know what they say: A man who don't work, don't eat."

"Right," I agreed.

On the long drive back, I thought about whether or not I should teach at the extension in the fall. Travis had decided that he wanted to go to medical school, and he had been accepted at Duke, so I wouldn't have my friend out there with me anymore. This was going to be a hard decision.

When I got back to my apartment, I sat down and looked through my picture albums. I had six photo albums, which started from middle school. I looked at a photo of Sophie, Catie, and me at our eighth-grade field trip to Great America. The picture had been snapped just after we'd gone on the log ride. We were all skinny back then, and Catie already looked self-assured. Sophie and Catie's ancestral genetics allowed their hair to tolerate the log ride and go easily into a ponytail. But my tribe was from Zimbabwe. Once my hair got wet, nothing could fix it but a hot comb and some pressing oil.

Glancing around my spotless apartment, I had to smile.

Mom would be so proud.

I thought about how she looked when I saw her earlier that day.

I need to be home. I can't be at the extension this fall.

The next week was slow. Due to exams, there were no classes, and Travis spent most of his time with Faye. I was happy for him, but jealous at the same time. He was my friend first! At the end of the week, I told Professor Klein that I couldn't teach at the extension in the fall, due to my mother's being ill.

"Are you sure?" he asked.

"Yes," I said, certain that I wanted to help Mom.

"If you need a little more time to decide, let me know," he offered. "The students, staff, and other faculty all raved about you. Your curriculum was outstanding. I was very impressed."

"Thank you," I said, delighted at the compliment. "But I feel I need to be closer to home right now."

I didn't realize how right my intuition was. Soon after I spoke to the professor, Ava called.

"You have a few minutes?" she asked.

"Of course. What's up?"

"Carmen called Mom. She said Sophie bolted from the program, and they haven't heard from her. Mom found out that the only reason Sophie went into the program in the first place is because Carmen and Terry had given her an ultimatum. They cut Sophie's allowance off."

"How long has she been missing?" I heard what Ava said but I still couldn't believe it. I had just spoken with Sophie and she seemed fine; like she was ready to move forward with her life and leave the past behind. I read her all wrong.

"I don't know. Mom couldn't remember that much detail. I think Mom's sick. Did you see her? Roscoe told me that you came by. Did he tell you she hasn't been to work in three days?"

"No, he didn't."

"Well she hasn't. I don't know what's going on, Ny. Something's wrong."

"I'm coming home in a few weeks," I said quickly.

"I didn't call you to have you rush home. I just thought you should know."

"No, it's the end of the semester. I had decided to come home anyway."

I had surprised even myself when I started making preparations to go home the very next day. I asked Octavia to come down and help me move out of my apartment.

She was good at packing and organizing, but that wasn't my primary reason for calling her. I needed her company. I didn't have a lot of stuff, because most of the furniture came with the apartment.

Octavia kept telling me how nice the place was. "And it's rent-free, you said?"

"Yep," I said.

"And *why* are you leaving, again?"

"I need to be home. There's a lot going on, and my family and friends need me."

"Oh," she said. "Where's your friend you told me so much about?"

"Travis? He's in L.A. with his girlfriend. He went down to meet her parents."

"They're serious now?"

"Seems like it."

"Didn't you say he was gonna be a doctor or something?"

"Yeah, he got accepted into Duke Medical School."

"Oh, you might have to hook me up."

I laughed. "I don't think Travis is your type. What happened to the fireman?"

"I'm just kidding. We still see each other. I like him a lot."

"Really?"

"Yes, girl." She giggled.

I was a little sad that Travis wasn't around to say goodbye.

"One more time," she said. "Why are you leaving this job?"

"I'm worried about my Mom. She's not well." I dropped down hard on the sofa while she packed my CDs. "I feel guilty being here while my family's struggling. They need me."

"You're only a short drive away. You don't think you can be there for your family and be here for your career, too? I haven't known you for very long, but all I've ever seen you do is be there for your family and friends. Canceling plans because your girlfriend needs a ride. Leaving work early because your aunt is having problems at home. You have a good heart; but long term, you can't be happy like that."

She disappeared with a box out to her car, then returned to dispense more advice. "For example, Morris takes good care of Malik. I appreciate that. I could choose to do nothing and live off of that, because it certainly is enough. But instead I want to live my life the way I've always planned it, to the fullest. That means saying no sometimes. Like my mama wants to come and live with me, but I'm not letting her. I don't want cigarette smoke and drama around my kid every day. I don't have patience for that. There comes a time when you have to put yourself first, girl. This is a good opportunity. When you get home, what are you gonna do?" She pointed a manicured finger at me.

"Look for a job," I said morosely.

"You already have a job." She lowered her voice. "Think about it. These opportunities don't come along every day, girl."

She started fussing about me not putting the CDs back in their covers, but I zoned it out. She had put more important things on my mind. I already knew that my friends and family were overwhelming. But I had never thought of myself as the kind of person who always put other folks first. It was clear from what Octavia said that I often did put myself last. When someone needed me, I was going to be there, and I didn't expect anything in return. Now, after finding a job I liked, which had a lot of responsibility, a furnished apartment, and nice incentives to pursue a graduate degree, I was turning it down. I thought my family couldn't take care of my mother without me at home.

I remember my mom saying once to me, "How in the world do you go to college smart and come out stupid?" I decided that the reason was that in college, it had rubbed off on me that it was okay to live however you wanted. There were no boundaries; everything could be questioned. I kept hearing students talk about life being what you make it, and about living life to the fullest. No talk of God. No talk of the consequences for sinning. But my mom believed in strict boundaries, and at home, it was not okay to say whatever you wanted or to wear whatever you wanted. And it was not okay to sleep with someone else's husband.

SIXTEEN

You can know somebody for an entire lifetime and yet stop knowing them in an instant. Sophie finally called me back. I had been worried sick about her since I heard she had run off from rehab. At first, I didn't recognize her voice. She asked me to meet her at the lake. She could have asked me to meet her on the moon, and I would have booked a spacecraft. I really needed to see her so I could know if she was okay. I hurried to the lake, fully expecting to have to wait for her. I was shocked to see her there waiting for me. She was sitting on a swing. She looked up and flashed a weak smile.

She looked like a completely different person. It wasn't just her emaciated features and dark lips. Nor was it the unkempt eyebrows and broken-out skin. It was the cigarette in her hand and the tired look in her eyes. She used to hate cigarettes; she said she hated the lingering smell.

Although the person in front of me looked like a stranger, she was my childhood friend, and I loved her. I hugged her as tight as I could. Through the confusion, frustration, and even the secondhand smoke, I held on to her. I fought tears, hoping and praying there was something better for her. Her frizzy curls framed her face beneath a multicolored cashmere skullie.

"How are you, Sophie?" I asked, wiping stray hairs off her cheek.

"I'm okay," she replied.

"Your hair's getting so long!" I turned her around a little and saw that it hung to the middle of her back.

She hardly ever lets her hair get that long.

"I know. I need to cut it," she said simply.

I sat down on the swing next to hers, looking straight ahead, unsure what to say to the stranger who had on the cutest riding boots I'd ever seen in my life.

"Love the boots," I said.

"I knew you would," she said, finally giving me what seemed to be a genuine smile.

"You smell like an ashtray," I said.

"I know that, too. I hate it. I keep smoking because I know I'll eventually hate it enough to stop."

"How long have you been smoking?" I asked.

"Don't know."

She sucked in her cheeks all the way when she inhaled, as if she wanted to draw all the carcinogens into her lungs that she could possibly get in one puff.

"Have you seen or talked to your parents?" I knew this was an untimely question, but so was everything else.

She didn't say anything.

"What happened to Family Day? I tried calling you."

"I didn't make it."

"How could you not make it? Don't you live there?"

She stopped in mid-puff and blew smoke my way. I almost slapped her.

"Please don't do that. Don't blow smoke in my face."

I moved away from her a little and looked out at the water.

"My bad, geez. What's wrong with you?" she said accusingly.

What's wrong with me?

I looked at her as if she had a third eye. I'd learned how to pick my battles a long time ago. I ignored her comment.

"Have you talked to Carmen and Terry?" I asked again.

She threw her cigarette down and stepped on it. I looked at her hands, with the tattered fingernails and two-finger skull ring.

I took her cold hands in mine and rubbed them. They were still soft. Sophie always had the softest hands I'd ever felt. When she trembled, I decided against asking another question. Instead, I just sat with my hands covering hers and tried desperately to sense her thoughts and feelings. Sophie was staring straight ahead at the geese that flocked near the water.

At this point, the only thing I'll be able to do is love her. I hope that's enough.

"Wanna come home with me?" I asked lightly.

She blinked her eyes.

"Why?" she asked, still staring at nothing.

"I don't know. We can hang out. Talk. Eat some of my mom's leftovers."

I think I saw a slight smile on her face.

"So?" I asked again.

"Nah, not today. I got stuff to do."

What kind of things can you possibly have to do?

"Like what?" I pried.

"How's Catie?" she asked, ignoring my question.

"She's okay. I haven't really been talking to her much. I think she has a new boyfriend."

"A boyfriend?" Sophie asked.

"Yeah, some guy. I'm sure she'll tell you about him."

"Wow. Doesn't that girl get enough dick in her life?"

"Sophie!" I exclaimed. "What is wrong with you?"

"I'm sorry, my bad," she shrugged.

I didn't reply. I was still shocked at what she had said.

I looked away, wondering what was wrong with her. When had she become so insensitive? I had already asked Mom and Roscoe if Sophie could stay a few days. They were both fine with it, but I wasn't sure what I was getting myself into. At that moment, though, I didn't care. Sophie needed help. Despite the differences with her parents, my parents loved her, and they would do anything they could to help her. After thirty minutes of sitting around and barely talking, Sophie agreed to come home with me.

"I need to get some clothes and stuff," she said. "I'll meet you at your house."

"I'll follow you," I said, not wanting her to disappear.

She paused, opened her mouth to speak, and then closed it.

"Okay," she agreed, and we walked to our cars.

Following Sophie was like following Catie. But I can't remember Sophie ever driving that terribly before. Eventually, we pulled up in front of a duplex on a neat street with pretty landscaping, and we walked through the yard.

"This is your place?"

"Anastasia's."

"Who's Anastasia?"

By now I was walking behind her, up the freshly painted steps of one of the duplexes.

"She's a girl from Summer Bridge who talked me into leaving," said Sophie.

"Is she nice?" I asked, not sure of what else to say. I was happy to hear her acknowledge leaving the program. I had been afraid to bring it up.

"Hell, no. She's a rude prude. And she's married to some eighty-year-old billionaire. His family's trying to get her cut off, though." I decided to engage the conversation later.

Sophie zoomed around the apartment, which was spacious but nearly empty. In the living room, there was a sofa and a large TV set. In Sophie's room, there was a mattress on the floor. The closet was maxed out with dresses, shoes, and purses. There were two ashtrays in the bedroom, both of them overflowing with cigarette butts.

I didn't sit down. I stood with my arms folded while Sophie packed her things. She was quiet for the most part, but every once in a while she would say a little something about how much she hated living there. I walked into the kitchen to see if there was anything to eat. The refrigerator was completely empty.

"Did you guys just get a new refrigerator?" I called to Sophie.

"No, we eat out a lot."

I started to get a bad feeling about this. Suddenly the front door opened, and I turned around to see a tall, sickly thin girl with jet-black hair and pale skin. She was at least six feet tall and had Cleopatra bangs. The rest of her hair hung down to her waist.

"Oh, hello," she said with a clipped British accent.

"Hello," I said. "I'm Anaya, a friend of Sophie's."

"You are . . . who?" she asked, looking confused. She was stylishly dressed, all in black—a black YSL t-shirt, leather skinny jeans, and some to-die-for patent-leather, black stiletto Louboutin booties. She wore bright-red lipstick and minimal makeup.

"Oh, *this* is Ny?" she called out to Sophie, who had walked back into the bedroom without having yet uttered a word.

"I'm Anastasia. I have heard so much about you," she said, leaning toward me a little. "Sophie speaks of you all the time. Gonna be a grand psychiatrist one day, eh?"

She smiled. Her teeth were perfectly straight but horribly yellow.

"I was, maybe. But I recently realized that I like teaching—"

"Good for you!" she said, cutting me off.

"Sophie dear, where *are* you going?" she asked, walking into the bedroom where Sophie was packing.

When she came back into the living room, she pulled a cigarette from a huge leather Coach bag, lit it, and puffed hard. Then she pulled her black wig off and stood there looking at me, with her cropped red hair.

"Sophie can be such a bitch!" she hissed as she tossed the wig onto the sofa. "Such a bloody little bitch!"

I didn't say anything.

Sophie screamed from the bedroom, "I heard that. What kind of idiot are you?" She charged into the living room, stopping directly in front of Anastasia. I had never heard her scream with such venom before, but Anastasia was totally unaffected. She remained cool, puffed her cigarette, and stared Sophie down.

"Did you steal my green scarf?" Sophie screeched.

"You're all over the gaff," Anastasia said. "Find it yourself, you ungrateful biddy."

"Ungrateful? What is there to be grateful for? Because you convinced me to leave Summer Bridge? Or because you brought me here and helped me snort more dope than I've ever had in my life?"

Sophie was hysterical, which frightened me. I didn't move and dared not say anything, not knowing if Sophie was ready to leave or ready to cut the girl.

She got right into Anastasia's face. "Maybe I'm supposed to be grateful for you using my credit card to buy those damn boots you have on your big-ass feet?"

Anastasia didn't break her stare or move a muscle. She looked at Sophie as if she were a little kid. She had a smirk on her face that made me uncomfortable.

"Sophie, let's go," I said, finding my voice. "Let's go!" I walked over to her and put my hand on her arm, but she only continued to stand and stare at Anastasia.

Anastasia snapped, "You're a wannabe, Sophie. You have no self-esteem whatsoever. You snort cocaine because you want attention. And you act out because, frankly, your parents just don't give a damn." She reached into her bag and pulled out some bills. "Here's your bloody nine hundred dollars. I told you I'd pay you for the boots as soon as I could get Franklin to send me some cash. Now, get all of your trash and get your ass out of my home before I drag you out of here by that horrid hair." She threw the wad of cash at Sophie.

"Don't you have nerve!" Sophie spit out. "You've spent most

of your life hustling people so you could get away from your stepfather, who cared too much about you. You're a phony!"

I pulled Sophie's arm a bit.

Anastasia turned toward me. "I don't know why a girl of your caliber would even bother with a girl like her," she said to me. "Get out!" she yelled to both of us, pointing to the door.

"Keep the money," Sophie said before heading out the door. "You'll need it."

We drove to my house in separate cars, with me following behind, just to make sure Sophie didn't veer off somewhere. Along the way, I called my mom to tell her that Sophie was staying over.

"Oh, thank God!" she said.

Sophie would stay in my room. She always did. I had a huge queen-size bed that she loved to sleep in.

Before we walked into the house, I said to her, "This is not a rehab facility, so there are no meetings and no restraints. You said you wanted to be here, so I'm letting you come. I can't babysit you, Sophie, and Mom's not feeling well."

"What's wrong with her?" she asked, looking concerned.

"We don't know. The doctor said something about her being critically anemic, and that the anemia is affecting her energy. She's changed her diet and started taking iron pills and some kind of steroid, so it's just a matter of time before she starts to recover."

"Thank you guys for letting me stay. I mean, with your mom being sick and all."

"Girl," I said, "you're family. We all love you. But try to go easy on her. She worries about you, and it's not a good time for her to be worried. You understand?"

"I got it," she nodded.

"That means you have to be on your best behavior. It also means we may have to cook for ourselves."

"Cook?"

When we got to my house, Sophie went into Mom's room and

watched TV with her. I did a few chores around the house that Mom hadn't done. When I went in to check on them, they had both fallen asleep.

The next morning, Mom went in for a checkup and was admitted to the hospital for further testing. I had never known anybody to be admitted to the hospital for being anemic. I went every day to sit with her. One night, walking through the hospital lobby, I heard someone call my name.

I kept walking. I was tired and wasn't in the mood for socializing with anyone.

"Anaya?" the voice said again.

I finally turned around.

"Carl!" I exclaimed. He sure was a welcome sight.

He came up and gave me a hug.

"What are you doing up here?" I asked.

"Dropped off my neighbor. What are you doing here?"

"Visiting my Mom," I said.

"Oh? What's going on? Is she okay?"

I couldn't hold it together. I started crying. Carl held me tightly in his arms.

"Take your time. Just take your time. I'm here," he said.

I managed to get small portions out. I told him how Mom had lost her stamina and had been going back and forth to the doctor.

"They'll figure it out," he whispered in my ear.

We sat in the lobby and talked.

"It's good to see you," he said.

"I certainly needed the company."

"It's all gonna work out. I believe that."

"Thank you, Carl. I believe it, too."

He had gotten a job as a counselor at a youth development center in San Francisco.

"It's a heck of a commute," he said. "But it's worth it."

"So, you like working with kids?"

"Yeah. It's where my heart is."

He talked with such passion about his job. I knew I was starting to feel that way about teaching, if only I could get Jeff out of my thoughts.

"Do you still live with your mom?" I asked.

"Nah, I got my own place. I'm a man. I need my own space. You feel me?"

"Need some privacy, huh?" I smiled.

"Yeah, something like that," he nodded.

After two hours of the kind of emotional connection I really needed, we finally walked to our cars and said goodnight.

After three days, Mom was to be released. The hospital said she had a liver infection. "Her immune system may have been compromised," the doctor told us. "It's very important that her surroundings be thoroughly disinfected."

We made sure of that. We cleaned the house from top to bottom before she came home. That was hard for Ava, because cleaning just wasn't in that girl's blood, so I assigned her the more straightforward and simple cleaning tasks. Sophie did the linen closet and all the blinds. Roscoe did the yard and the garage, and Catie did the floors.

"I don't even do my own floors," she said.

"That's what makes it so special," I smiled.

Aunt Marie offered to bring Mom home, and that plan gave us more time to get the house together. When she walked through the front door, I saw her look at the table in the entryway for the mail, but I had already moved it to my room in order to pay the bills.

Aunt Marie walked in behind her with a look of exasperation. She set Mom's bag down near the stairs, and Roscoe took it up. Aunt Marie put a hand on her hip and sighed. Mom must have driven her crazy in the car.

We welcomed her home with a cooked meal. When we followed Mom into the kitchen, she looked around for a minute and then sat down at the table. For once, there was nothing for her to complain about.

Aunt Marie put Mom's pills on the table, one by one.

"Don't forget to take one blue one before bed," she advised, "and two of these in the morning."

"I don't need instructions, Merle. I can take my own medicine."

"I know. I just thought Roscoe and the kids should know what you take, how much, and when."

"Well, I don't need anybody monitoring me and telling me what to do," Mom hissed. She was in a critical mood.

Ava looked at her with compassion, seeming to understand that Mom was tired. It was nice to see Ava maturing, although I'm not sure who else noticed. She was no longer so judgmental.

Roscoe was sober, but he probably needed a drink.

We sat around for a while after dinner and talked until it was time for Mom to go to bed. She was better, but she was still low on energy.

When Sophie came back from her meeting, she went straight to the computer in my bedroom. I didn't have much privacy, with her sharing the bedroom with me, but I preferred the coziness to being worried about her.

"Are you going back to school?" I asked.

"I don't know," she said, yawning. "I didn't like school. I was almost flunking out."

"What do your parents say?"

"Nothing."

"What do you wanna do?"

"I thought about going to a trade school for fashion design and starting my own clothing line."

"Really?" I was shocked, because I had never heard her even mention a dream career before.

"I don't know if it would work. But I love clothes, and I've always wanted my own line."

That certainly made me sleep better, to know that Sophie had a passion for something. The next day, she kept me company as I drove around inquiring about jobs at several of the surrounding schools. We stopped at a local community college with fashion design courses, and Sophie eagerly brought back a course list. But when we returned about four, Sophie and I found Mom passed out on the kitchen floor, not answering our pleas to wake up. I called 911, and an ambulance arrived in less than five minutes.

When they arrived, I was down on the linoleum with Mom. "Step back," ordered one of the paramedics. As Sophie and I watched from a distance, I was scared but didn't cry. Sophie was sobbing.

"It's gonna be okay," I said, holding her hand.

Mom was quickly brought to consciousness. The paramedics carried her out to the ambulance, and we followed them to the hospital. On the way, I called Roscoe and Aunt Marie on my cell and told them to meet us there. Sophie and I were in the waiting room for twenty minutes before a doctor came out to talk to us. He didn't look worried.

"Miss Goode?"

"Yes?" I said, standing up.

"Your mom's going to be fine. She overexerted herself. She must take it easy. Don't allow her to do housework or anything strenuous."

"Okay," I promised.

"We took some blood tests and are waiting for the results now. They should be in soon."

"Will she have to stay here?" Sophie asked.

"We have to see the results to make that determination, but I'm sure she's fine. If everything pans out okay, she can go home tomorrow morning."

"Can we see her?" I asked.

"Of course," he said.

When Sophie and I went in Mom's room, we saw that she was sitting up in bed with a scowl on her face.

"I'm not in the mood for this," she fussed. "I wanna go home."

"Mom, you will go home, as soon as they get the results of your blood test."

"I'm *tired* of waiting for results. I wanna go home now," she wailed.

Roscoe and Aunt Marie arrived ten minutes later. I saw the doctor talking to them out in the hallway, and that conversation lasted a lot longer than the one he had had with me.

When Roscoe came into the room, I gave him a hug.

"Where's Merle?" Mom asked.

"Getting you some ice," he said.

"I'll be right back," I said, and I searched for Aunt Marie out in the hallway. When I saw her coming toward the room, I asked her, "What did the doctor say?"

"Ah, honey, just talking about the results. They wanna keep your mom a little longer."

"Why, what's wrong? Isn't she getting better?"

"No, honey, she's not. The test results aren't helping them figure out where the fatigue and lack of appetite are coming from. They're gonna do a colonoscopy tomorrow, and if she still isn't eating, they're gonna probably put her on a feeding tube."

I felt as if the wind had been knocked out of me. Colonoscopy? Feeding tube? How did Mom's diagnosis go from having menopause to possibly having something intestinal? I looked in the room and saw Roscoe talking to Sophie. Mom had her eyes closed, but she was awake. She did that a lot lately, complaining that her eyelids were heavier than usual.

"Does Mom know all this?" I said, starting to get scared.

"They tried to talk to her, but your mom is stubborn. She thinks she needs to go home to rest. It's gonna take a lot more than just rest, though."

Just then, Catie walked up and gave me a big hug.

"Hey, girl, how's your mom?"

"She's doing okay."

Aunt Marie, Catie, and I walked into Mom's room, where Roscoe was telling Sophie a fishing story. Mom was smiling at the memory, but she had her eyes closed.

Catie went over and kissed her on the forehead.

"Hey there, pretty girl," Mom said, opening her eyes to look at Catie.

"Hi, Mom."

When Mom took her hand, I saw Catie blink, fighting back her tears.

"How you been, Catie?"

"I'm good! Just living life and having fun. You know me."

"I know you. You take care of yourself, Catie, you hear me? Respect yourself and demand respect from others. You're a beautiful girl, inside and out. Take care of yourself."

Catie lost it. She reached down to hug my mom and cried like a baby.

"I love you," she told my mom.

"I love you, too, baby. You promise me you'll take care of yourself?"

"I promise, Mom." Catie stood up, wiped away her tears, and fixed Mom's short bangs. Mom had gotten a haircut a few weeks ago. It was a really short haircut, which wasn't Mom's style. It looked really nice on her, though.

"You like?" Mom asked.

"Actually, I do. Short hair looks good on you."

"I agree," Aunt Marie said.

Mom's nurse walked into the room. "We need her for about an hour," she said. "Gonna take a little blood from her, and get her all cleaned up."

"I'll call Allen and have him pick Ava up from the house," Aunt Marie said. "She should be home from school by now, right, Ny?"

I nodded.

After Aunt Marie called Uncle Allen, she and Roscoe went down to the cafeteria, while Catie, Sophie, and I went to the lobby to get a change of scenery and sit in more comfortable chairs.

I rested on a small sofa and laid my head back. "I'm exhausted," I said.

"Ny," Sophie said, "you need to go home and rest. I can stay here with Mom and Roscoe."

"Yeah, you wanna go get a massage?" Catie suggested. "My treat, of course."

"That sounds like a good idea, Ny," Sophie said. "You should go."

"No, I'm gonna stay."

Just then, Uncle Riley and Miss Troy walked in.

"Ny-Ny," Uncle Riley said, hugging me. "Are you okay?"

"I'm okay."

"And Anita?"

"I don't know, Uncle Riley. Tests and more tests. I really don't know what's going on."

"What happened?" Troy asked.

"She passed out at home."

"Where's Ava?" Uncle Riley asked.

"Uncle Allen's gonna bring her up here."

"Can Anita have visitors?"

"Sure, but not for a little while. They're taking some blood and cleaning her up right now. We were just about to leave to get some fresh air and some food. You guys are welcome to wait here until Mom's back in her room."

Catie had been digging in her purse for her car keys, but she shot a look up at Troy when she heard her voice.

On the way out of the hospital, Catie asked, "When did your uncle start dating transvestites?"

✳

When we came back, Mom was sitting up in bed. Uncle Allen and Ava were there.

"Good thing you have a room to yourself, Mom, and don't have to share," Ava said.

"Yeah, there's a lot of sick people in these hospitals," Troy joked, a little too loudly.

"Don't get us kicked outta here," Uncle Allen said.

"Well, if they kick y'all out, they gonna have to kick me out, too," Mom said.

We all laughed.

After a while, Uncle Riley, Troy, and Uncle Allen left.

"No more visitors," Mom said. "Tell folks to come see me when I'm home."

"Mom," Ava said, "people are here to support you."

"She's grumpy 'cause that's how Venus responds to a change in body function," Aunt Deb said, as she walked into the room.

I hugged Aunt Deb.

Mom sighed. "Deb," she said, "no palm readings today. I'm not in the mood."

"Hush, Anita, you need the favor of the gods right now."

"Aunt Deb," Ava insisted, "she only needs the favor of *one* God."

"Well," Deb acquiesced, "whether it's multiple gods or one, she needs a favor." She walked over to the bed and hugged Mom.

"Deb," Mom shook her head, "what am I gonna do with you?"

Deb shrugged. "The stars don't lie, Anita. Your house of health is being challenged for some reason. We have to get that balanced out."

Ava rolled her eyes. Aunt Marie chuckled.

Mom's nurse came to the door and motioned me outside. "There's a young man at the nurses' station, asking for you," she said to me. I left the room quickly before anyone could ask questions.

When I looked down the hallway, there stood Carl with his hands in his pockets. I was glad to see him. I walked slowly toward him, wondering what my hair looked like. I hadn't tried at all to look cute.

"How are you?" he asked, putting out his arms to hug me.

"I'm okay," I said, hugging him longer than I ever had before. There were a few moments of silence. I wasn't quite sure what to say or why he was there.

"Do you want to go to the waiting room?"

"Sure," he said, with a tender look on his face.

"I wasn't expecting you," I said.

"I know. When you texted me that your mom was in the hospital, I wanted to come and check on you. How is she?"

"She's weak. She's awake and talking, but she's not herself. They have more tests to run, so we hope they'll have an answer for us soon. It's a lot, but it's going to be fine. I know it is."

He held me close again, and that felt good.

"Thank you for coming," I whispered, and I started sobbing.

"It's gonna be okay, Anaya."

"I'm scared."

"I know."

We stayed in the waiting room for a while, with Carl doing his best to comfort me. When we were there, Aunt Deb came in to say goodbye.

"And who is *this* young man?" she asked.

I introduced them.

"Ah, Carl. One of my favorite authors is named Carl . . . Carl Jung. He once said, 'The sole purpose of human existence is to kindle a light in the darkness of mere being.' That man was a genius . . . It's a pleasure to meet you, Carl."

"You, too, ma'am," he replied politely.

"Oh, don't ma'am me. I'm much too young for that. 'Aunt Deb' will do just fine."

"Okay, well it's nice to meet you, Aunt Deb."

"Oooh, your intercosmic vibes are so strong!" She turned to me and winked. "I can feel them from here!"

"Thank you," Carl said tentatively. Surely he had no idea what Aunt Deb was talking about. I certainly didn't.

"Well, I better be going," Aunt Deb said. "I have to get home and feed my cats. They get upset when I'm late to feed them. Ny, I will be back tomorrow. Call me if you need anything, you hear?"

"Yes. Thank you, Aunt Deb."

"Take care, you two."

After Aunt Deb left, I looked at Carl and shrugged my shoulders. Before he could respond, Catie walked up to us.

"Ah, the Hershey bar from the festival. I remember you. What brings you here?"

Carl blushed.

"He's here to see me, Catie."

"Aw, handsome *and* supportive. Good for you. What's your name again?"

"Carl."

"Carl, yeah, that's right. Well, I hope you're giving my friend some. It's been ages, and she's turning into an old maid."

"Catie!" I exclaimed.

"What? It's the truth. You got cobwebs in that coochie of yours." She laughed. Then, seeing that she was the only one amused, she said, "Okay, I'm outta here. I'll be back tomorrow. If anything changes with Mom, or you need me, call." She gave me a hug and a big kiss on the cheek. "Carl, it was very good to see you." She winked at him and walked out.

As if on cue, Roscoe walked into the waiting room. I introduced them.

I was trying to spend a few minutes with Carl, and it had turned into a family reunion.

"I've heard nothing about you," Roscoe started. "Who are you?"

Carl tensed up, but he didn't say anything. *That's the way to charm a perfect stranger, Roscoe.*

"He's my friend, Roscoe," I explained.

"Well, you know what they say about friends, don't you, Carl?" Then *I* tensed up, afraid of what he would say.

"No, sir, what do they say?"

"They say if you aren't a good and respectful friend to my daughter, I will put your head on a platter. You heard that one?"

Wow.

"Um, no, sir, I haven't."

"Well, now you have." He turned to me. "Ny, can you drive Ava home? It's getting late, and she needs to get ready for school tomorrow. Marie and I are gonna stay here a while longer."

"Of course. I'll just go in and say goodbye to Mom."

"Okay. I'm gonna go down and get me some coffee. Carl, you take it easy."

"Um, you, too, sir. Thank you."

Roscoe had already started walking away.

"I'm going to say goodbye to my mom. Did you want to come in and meet her?"

He nodded and followed me to Mom's room, taking a nervous glance back toward Roscoe. "Don't worry," I confessed. "He's harmless."

Mom was talking to Ava and Aunt Marie when we walked in.

"Hey, Anaya!" she called.

"Hey, Mom." I looked across at Ava. "Roscoe asked me to take you home."

Ava groaned, but she didn't object. She started gathering her things.

"Hello, young man," Mom said to Carl.

"I'm sorry," I said, and introduced everyone.

I wasn't as worried about this group embarrassing me as the others had.

"Carl, it's a pleasure," Mom said, extending her hand.

"The pleasure is mine, Mrs. Goode. Anaya says so many great things about you."

"Funny. She's never said a thing about you." Mom looked at me.

Perhaps I had jumped the gun. I cleared my throat.

Carl seemed a little uncomfortable, and I felt terrible. Although it was horrible to admit, Mom was right. I hadn't mentioned Carl to anyone.

"Hey, Carl!" Sophie called, waving from across the room.

Thank goodness for the distraction.

"Oh, hey, how ya doin'? Sandra, right?"

"No, Sophie. Close, though."

"Right. Yeah. It's good to see you again."

"Good to see you, too . . . So, you and Ny are dating now?"

"Sophie!" I snapped.

"What? I'm not asking for intimate details. I just wanna know if y'all dating or not. Good grief!"

Mom and Ava chuckled.

"That's nobody's business but Carl's and Anaya's," Aunt Marie said, walking over to Carl.

"Hello, Carl, I'm Anaya's Aunt Marie." She gave him a hug.

"Hi, Aunt Marie."

"So, Carl," Mom said, "tell me about yourself. Where do you work?"

"Well, ma'am, I work as an education counselor for at-risk youth in San Francisco. I've always had a passion for working with young people."

"That's impressive," Aunt Marie said.

"I'll say," Mom agreed with a little smile. "Are you from the Bay Area?"

"Yes, ma'am, I am."

I had never seen Carl look shy before. It was cute.

"And your parents live here, too?"

"My mom's here in the Bay Area. I don't know my dad."

I figured it was as good a time as any to cut in.

"Okay, Ava," I said. "Let's go."

"I'm coming, too," Sophie said.

We all kissed Mom goodbye.

"It was nice meeting you, ma'am," Carl said to Mom. "And you, too, ma'am," he said to Aunt Marie.

"It was very nice meeting you, Carl," Mom said.

"Very nice," Aunt Marie added.

Out in the parking lot, Ava and Sophie waited in the car while Carl and I said goodbye.

"Call me when you get in the house," he said.

"Okay, I will."

He kissed me on the forehead.

"Everything's gonna be just fine, okay?"

"Okay," I said.

I hadn't even put on my seatbelt before the interrogation began.

"So, when did you guys hook up?" Sophie asked.

"You aren't fornicating, are you, Anaya?" Ava chimed in.

"Of course, she is! You saw him."

"Fornication will not get you into the Kingdom of Heaven," Ava said.

"Neither will nonsense. Shut up, Ava, and let her tell us," Sophie urged.

"We just started talking again. And no, I'm not sleeping with him."

Sophie sighed, and Ava smiled.

"Good for you!" Ava said. "The Bible says, 'When a man findeth a wife, he findeth a good thing.' It doesn't say anything about sleeping with men for fun," Ava said defiantly.

"Shut up, Ava," Sophie and I said in unison.

"If he makes you happy," Sophie said, "that's all that counts. You deserve to be happy."

"And you deserve to be put first," Ava said.

They were both right. Being with Carl felt so different from being with Jeff. No hiding and insecurity. No second place. It felt much less complicated.

SEVENTEEN

Before I knew what happened, Carl was a regular at the hospital. He fit right in. Everyone loved him. Even Roscoe started to like him after he found out that Carl was a diehard Lakers fan.

One night, while we sat in the hospital waiting room, Carl walked in, carrying coffee and sunflower seeds.

Gotta love that man.

"Aw, isn't that cute?" Catie teased as Carl gave me a hug. "Mister Coffee and Sunflower Seeds is here."

"What?" Carl asked with a grin.

"You!" Catie said. "Coming up here every day to take care of my friend. That's cute."

"Adorable," Sophie added.

"I do what I can," he said. "I just want her to be okay."

"And she will be, as long as she has you," Catie said. "You got a brother?"

We all laughed.

"I do," Carl said. "But you don't wanna meet him."

We laughed again.

"Well, what about an uncle? I don't mind 'em a little bit older."

"Catie!" Sophie and I shushed in unison.

"What? I'm thinking about the future!"

Carl smiled and looked at me. "How's it going today? Any news?"

"No news, no changes."

He rubbed my back a little as I sipped my coffee.

"Carl," Sophie said, "the next time you come up here with only one cup of coffee, you might have a little problem. There are *three* of us."

"Aw, that's my bad. You want me to go and get you some coffee?"

"No," she said. "I'm just giving you a hard time."

"So," Catie said, "I can't ask about the hookup, but you can solicit coffee?"

"Shut up, Catie!" Sophie said.

"You wanna go in?" I asked Carl.

"Is she awake?"

"Yes."

"Okay."

"We'll be back, guys," I said to Catie and Sophie.

"I'm gonna take off and come back in a little while," Catie said.

"Okay, see you when you get back." I hugged her.

When Carl and I went in Mom's room, she looked up and smiled.

"Hey, you two."

"Hi, Mom."

"Hi, Mrs. Goode."

Carl sat in a chair, and I sat next to Mom on her bed.

"How are you feeling, Mrs. Goode?"

"I'm hanging in there."

He didn't seem to know what else to say, but he didn't need to say anything, because Mom kept on talking.

"Are you treating my daughter right?"

"Oh, yes, ma'am. Of course. Your daughter's a special girl. I like her a lot."

"Make sure you do. If you ever decide you don't wanna be with her anymore, you tell her. Don't play games with her, just tell her the truth."

It was funny how my family had put Carl and me together. Although we had been spending a lot more time together, the majority of that time had been spent at the hospital. We talked on the phone and texted in between hospital visits, but that was about it. When I wasn't at the hospital, I was taking care of the house. My mom would never forgive me if I didn't keep the house up, and I knew Ava and Roscoe wouldn't.

I also tried to keep an eye on Sophie, who hadn't disappeared once since she'd been staying with us. She was looking healthier and seemed to be doing much better. It was truly a burden lifted off of me.

"Oh, definitely. One thing my mom taught me was to be honest. She always said it only makes things worse if you lie."

"Smart woman," Mom said, smiling.

I cringed, because she should have been having that conversation with me. I was the one with the problem about honesty.

Mom turned to me as if she had read my thoughts.

"The same thing goes for you, young lady."

Carl cleared his throat loudly.

"Yes, Mom," I said.

"See, Carl, she wants a man like her dad, a provider, hard-working, and loyal. If you fall short of that, you may not be able to keep a relationship with her. She's spoiled in a lot of ways, but she's got a good heart. She's a good girl. Don't take that for granted."

"Never. I respect Anaya. She has a good head on her shoulders, and she knows what she wants. I promise I won't take that for granted, ma'am."

"And don't ever put your hands on her in anger. If it comes to that, just leave the relationship. Because if you make that mistake, you got a lotta folks who'll come looking for you."

We all laughed.

After we had left Mom's room, I told Carl, "My family and friends all seem to like you."

"That's cool. I like them, too."

"Oh," I said.

"Oh, what?" he said.

"What do you mean, 'Oh, what?' There's no *what* after the *oh*," I said.

"You have an attitude, girl."

"No, I don't, boy."

"Seems like it."

"I'm sorry. I just sense that something's bothering you."

"You're going through a lot, and I'm your friend. Whatever issue I may or may not have with you can wait. This is about you and your mom right now."

"Please tell me."

I grabbed his neck and kissed him. I don't know where that came from, but it was a long, passionate kiss. Finally, he pulled back a little.

"Why was I never good enough for you?" he asked.

"What are you talking about?" I replied, taken aback.

"You know what I'm talking about. We hit it off at first, and I really thought we had potential. Something special. I looked forward to your phone calls. Man, a brotha was trying to come up with new ideas for dates and everything. I was into you and I could swear you felt something for me. But you just stopped calling me back. Then you just stopped calling, period. No rhyme or reason. Just disappeared off the scene."

I sighed.

"At the time," I said, "I had things going on, and I couldn't fully commit to a relationship."

He looked at me without saying anything. I tried to find an explanation in his face, but there was nothing. He was expressionless. But if I looked really hard, I could see hurt in his eyes. After all this time, I wasn't sure what I should tell him, but I figured the truth would be best, so I wouldn't get caught up in my own web of lies.

"Why?" he asked firmly.

"What do you mean, why? I had a lot going on, Carl."

"Like what?"

"Like life."

"What else?"

"I was seeing somebody else, okay? Is that what you want to hear?"

"I want to hear the truth," he said.

"I . . . I wasn't able to tell you the truth at the time."

"Why couldn't you have told me that? Why did you waste my time? You knew how I felt about you, but you played me."

"I'm sorry, Carl."

"When did you have time to see somebody else, anyway? We were together all the time."

"We were not together all the time. And it's not the quantity of time you spend with somebody, it's the quality."

Wow. The power of word vomit. That wasn't a nice thing to say.

"Quality," he repeated dryly. "Okay. Were you in love?"

I had never known him to be so forward.

"No, I wasn't. Do you believe me?"

"I believe you. Up until now, you've never given me any reason not to believe you."

"I cared about you, and I liked spending time with you. I was going through something, and it wasn't possible for me to devote all my time to you."

"Because you were spending your time with that lawyer."

My tongue felt numb. I blinked hard.

"Excuse me?"

"Nothing. I merely want you to know that I cared about you for you. I didn't expect anything from you, and I didn't need you to fill in for anybody, either. I wanted to be with you and get to know you a little better. I'm still struggling through school, trying to get it together. I don't know everything, but I cared about you and I put you first. Before everything and everybody. You hurt me, Anaya."

I put my hand on his cheek.

He smiled generously at my affirmation. "I respect you—mind, body, and soul—and I want to take care of you and make you smile when it hurts. But I also want you to want those things for me."

"I do," I said.

"No, you don't." He remained unconvinced.

I looked him square in the eye. "Why do you always shut me down when I try to tell you how I feel?"

"I don't," he said.

"You do! I wanna give us a try. A real try this time. I've always liked you, and I see a lot of things in you that I respect. Can you give me a chance to prove to you that I want to try?"

"I guess. I'll give you some time to think about it. I'm also gonna give you a little space. I know I've been crowding you a bit."

"No, you've been great."

"Simply trying to be a friend."

"I appreciate that more than you know."

He kissed me and it felt good. I scrunched my toes in my sandals and kissed him back.

"Call me later," he said, stroking my cheek.

After he left, I sat in Mom's room, replaying the conversation for hours in my mind.

When did Carl figure out about Jeff? Why didn't he say anything? Why did I choose Jeff over Carl?

The hospital visits were hard for me, watching Mom so ill every day. I felt as if we were losing her. When I came home each night, I was tired and upset. I was grateful that Sophie was helpful at the house. She did dishes, cleaned the bathrooms, took out the trash, and helped with anything else she could think of. But she was a terrible cook, so Mom, although stuck in the hospital, forbade Sophie to do anything in her kitchen except eat and wash the dishes. Sophie had stopped smoking, so she had put on three needed pounds and actually looked like herself again. She enrolled in the local community college for fall semester.

After a week, Mom seemed much stronger, so they let her come home. Aunt Marie came by the house every day to check on us. Although Mom wanted to do some cooking and fussing as usual, she wasn't able to drive or do housework because she got tired so fast.

Meanwhile, Aunt Marie was getting thinner. When she got stressed, she didn't eat. She and Mom kept their feud going, but it was tamer now. Neither of them had the energy for much more. But one afternoon, Aunt Marie brought Amber to visit, and a lot of frank things got said. I felt lucky to be able to hear them from the kitchen.

"Hi, Auntie," Amber said to my mom, who was resting on the living room couch. "You okay today?"

"Girl, your auntie is just fine. Just a little tired is all. Nothing a bit of rest can't fix. How's school?"

"Good," Amber replied.

"And cheerleading?"

"Mom doesn't let me—" Amber started to say.

"Amber!" Aunt Marie interrupted. "Go in the den and do your homework. Your dad will be here soon. Anita, can she use the computer in there?"

"Of course," Mom said. "Make yourself at home."

When Amber had left, Mom said, "Merle, stop smothering that girl."

"I'm not smothering her."

"Yes, you are. Did you make her quit the squad?"

Aunt Marie frowned.

"You know how much she loves cheerleading."

"She lies, Anita! Tells us she has practice when she doesn't, and tells us she doesn't have practice when she does. I'm not gonna reward that kind of behavior."

"But cheerleading keeps her busy. If she has too much idle time on her hands, she's gonna really get in some trouble."

"Well, if she gets into any trouble, she'll have to pull a magic trick. We don't let her out of our sight."

"Well, Merly, if that's the way you want to handle it, go ahead. I can't tell you how to run your house. I will tell you, though, you're making a big mistake. If you hold on to that girl too tightly, she's gonna rebel."

"We've already been through the rebellion."

"You ain't seen nothin' yet."

Aunt Marie sighed.

"Where's Adam?" Mom asked.

"Basketball," Aunt Marie said. "He's always at some tournament. I'm not sure it was such a good idea to put him on this new traveling team."

"Leave him alone, Merle, he's a boy. Boys are supposed to travel."

"Who's traveling?" Uncle Allen asked, coming into the living room.

"We were just talking about Adam," Mom said.

"Hey, girl!"

"Hey, Al, how you doin'?"

"I'm fine. How are you?"

"They can't keep me down, Al."

Just then, Roscoe walked into the room, and he and Uncle Allen did the man-hug.

"How's work?" Roscoe asked him.

"Aw, man, I can't get folks to be accountable. Everybody wants to point the finger instead of figuring out solutions. It's sickening."

"Well, Al, let me tell you something," Roscoe said, moving in closer to him as if he were getting ready to reveal a government secret. "In life, people are either shovels or rakes. If a problem comes up, they'll either rake the problem to themselves and solve it, or shovel it off to someone else."

Uncle Allen paused a moment before finally saying, "Right, Roscoe. You're absolutely right."

"Amber's in the den on the computer," Aunt Marie said.

When Uncle Allen went to get Amber, Mom said, "Merle, you don't greet your husband when he walks into a room?"

"I did greet him," Aunt Marie said, sounding shocked.

"No, you didn't," Mom said.

"Aw, Anita," Roscoe said, "you don't always greet me, so why you worried about how she greets Allen?"

"I wasn't talking to you, Roscoe Goode."

When Allen came back with Amber, Mom said, "Come give your auntie a hug."

"Love you, Auntie," Amber said.

"You be good, you hear?"

"Yes," Amber promised.

"Love you, too, sweetie."

"You take care, Anita," Allen said.

"I'll be fine if you take this wife of yours home with you!"

Uncle Allen laughed.

As he and Amber were leaving, Marie called, "Make sure you do your homework, Amber . . . And no phone!"

Amber groaned.

After this, Aunt Marie started to braid Mom's hair, which she did once a week because it had started thinning.

"You can't smother the child, Merle," Mom said. "She'll rebel against that."

"She can rebel all she likes, but she'll do it in my presence."

"She's not always gonna be in your presence, Merle. You have to give her a chance to prove herself, before you tie her to the ball and chain. She's miserable."

"She's not miserable. That girl has a great life. You know that, Anita. The girl's lucky to see the light of day. We should have punished her more."

"You're punishing her by dragging her all over town with you, Merle. The girl's getting into her teen years. You can't change her, and you can't force her to do anything. You can groom her and raise her—that's it. If you hold on as tight as you are now, you are gonna lose her, 'cause she'll feel like your expectations for her are so low. You guys are gonna have to get past this one, Merly."

"I'm scared, Anita. Kids these days—you see how they are. I don't wanna lose my baby to drugs, or AIDS, or gangs. I just wanna love her, Anita."

She started crying. Aunt Marie cried so easily. I could tell she had been doing it a lot.

Mom just let her cry for a while. Then Mom said, "Let it go, Merly. You spending all this time watching Amber like a guard dog. What about Adam? Who on Earth is paying attention to him?"

Aunt Marie started crying again. When Aunt Marie blew her nose, Mom said, "Good Lord, Merle, you gonna bust a vessel!"

"I just don't wanna lose her."

"I understand that, but you have to let the girl breathe. You have to, or she's gonna break your heart. Just hold her close, while letting her go. Can you try to do that?"

Aunt Marie let out a loud howl. After crying for a few minutes, Aunt Marie composed herself.

"You were always the wise one, Anita."

"I was always the pretty one, too," Mom added.

EIGHTEEN

Mom had ovarian cancer. Apparently, ovarian cancer and menopause have identical symptoms. Once she was diagnosed, everything went blindingly fast. Roscoe took her for chemo treatments three days a week, she started to be sick and lose her hair, and he started to drink again.

When Ava found out, she advised, "We need to fast and pray." I didn't feel much like eating anyway. My mom had always been the rock for everybody else. I wanted to be strong, too, for our family; but how could I do that when my mom was fading away before my eyes?

The doctor told us that the chemo would probably make her sicker and we should be prepared for changes in her mood.

When I walked into Mom's bedroom one day, she was crying. She sat at her vanity and rubbed her hands across the peach fuzz on her head.

"Mom?"

She turned to look at me with tears on her cheeks.

"We need to go to your MRI appointment."

Mom was claustrophobic and would probably panic from being confined inside an MRI machine. We got there early, so that the doctor could give her Valium a half hour before the appointment. Aunt Marie met us at the hospital. While the nurse led Mom away, Aunt Marie, Roscoe, and I waited in the lobby.

"It's gonna be fine," Aunt Marie tried to reassure me.

My cell rang.

"Hey, hon," Octavia said. "How you doin'?"

"Hey," I said, moving away from my family for a little privacy. "I'm doing okay. We're at the hospital with Mom."

"I don't wanna hold you up. I just want you to know that if you need anything, don't even think twice about calling me. You hear?"

"Yes," I said. I was overwhelmed by how nice and compassionate she was. Everyone was being so helpful to us. I'd never been in a situation before where I needed anyone other than my parents. The support felt good. It made me realize that I didn't need to be in control of everything all the time. I had a support system that I could lean on, which was invaluable.

Octavia and I caught up some, and she said things were good with the fireman. I wanted to ask about Jeff; but I didn't, and she didn't mention him, either. After that call, I went to the cafeteria to get coffee. When I returned, the doctor had just come into the waiting room.

We looked at him hopefully.

"Mrs. Goode fell asleep during the procedure," he said, "so we're going to let her rest a while."

"What did you find out?" Aunt Marie asked impatiently.

"Well, she's not responding to the chemotherapy. The cancer's spread to parts of her liver and kidney. She is too weak to endure surgery."

My head was spinning, and all I could hear were muffled voices. My heart was pounding while Aunt Marie said something about getting a second opinion, and the doctor offered to support anything we wanted to do.

"There's an intense type of radiation treatment," he said. "But I think that it would be too much for her."

"Now what?" Aunt Marie suddenly said, stricken.

"She wants to go home," the doctor answered.

"Does she know?" Roscoe finally asked, his voice cracking.

"Not yet."

"How can she go home? Doesn't she need treatment?" Roscoe asked.

"All we can do now, Mr. Goode, is make her comfortable. We can send her home with morphine, or . . ."

"Or what?"

"Well, there's hospice," the doctor said quietly. "I'm really sorry."

This was the first time I'd ever seen Roscoe cry.

"God help us," he said.

We brought Mom home the next day. She had an oxygen tank next to her bed and a small machine filled with morphine. We didn't tell Ava how bad off Mom was, but she knew things weren't good. Uncle Riley and Aunt Marie practically moved into the house. I was grateful, because we needed them. People called to offer support, and visitors dropped by with food, flowers, and cards, but Aunt Marie wouldn't let anyone see Mom.

Sometimes, I would go into Mom's room and watch her sleep. One morning when I walked in, I found Ava reading the Bible to Mom while she slept. When I came over to the bed, Ava immediately stood up and hugged me tight. We cried hard together.

"I'm not giving up," she said.

"None of us are."

"She's going to be all right, Ny. God has the final say."

"Yes he does, Ava."

"What's going on here?" Aunt Marie walked into the room.

We didn't answer because neither of us knew what to say.

Aunt Marie ushered us out of the room quickly. Once we were outside, she said, "Don't express negativity around her. Okay?" Aunt Marie's tone was sharp, but hushed. "She can hear you and sense your feelings. Don't do that. It doesn't help anything."

She walked away, leaving us dumbfounded.

We tried to keep ourselves busy. The days and nights ran into each other, and sometimes I didn't know what day of the week it was. I had put my own life on hold. I didn't have a job or any prospects for one, and I knew Mom wouldn't like that.

I started thinking about what was next. I enjoyed teaching on the faculty campus more than I ever thought I would. During my spare time, I searched for jobs, and I had received calls for interviews. Two were teaching jobs, and one was a job working as a paid intern for a local congressman. The thought of getting back to life and having some direction felt good. I knew that at the moment, moving out wasn't an option.

One morning, Mom started throwing up and had a high fever. We rushed her to the hospital, and they admitted her to the ICU immediately. The waiting room was filled with family and friends: Ava, Uncle Riley, Aunt Deb, Sophie, Catie, and me. In the ICU, visitors were limited to three per room at one time. When three of us were in the room with Mom, the rest of us just kept each other company.

The hospital had become our second home. After Mom was admitted with the fever, the doctors told us they wouldn't release her until the fever came down. Once the fever came down, they didn't want to release her until she "stabilized."

"She's never coming home, is she?" Ava worried.

"I don't know. Whatever happens, we are going to be okay. Just like we were when Andrew went away. It will be hard, I won't try and kid you, but we will be all right. We have each other." I hugged her tightly.

I suppose I was talking to myself as well. With all the sad things that had happened over the past few months, I knew that life goes on. I was certain that Mom wouldn't want us to just crumple up and die with her.

Travis came to visit me one day, and we went out for lunch. I was happy to see him and grateful for the break away from the hospital. I hadn't talked to him much since I left campus. We e-mailed occasionally, but it was great to actually see him. He was as chunky as ever. We talked a little bit about Mom, but I got too emotional, so I switched subjects.

"How's Faye?" I asked.

"She's good. Getting a little nervous about the move, but she's cool."

"She's going to North Carolina with you?"

"Yep." His smile was so big that I had to laugh.

"You must have made quite an impression to make a girl move across the country to be with you," I said, teasing.

"Well, what can I say?" He joked with that charming bright smile of his that made him look so handsome.

"You can say you'll keep in touch."

"I promise I will." He took a huge bite of pizza. "So, you know what I'm going to ask you, right?"

"Nope," I lied.

"Yes you do. What's up with Jeff? Have you handled things like a big girl?"

"Haven't talked to him." I looked down at the uneaten pizza on my plate.

"Why not? You need closure. We talked about that," he reminded me.

"We talked about it, but I didn't agree to talk to him. Wipe your mouth."

"You need to talk to him. You can't walk away from your feelings."

"I said I didn't talk to him. I wrote him an e-mail, though."

"An e-mail? Come on, you know that both of you deserve better than that."

"That's all I could do!" I said, raising my voice. I looked around and smiled at the people in the restaurant who were looking back at me.

"What's the point? We won't be together. We can't be," I said in a much lower tone.

"What did you say in the e-mail?"

"I apologized for the disappearing act. Apologized for anything I'd done to hurt him and his family. I told him I harbored no negative feelings toward him. It was the release I needed to move on. The chapter I needed to close to free myself," I said, fighting tears.

"You still love him, don't you?"

"I do." At this point, I simply cried. "But he belongs to someone else, and I can't compromise myself for a relationship that never belonged to me in the first place."

"What did he say?"

"I said I wrote him an e-mail, I never said I sent it," I confessed.

There was no denying my feelings for Jeff and sending that e-mail would force me to face those feelings once and for all. I tried to put on a brave front and tried to stay strong, but I was hurt and I needed closure. Mom's illness made me realize how precious both life and time can be. I spent a lot of time making sure other people were okay but I hadn't done the same for myself. Mom will need me to be strong and help her take care of things around the house when she comes home and I can't do that if I'm emotionally overwhelmed. I had to get the thing with Jeff behind me. As I began to cry, Travis reached over and held my hand. I wanted to be as good to myself as I had been to other people. I was going to send the e-mail as soon as I got a chance.

"Have you talked to any of your former students?" I asked, eager to change the subject.

"I have," he said, filling me in on the latest news from campus. Lunch lasted more than two hours. We both hated to leave, but he had to get back.

"It was good seeing you, Travis," I said. "I'm so happy for you and Faye."

"It was good seeing you, too, my friend. I'll be in touch."

He picked me up and squeezed me.

"Ow!" I joked.

"I'm gonna squeeze you even harder than that if you don't call Jeff," he promised.

"I'll talk to him."

"I'm here for you, and I love you," he said, kissing me on the cheek.

"I love you, too, Travis," I replied.

When I returned to the waiting room outside the ICU, all of my family members were still sitting there, looking glum. I sat down next to Sophie just as Aunt Marie came out.

"She's resting now," was all Aunt Marie said, sitting down wearily.

We had questions, but it was Catie who asked, "Is she okay?"

"We hope so, Catie," Aunt Marie said. "We hope so."

Aunt Marie seemed heavy with despair. She and Mom were best friends, although they would never admit it. When Mom went into the hospital this last time, Aunt Marie had stayed in the room with her more than anyone else. She usually came in the morning and sat with Mom until evening. Roscoe had to work, so he didn't make it to the hospital most days until after five.

Aunt Marie usually told Mom all the latest family and celebrity gossip. She talked on and on, as if she were certain that Mom could hear. Sometimes Mom responded, and sometimes she didn't.

Occasionally, some of Mom's coworkers would come up to the hospital to visit her. In the beginning, Aunt Marie allowed them in, until Mom was too tired for any more non-family visitors. They all understood.

On most evenings, family members gathered in a small room that the hospital staff let us use. We would sit around, drink coffee, and sometimes talk. I saw one evening that Jeff had replied to my e-mail with a simple, "I will always love you."

Mom's illness had a more profound effect than anyone could have imagined. Sophie, Catie, and I reconnected during our long hospital visits. Catie shared how unhappy she had been with her life. Even with all the grandeur of couture and luxury, she admitted to being completely miserable. The emptiness she felt when the Johnson's died apparently resulted in her being afraid to get close to anyone again, for fear of losing them. I knew she suffered, but I really had no clue how deep it was and how much she had kept to herself.

"I can't believe you held all of that in for so long," Sophie said between sniffles.

"I know. Sometimes I didn't even realize it. I just tried to put it out of my mind. Tried to pretend I didn't hurt and that all of the things that I had were enough. But now . . ." she said with tears in her eyes. "Now . . . looking at Miss Nita in that hospital bed makes me realize that no matter how much I try to pretend, it's possible that I will lose somebody else again in this lifetime. That's just how life goes. In the meantime though, I wanna live. Really live. I want a family and a real job and I want to have dinner parties and a real relationship. I'm worth that. I deserve that."

Sophie and I were speechless. We cried and hugged. No one thought it was unusual, and probably thought we were crying about mom.

After we composed ourselves some, I looked up and saw Terry Beat standing in the doorway. My heart jumped and Catie did a double take. Sophie stared open mouthed at her dad and new tears welled in her eyes. As I hugged him, I noticed that he still wore the same cologne from when we were kids. It made me emotional all over again as I thought about how close our families used to be.

"Ny!" he said, hugging me tight.

"Hi, Uncle Terry," I said and immediately started crying. He held me for a long time.

"Catie?" he said.

Catie smiled.

"Hi, Uncle Terry," she said, standing to hug him.

It's sad that it takes tragedies to bring friends together again, but seeing Terry really made my day. When he looked over at Sophie, she finally walked over and gave him a hug. She hugged him and cried in his arms. Her body shook in her dad's arms and he held her tighter. He whispered something in her ear and she cried harder. Catie and I moved away to give them as much privacy as we could in the small room. Terry held on to Sophie for what seemed like forever.

"I'm a little better now that you are here," Sophie said, wiping her nose with the back of her hand.

"You know I love you."

She nodded.

Just then, Roscoe walked into the room. When he saw Terry, he squinted, as if to make sure his eyes weren't deceiving him.

"It's good to see you, man," Terry said.

Sophie backed away from Terry and Roscoe, and she sat down quietly.

"It's good to see you too, man," Roscoe said. "This is gonna make Anita's day."

"I had to be here," Terry said. "How are you holding up, man?"

"It's pretty scary, thinking my sunshine may be leaving me for good."

Terry put his hand on Roscoe's shoulder.

"Thank you for coming, Terry."

As they embraced, Terry nodded to Uncle Riley and Aunt Deb, and smiled to everyone else. Then I got up, hugged Terry again, led him by the hand to Mom's room, and we both went in. I could feel the sweat in his palm.

Aunt Marie looked up when we walked in. "Terry!" she exclaimed. She stood and threw her arms around him.

To my surprise, Mom was awake. She smiled as much as she could. "Beat Man!" she whispered weakly. "What's up, boy?"

"What's up yourself, Sassy?"

He bent over to hug her. Aunt Marie motioned for me to leave the room with her. When I looked back, Terry and Mom were still embraced.

Terry visited with Mom for a while. I don't know what they said to each other. I was just happy that he made it in time. When he came out, Aunt Marie went back in. Catie announced that she needed to leave. I walked Catie to the elevator and gave her a big hug. I was still overjoyed on the inside. We cried once more before I let her go.

"Love you, girlie," she said quietly.

"Love you, too. You know everything's going to be okay, right?"

"I do. I really do," she said. "You know everything's going to be okay too, right?"

"I do," I said.

"We got this," she said giving me a fist bump. With that, she disappeared behind the elevator doors.

"Would you guys like to get something to eat?" Terry asked Sophie and me.

I explained, "My friend Carl is coming to pick me up."

"Sophie?" Terry asked, looking at his daughter.

"Um, I guess I'll go with you," she said slowly. "But we'll wait with you here, Ny, until Carl picks you up."

While we waited, we talked about Mom.

"She's always been there for me," Sophie said. "I don't understand why this horrible thing has happened to such a beautiful person."

Tears filled my eyes.

"Are you okay, Anaya?" Terry asked.

"Yeah, I'm okay. Go ahead, Sophie."

"I was gonna say that she always told me that no matter what anybody said, that I would be fine. And you know what, Daddy? She's right. I am gonna make it."

Terry put his head down, obviously ashamed of the way he had neglected his wife and daughter. It was understandable that he had a demanding career but it seemed that he had all but abandoned them. After his music career skyrocketed, his presence became less while Sophie's defiance increased. I felt sorry for all of them. It was a sad situation for everyone. I am sure that's why Sophie turned to drugs. Much like Catie, she was trying to numb the pain of losing her father. They used to be so close and now their relationship was almost nonexistent. As I watched Sophie interact with her dad, she looked more content than I had seen her in a long time.

"I messed up, Sophie," he said.

"Yes, you did," she said.

"I can try to do better."

"There's more you can do. But before you do anything, you have to want to do more."

Terry put his face in his hands. I started to leave.

"Don't go, Ny," Sophie said, holding out her hand to stop me. "This is a family moment, and you're family."

I sat back down.

"I'm not mad at you anymore, Daddy," she acknowledged. "I learned to let that anger go. It was hard, but I did it. You left me when you knew I needed you. I stumbled and fell, but I got back up. On my own."

Terry rubbed his eyes.

"I love you, baby," he said.

"I know," Sophie said.

She had come a long way, and I was proud of her. Mom was right—Sophie was going to be just fine.

When Carl came to pick me up, I was feeling good. The conversation with Catie did me good. And Terry and Sophie finally connecting made for an even better night. I knew they still had a ways to go, but it was so wonderful to see them taking the first steps. They deserved happiness and it was right in front of them. All they had to do now was have a conversation with Carmen. It was obvious that Terry didn't want to be married to her anymore, and he needed to find a way to separate his relationship with Carmen from his relationship with Sophie. Just because he and Carmen weren't working out didn't mean he had to leave Sophie behind. He hadn't said it, but looking at him with his daughter, made me think he finally understood that.

Carl and I were doing great, considering the circumstances with Mom. Most of our "dates" lately were in the hospital cafeteria or at a nearby deli. I was sometimes overwhelmed by how supportive and comforting he was. After all we'd been through, he was still a good friend to me. As soon as we were away from my family, I gave him a big kiss.

"Mmm. What was *that* for?"

"For being you."

"Well, I guess I oughta be me more often."

We kissed again, and this time he kissed me more seriously than ever before. My toes were tingling.

"Wow!" I said, catching my breath.

"What?"

"Nothing. Just wow."

"Didn't know I had it in me, did you?"

"I suspected."

"I tried to give you a lil' taste in Arizona, but you were too scared."

"Scared? Who was scared? You fell asleep!" I laughed a little, but I stopped when I saw that he was serious.

"You were scared," he repeated. "Either you were scared, or you just weren't feeling me like that."

"Carl, it wasn't the right time."

"Okay," he said shortly.

I knew where he was coming from, and I knew how frustrated he had been with me. I put my arm around his as we walked toward the car, but he just looked straight ahead without saying anything.

"It's cool," he finally said.

"You always say that."

"Stop whining. I said it's okay. Your priorities are your priorities. It's clear they don't include me."

It was hard to nurture a relationship in the middle of everything else that was going on. But I was committed to doing my best, and Carl was steadfastly patient. I knew Carl had issues with our past and had things he needed to talk about, but I loved him so much for holding those things back, for the sake of my situation. He was a great guy. Rather than argue, we were silent on the way to the deli.

Terry came to the hospital again the next day. He took turns visiting with Mom and sitting in the waiting room with the rest of us. There weren't many visitors—just me, Catie, Sophie, Terry, and Roscoe. Aunt Marie was with Mom.

"So, I heard you won a Grammy," Roscoe said.

"I did," Terry said humbly.

Sophie was sitting right next to him, seemingly happy to have him around.

"Terry," Catie said, "I miss your parties, man."

"Yeah, Dad, we used to have fun at those parties," Sophie said.

"That's an understatement," Catie went on. "Those parties were—"

She was staring at something. I followed her glance to see Carmen standing in the doorway.

I had forgotten to call Carmen back. She had called the house a few times to see how Mom was, but she had not visited the hospital. I was surprised to see her.

She walked slowly into the room. Catie and I immediately stood up and hugged her. Then she walked over to Roscoe and hugged him.

"How is she?" Carmen asked.

"Hanging in there," Roscoe said quietly.

Carmen looked over at Sophie and Terry, who had both remained sitting. "I didn't know you were in town," Carmen said to Terry. Then she looked back and forth between Terry and Sophie, as if trying to figure something out.

She doesn't know they've been spending time together.

"Don't start," Sophie said.

Carmen ignored Sophie and continued looking at Terry.

"Look, Carmen," Terry said quietly, "I didn't have a chance to call."

"You didn't have a chance to call?" Carmen said sharply. "When did you get in town?"

"Not here, Carmen," Terry said. "Have some respect." He tried to put his hand on her arm, but she pulled away.

Carmen fumed and launched into a tirade. "Not here? Then, when? Huh? When you're on the road? Not then, 'cause you don't have time. Oh, maybe when you're in the office? No, that's not good, either, 'cause you're too busy. Maybe on our anniversary? You'll find some time then, won't you? Oh, wait. That would have been yesterday. Guess you didn't have time then, either."

"I'm sorry," he said, stone-faced. "Anita's family's here. They need us. Please, Carmen. We can discuss this later."

Sophie had her arms crossed, glaring at Carmen.

Why is Sophie so angry with Carmen? Terry's the parent who hasn't been home.

"Carmen," I said, "do you wanna see Mom?"

It took her a moment to respond. "Yes, I do." I showed her which door, and we entered together.

When Mom saw Carmen, she smiled. Carmen immediately started crying. That upset Aunt Marie.

"Hi, Carmen," Aunt Marie said, walking over toward her.

She gently pulled Carmen away from Mom and hugged her. Aunt Marie didn't like any negative energy around Mom. She said it wasn't good for her. I could understand that to some degree, but, hell, we were sad. We were going to cry and experience pain, and that's not always easy to keep in. I had cried so much already, that I wondered if I had any tears left. I promised myself that when Mom came through this, I would tell her how much I appreciated her.

Carmen cried some more, and Aunt Marie consoled her.

Mom looked away.

When Carmen got herself together, Aunt Marie pulled a chair close to Mom's bed for Carmen to sit on.

"I like your hair, Anita!" Carmen exclaimed.

Mom ran her hand slowly across her head.

"Do you? It's growing on me, too."

We all laughed.

Carmen held Mom's hand and said urgently, "You will always be my friend, you know that? I love you."

"I love you, too," Mom said gently.

"You did such a good job with the girls. I've always been jealous of the way you handle them. I can never get Sophie to respect me like your girls respect you."

I knew that this entire line of conversation irritated Aunt Marie as being inappropriate.

"I saw Terry's stupid ass out there," Carmen said.

"Ah, yeah, Beat Man. It was good seeing him." Mom smiled.

"Speak for yourself. That *hijo de la chingada* didn't even call me when he got to town."

"You two need to talk."

"It takes two to talk," she said loudly. "I can't talk by myself."

As Carmen's voice rose, Aunt Marie's eyebrows almost shot through the ceiling. She was two seconds from showing Carmen *la puerta*.

"I know, but he's here now, and there's no way for him to avoid it. He knows it's time."

"Has he said something to you?" Carmen asked.

"No, but I know he wants to make things right. I saw it in his eyes."

"*Cabrón!* I hate him," she snarled.

"Carmen, you have to calm down. This is not all about you. Sophie needs you. She needs both of you, and you're gonna have to put your anger aside for her sake. I won't be here to take care of her anymore. She'll need you."

Mom's words stung all of us, and the room was painfully silent. I stood up and walked to the window, feeling cold. I tried to accept the fact that my mom might not live, but I couldn't. How could I go the rest of my life without her? I wanted her to see me get married, have kids, tell me how to feed them, how to hold them. In that moment, I realized that I did want kids, after all.

I saw Aunt Marie stand up. "Carmen, dear, perhaps you should get some fresh air or something."

I knew it.

As Carmen stood up, Ava walked into the room. She went over and kissed Mom.

"Hi, Mama," she said as cheerfully as possible.

"Hey, baby. How was your day?"

"It was okay."

Ava was more emotional than I was around Mom, and I didn't want to watch it today, so I decided to go back to the waiting room with Carmen. As I walked down the corridor, I fervently prayed for God to heal my mom and let her come home to us.

These days at home, things were chaotic, but we were managing. After Mom took ill, Uncle Allen stepped up in full support of Aunt Marie and was there for all of us. Aunt Marie seemed to appreciate his help and leaned on him a lot emotionally. Terry brought food to the house and hung out. His presence was good for Sophie. Terry even went to a couple of family meetings at Summer Bridge with her. I knew that Terry had asked Carmen for a divorce. But although Terry was in town, Sophie still lived with us, and he stayed in a hotel. She explained to me that she felt useful at our place.

One night I asked her how she felt about Terry being back.

"Whenever I see him, it makes me realize I'm not so screwed up, after all," she said.

Within the week, the inevitable happened at the hospital. Aunt Marie and I were sitting in Mom's room, talking about celebrity gossip, when I noticed that Mom's color had changed from her medium brown to ash grey. While Aunt Marie talked on about who was pregnant and who had broken up in Hollywood, I fought back tears. Then I rushed out into the hallway to call a nurse.

"Help me, please! Someone!"

A nurse followed me back to the bed and checked Mom's pulse.

I looked over at Aunt Marie, who was sitting straight up on the edge of her chair.

"I'm sorry," the nurse said. "She's gone."

The words felt like a punch in the stomach. I couldn't breathe. My hands shook as I grabbed my aunt. I could hear the nurse doing something behind me, but I had no idea what it was. Finally, I let go of Aunt Marie and walked over to my mother. She looked so peaceful in her white nightgown. Her hair had been growing back, and the Caesar cut looked good on her. There were no bruises anywhere on her body. She looked like she was sleeping, just as Andrew had looked.

"Mom?" I questioned softly, letting the tears fall out of my eyes, down my face, and on her gown. I kissed her face. She was still warm. "Mom?"

Aunt Marie led me out of the room and called Roscoe on his cell phone.

"Come now," she said to him.

The next few days after Mom died were hazy. Aunt Deb helped Ava and me to pick out something for Mom to wear. We chose a peach-colored silk dress that she had worn when she and Roscoe renewed their vows on their fifteenth anniversary. Next, we had to choose if we were going to put a wig on her, but we decided that the short little Caesar cut would be what she would have wanted.

The ceremony was beautiful. Ava's pastor had come to the house a few days earlier to meet the family. He asked us to tell him about Mom so that he could prepare her eulogy, and he actually did a great job. He spoke about Mom's energy, and her passion for her family and her work. He mentioned her cooking, her sassiness, her relationship with Roscoe, and even her struggle with Andrew's death.

Roscoe looked handsome but sad in his black suit and peach tie. Usually his family didn't come around much, but a few of his relatives did come and discuss Mom's legendary cooking skills.

When Uncle Riley went to the casket to view his sister one last time, he put up his hands and cried, "Oh, Anita!"

My heart and throat were burning. I had been crying for so long that I could hardly breathe. I kept thinking about the last time I saw Mom healthy. She had been cooking and fussing in the kitchen. What had happened in such a short time? Why did God take her? I had so many things to tell her. I never got to tell her about Jeff. I never got to tell her how smart and beautiful she was. I wanted her to see me get my master's degree. I wanted to share with her that I had decided to teach. We still had so much to do together.

The ceremony at the memorial park only lasted a few minutes. Ava's pastor said a short prayer and turned the casket over to the groundskeepers. Most of us, including Carl and I, stayed until the body was actually lowered into the ground, but Ava went ahead to Aunt Marie's house with Uncle Allen, Adam, and Amber. None of them wanted to be there for the final moment.

As everyone hugged and consoled each other, I left the group for a minute to take home some of the flowers. That's when I saw Jeff standing on the other side of the chairs. I literally caught my breath, because it had been so long since I had seen him. I knew I loved him more than I could ever love a man again. I wanted to run up to him, hug him, and tell him how much I missed him. But I knew I couldn't do that. I walked over to him very slowly.

He gave me a strong hug. It was wonderful to be in his arms again. He still felt warm and smelled good. Now I remembered why I had to run away from him: It was so hard for me to resist him. For the briefest time, I forgot my surroundings, the sad occasion, and the fact that Carl and my family were nearby.

I let go of his hug and looked up at him.

"I'm sorry about your loss," he said gently.

"Thank you."

"How is everyone? How's your dad?"

"He's holding up. Everybody's trying to be strong."

"How are you?"

"I'm hanging in there."

"If you need anything, just let me know."

"Thanks."

"I'm serious. Anything, just call me. Even if you don't need anything, you can call me."

"Thank you. I'm sorry for disappearing the way I did. I was hurt. I didn't know what else to do."

He held up his hand. "You have nothing to apologize for. I miss you like hell, but I'm not angry with you. I don't know how to be angry with you. I understand."

"You do?"

"Yes." He hugged me, and I felt warm inside.

"I love you," he said, an admission that momentarily paralyzed me. "I wanted to see you in person and give my condolences. I know how much your mom meant to you."

"Thank you, Jeff," I managed to say.

"It's the least I could do."

Carl walked over, shook Jeff's hand firmly, and put his other hand around my waist.

I immediately felt guilty for having walked away from Carl so abruptly.

"Hi, Professor," Carl said.

"Hey, Carl." Jeff looked a little confused. I'm sure he was surprised to see Carl at my mom's funeral—especially with his arm around my waist.

"Everybody's ready to go," Carl said to me.

After a few awkward seconds, I said, "I'll be there in a minute, Carl."

"Okay," he said, smiled to Jeff, and left.

"We're going over to my aunt's house to eat. You're welcome to come."

"No, I won't do that. I just wanted to pay my respects. I tried to talk to you at the funeral, but you were surrounded by so many people. It was a beautiful service. Your mom touched a lot of lives. I see where you get it from."

"Yes, she did. Thank you for coming, Jeff. It means a lot to me."

"If there's ever anything I can do, ever, I'm here."

"I'm sorry I left without saying anything."

He held up his hand. "Stop it. No apologies here, just life and moments that we share."

"Thanks," I said. "Take care."

"You, too . . . Anaya?"

"Yes?"

"You look *amazing*!"

I smiled and turned to leave. But then I had a thought. Turning back, I said, "By the way, boy or girl?"

"Girl."

I smiled, despite the spear that slashed at my heart.

On the way back to the car, I tried to picture myself in the delivery room having Jeff's baby. The picture was blurry, though. And with good reason: We would never be together again.

When I got to the limo, my family was already sitting inside. As I climbed in, Aunt Marie gave me a small, knowing smile.

I saw Jeff sitting in his car as we drove down the hill toward the freeway. He didn't look over when the limo passed, he just sat staring straight ahead. I looked over at Carl. He smiled. I nudged his leg with my foot.

On the ride home, I replayed in my mind the few minutes with Jeff. The old feelings came rushing back. It all happened so fast— the relationship, the breakup, Sophie's addiction, Mom's death.

Aunt Marie's house was full. I'd never seen so many people in there before—cousins, aunts, and uncles I hadn't laid eyes on in years. Some, I had never seen.

Aunt Marie had a black-and-white photo of Mom blown up and placed on an easel near the front door. I had taken it one day while Mom was cooking in the kitchen. Something about the way she looked had made me want to take her picture; she was cheerful and beautiful. I remember asking her to look at the camera, and she raised her head up high, lifted her spatula in the air, and gave me a big smile. It was the perfect picture of her. As I listened to people telling old stories about Mom, nothing could take away the raw pain of losing her, but the picture was comforting.

I hugged Roscoe as I passed him in the hallway.

"I'm going to head home soon," he said to me.

It made me realize that, in a few days, it would be just Ava, Roscoe, Sophie, and me. Our house had been busy with relatives and friends for the past few weeks, so we hadn't had time alone in the house since before Mom died. But soon, the company would be gone. We'd be alone with all the memories of Andrew and Mom. I pictured Mom in heaven, fussing at Drew.

Go easy on him, Mom.

How could I not have seen before how short life is? We get only a certain amount of time. I had decided to accept the interviews for the teaching jobs and go directly to graduate school. Why wait? I would use the money from my parents to help me get through graduate school. My independence had long awaited my arrival. I looked around at the people I thought needed me so much. They were all fine—I was the one who needed to get moving.

Ava didn't cry much, but I knew everyone grieved in different ways. She was steadfast in her faith. With all my new plans for the future, one thing would remain the same. I would still be living at home with my sister and my dad. Along with my newfound independence came the ability to make decisions, and I knew without a doubt that I wanted to stay home for a while longer.

I got a phone call from Judy. "Your mom was a wonderful woman," she said. "She loved you a lot, and she was proud of you."

"Thank you, Judy. And thank you for calling."

"When are you coming to see me?" she asked.

"When's a good time?"

"Anytime soon," she responded.

Aunt Marie walked into the living room to put some refreshments on the table and pick up a couple of empty cups. I could tell she was tired, but she looked as beautiful as ever. Uncle Allen walked up behind her and took the cups. She thanked him and gave him a kiss. They had reconnected, or rekindled, or whatever it is couples do when they need to get the spice back in their marriages. It was a beautiful sight, and I felt happiness for Aunt Marie.

Sophie and Catie were on a couch, with Antoine sitting between them. I wasn't surprised to see him at Mom's funeral, but I was surprised to find out he had come with Catie.

Sophie looked content. Her complexion had cleared up, and she had gotten a haircut. When she laughed at something that

Catie had said, she tossed her curls out of her face in the way that I found so endearing.

"Love you," she mouthed to me across the room.

"Love you," I mouthed back.

Carl looked incredibly handsome in a suit. I knew I loved him, even if it wasn't the passionate, aching love I had for Jeff. I once heard someone say that you're supposed to be with the one who loves you, rather than the one you love. I don't know who makes up that crap. What I do know is that it feels good to have a man who is totally mine. What I have with Carl can grow, and but what I had with Jeff had no way to change.

I walked over to Carl and squeezed his knee. He reached over and kissed me on the forehead. As I sat down next to him, I closed my eyes. Later tonight, I'd finally tell Mom about Jeff.

"Always be prepared for anything," she said. "But I'll never leave you."

I thanked her, and I put my head on Carl's shoulder.